TEROVOLAS

The Van Helsing Papers
(1891)

By

Edward M. Erdelac

JournalStone

San Francisco

JournalStone books may be ordered through booksellers or by contacting:

JournalStone
199 State Street
San Mateo, CA 94401
www.journalstone.com

The views expressed in this work are solely those of the authors and do not necessarily reflect the views of the publisher, and the publisher hereby disclaims any responsibility for them.

ISBN: 978-1-936564-54-5   (sc)
ISBN: 978-1-936564-55-2   (ebook)

Library of Congress Control Number: 2012949586

Printed in the United States of America
JournalStone rev. date: November 16, 2012

Cover Design: Denise Daniel
Cover Art: M. Wayne Miller

Edited By: Norman Rubenstein

For Adonai and my family

FORWARD

I first met Professor Abraham Van Helsing in Natal in 1877 while doctoring for the army. By the end of that year I was best man at his wedding, which will indicate the regard with which we held each other. I loved and respected the old man dearly. We passed through hell together at Intombe, beneath the churchyards of London, and beyond the Borgo Pass. Thus it was with an outraged heart that I watched the deterioration of his private and professional life in the years following the publication of the Dracula papers.

That this paragon of wisdom, so like a Faust in the totality of his learning, should have met with professional scorn to…I was about to write *'to the end of his days,'* but that would be a lie. Abraham Van Helsing is mostly forgotten. The world turned away from him as a schoolyard bully turns at last from a righteous underdog who refuses to fight. He passed away quietly last year in his little cottage in Holysloot, and no ill-timed clamoring of detractors marked his passing. There was only a feeble local obituary reciting the string of titles after his name, hinting little of his exploits. Perhaps he would have thought this correct.

Thanks to his portrayal on stage and in the motion pictures, most schoolchildren know the name Count Dracula, but are unfamiliar with Abraham Van Helsing, except as a footnote to that fiend's story.

This, I am sure, he would *not* have found correct.

It is with this terrible loss to posterity in mind that I present the current volume, a collection of the late Doctor's private papers detailing his heretofore largely unknown career. It was my honor to be assigned the task of publishing this work by the man himself, whose will stipulated that I, as his friend, edit his writings and that they not be submitted for publication until one year after his death. The reasons behind the former request I have already stated. As to the latter, I can only surmise. Was it to protect the identities of persons described within, or to save himself from further censure by the academic community whose universal scorn cost him his tenure? I do not know, so it is likely that no one ever will.

In reading through the voluminous records Van Helsing kept, I have chosen to publish these particular papers first as I believe they may hold some interest to the public. They cover the period directly following the events of *Dracula*, which has seen print elsewhere and continues to enjoy popularity (albeit as fiction, which the parties behind its publication perhaps wisely, if falsely, touted it as). Although I myself was not personally witness to the events described here within, having been wholly engaged in my work in Purfleet at the time, knowing Van Helsing as I did, I believe every word of it. He was not the sort to record exaggerations, nor to give himself over to self-promotion.

Personal endorsements aside, I have included with Van Helsing's journal entries numerous accounts corroborating the Professor's claims. Whether this work will bear fruit in the vindication of Van Helsing's great and slandered name, I doubt. Like him, I have come to view today's scientific community as a jackass who will starve for want of feed while standing in a field of tall grass. But that is another matter entirely.

Instead, it is my hope that a reader astute enough to crack a book with Abraham Van Helsing's name on it will glean some modicum of the truth the old man always sought to bring to light himself. That, and wonder as I do at the astonishing career of a man who by wit or by providence found himself again and again in the path of fantastic forces, and never flinched.

It is to them, the seekers of truth, that I dedicate this volume.

Dr. John Seward
London

May 19, 1935

CHAPTER
1

The following entries have been transcribed from a series of handwritten documents found among the personal effects of Mr. Buckner J. Tyree of Callahan County, Texas, United States of America. Any peculiarities of diction or deliberate omissions have been included in the interest of preserving the original source material. –J.S.
Aug. 13th, 1891.

Picker told me to say nothing about what we done, but I feel like if I don't tell somebody I'll bust. I know he's probably right though, on account of he's got a better head between his ears than I got, so I'm just gonna write down in this book what I swore by the moonlight and my Mama's good name that I wouldn't tell nobody.

Picker and me was rangin' out back of the Morris place, where we could see the light of the big house and the back porch real clear. Cole told us he didn't wanna see us back there no more, on account of the trouble between him and the Norgies that bought the Judson spread after Old Man Judson went toes up. Cole told me one night he might come out and blow holes in us thinkin' we was them Norgies tryin' to steal his cows. But Picker said Cole and his boys was campin' down on Busted Elbow Creek huntin' up the mountain lion that's been at his stock, and anyway it'd be alright so long as we didn't make no trouble.

We wasn't doin' nothin' wrong back there. Maybe we had a jack of Injun whiskey between us, but it gets cold at night and Picker says a man has got to have something to keep the blood movin' up and down his limbs, else they'll ice up and drop off. I been sayin' how it's been real sparse for wolfin'- Picker has too - for the past couple years. You'd think somebody had gone and shot all the god___d wolves and coyotes, just like they done all the d___d buffalo. We needed the work, and Picker said even if Cole caught us on his land and run us off, we'd still be able to hawk any hides or bones we got.

We'd left a couple chaws of jerky sprinkled with arsenic out on the range yesterday to catch some wolves whilst Cole and his boys was out on the north forty lookin' over some cows that got mauled by the lion. Well, me and Picker plain forgot about that pair of hounds Cole had just picked up on his last trip to Bastrop (he done it to keep varmints from settlin' in under his porch), and Picker come by my place and said,

"Hey Buckner, we ought to go and make sure we ain't pizened them dogs."

I wish to the Lord he hadn't.

We was out in the dark feelin' around for the spot on account of we didn't dare use no light for fear of Cole's Mex cook seein' us from the house and maybe takin' the scattergun to us, when right sudden Picker told me to stop movin' and get quiet. I did, on account of Tonks got real good hearing - better than any white man's. At least that's what Picker says.

At first I thought we seen one of Cole's dogs go runnin' across the yard, but Picker told me he'd got a look at them dogs earlier and they wasn't near as big as whatever it was we seen. Well, I got real scared then, 'cause right away I figured it must be that mountain lion that had been at all the cows. I figured it must've doubled back from Busted Elbow Creek to avoid the hunters and come back near the big house where there weren't no men, but lots of calves to pounce on.

Then the back door of the place banged open and we seen them two dogs of Cole's come barkin' and skitterin' off the porch after the whatever it was, on account of they seen it too. I'd been afraid that maybe one of them dogs had been at our pizen jerky and crawled under the porch or back up into the house to die, but now I seen 'em both, and Picker was right, they weren't near as big as the whatever it was we seen. From inside the house I heard that Mex cook start to cussin.'

Them dogs was mad as h__l and they made a bee line right for the lion. We couldn't hardly see nothin' in the dark, but we heard 'em tear into somethin,' and that somethin' let out a noise that weren't nothin' at all like no mountain lion.

Me and Picker stayed there where we was, listenin' to the fight, and I seen Picker had with him that gun he bought from Old Alkali Firebaugh. Lord, I wish he hadn't brung it, but sometimes when we come across a lobo that the pizen ain't done for yet, it takes a bullet. I always told Picker it was a waste, and that we could've just as soon bashed it with a stick of firewood, but Picker always told me to stow it. I think he likes shootin' that gun whenever he gets the chance.

One of Cole's dogs let out a yelp and I seen it go flyin' just like it'd been picked up and throwed. It hit the corner of the house and lay there whinin.' I don't know what happened to the other one, but I guess it died, 'cause the next thing I heard was a lot of cracklin' and wet noises like it was being et. I asked Picker what we ought to do, and I thought I said it quiet enough, but Picker hushed me.

Then the noises stopped, and we could hear the whatever it was we seen, plain as day, sniffin' the air. I don't know if we was down wind of it or up. I didn't feel no wind at all, but all of a sudden the thing growled real low, and come tearin' right towards where we was. I could hear it cuttin' through the grass, and in a minute I seen it - or at least part of it. Big and dark it was, and the hair on its back was all up and it had long sharp ears laid flat against its head.

Then Picker put up his gun and shot at it. I heard it make a noise, but it didn't stop comin.' I don't know if Picker hit it the first three times, but he must've got it the last three, 'cause it went nose down in the dirt and slid to a stop right in front of us.

Me and Picker was right happy, and not just 'cause we was alive, but 'cause we figured Cole'd be pleased as all h____ with us 'cause we kilt the critter that had got his dogs, and probably all the calves and cows that'd been turnin' up missing too. Picker got out his skinnin' knife and said he was gonna take the pelt. He handed the whiskey over to me, and in between swallows I got to wonderin' aloud what we ought to do with the carcass till Cole got back. Then Picker stopped cuttin' and he took out a match and lit it.

To this very minute I can't get it straight in my head. I don't know if it was that Injun corn or all that dark and the blood pumpin' in my ears, but when I looked, Picker had the hide peeled halfway back, and underneath there was a bare naked human man.

The match went out, and I guess I must've had one of my spells, 'cause the next thing I knowed Picker was shakin' me, and that Mex cook was in the light of the back door, holdin' up his britches with one hand and totin' the scattergun in the other, and hollerin.' Picker got me up, and we set to runnin,' whilst the cook yelled after us and let loose with the shotgun over our heads.

When we struck the old road that goes by my place, I was near out of my head for fright, but Picker shook me and made me promise not to tell nobody - not Alkali, not Cole, not nobody, what we seen or done. I don't remember how I got here back in my little shack. I guess Picker must've brung me. I just knowed I had to write it all down before I forgot. It's near daylight now and I'm real tired and drunk. I can hear my birds scratchin' on the roof wantin' to be fed. Maybe it was a dream I had. I got to ask Picker when I see him...

* * *

From the Journal of Professor Abraham Van Helsing (translated from the original Dutch)
5th July.

Thank God I am sane.

Those were the last words I wrote concerning my previous expedition to the Carpathian Mountains. How much has happened since I wrote those words, and in such a short time! Eight whole months have passed. Where to begin?

I will tell of how I came to be diagnosed with lycanthropy.

Following the series of events which took me away from my teaching at the University in Amsterdam to London, and at last to the mountainous region of Wallachia, I deemed it necessary that I should submit myself to the observation and care of my old friend Dr. John Seward in his asylum in Purfleet. The particulars of my stay I will not here recount. If John has learned anything from his old mentor it is the value of copious notation, and thus it would be mundane to relate here what has probably been more thoroughly documented on his phonographic records.

I know now that the specific reasons behind my decision were conceived in certain deeds which I was forced to commit in my pursuit of Count Dracula. In particular, I believe that the seed of my instability was planted by his wives - those three beauteous ladies with whom I dealt so harshly whilst they lay in their ghastly repose. I do not know how much of my current mental state is the product of whatever preternatural bewitchment almost stayed my hand in their execution, and how much is the perfectly logical after-effect of prolonged mental stress and fatigue.

Whichever, not long after the funeral for our heroic Mr. Quincey Morris, I privately confided in John that I had begun to harbor some very unsettling, violent fantasies centering around our beloved Madame Mina Harker.

I was possessed of an unusually keen paranoia concerning her safety. I could not sleep for wont of assurance that she was at all times secure. I was at the Harkers' nearly every day, and I am sorry to say I made quite a nuisance of myself. When at last Jonathan spoke frankly to me about my peculiar habit, I took to visiting the Harker home unannounced by night, watching from the silent shadows of the courtyard until the last lamps in the house were extinguished.

I would find myself passing cemeteries, which were not on my usual route. A ghoulish compulsion began to grow within me, that I should enter the graves within and subject the innocent corpses to the same *maschalimos* treatments I had prescribed for the vampires. I took to carrying my implements with me: my mallet and stakes, vials of blessed water, and garlic cloves. I knew the bodies in those plots were not the creatures that my imagination was telling me they were, and yet I was overwhelmed with a desire to do them violence.

I also had terrible nightmares in which I would pry open the tomb of Miss Lucy Westenra-Holmwood, thinking to find Dracula's favored bride there - the very lovely, dark haired one whose coffin had commanded such a special place in his ossuary. When I flung aside the sarcophagus however, it was always Miss Mina who would leap from the casket, slavering and hungry for my blood. Sometimes these terrors ended with my death. Quite a peculiar thing, for is it not speculated that those who die in dreams die in life? Other times, they ended with hers - and if it was hers, it was always a prolonged, bloody end, and my phantasmic alter ego would perform acts of lustful malice upon her too vile even to recount here.

In a moment of clarity I saw that it would not be long before I was apprehended in the midst of some atrocity that would bring myself and my loved ones much shame. It was with no small relief that I surrendered the care of my body and mind to my friend John.

I have been on extended leave from my teaching for far too long, but I am grateful to the understanding of my colleagues, who have written me with assurances that I can return whenever I am able. It is good to feel needed.

I also take comfort now that I am once again the man that I was, and am pursuing an active role in my emotional convalescence. I feel that my return to these notes, which are evolving into a kind of journal, is somehow a part of it. John tells me that there was a time when I would place this book within a circle of holy water and bury it in sprigs of fresh cut roses, and cower in the corner of my room, not daring to look at it, fearing the entries scrawled within. I have no memory of this, and it seems humorous to me now that I should have been so foolish. I hope that John will share his documentation of my case with his grateful patient one day, if only to amuse an old man.

It was John who diagnosed me with *melancholic lycanthropia*. I was of course already familiar with the condition. It has been in the physician's lexicon since the fifth century, though with the advent of modern medicine and the eradication of humoral theory, the *melancholic* has been mostly done away with, leaving the lycanthropy (the Greek *lykos* –'wolf' and *anthropos* - 'man') alone intact.

In folklore of course, it is the name given to the werewolf—the man or woman who assumes the shape of a wolf, usually by night. The means by which this is achieved are numerous, and include everything from wolf-hide belts and imaginatively composed unguents, to the ubiquitous pact with Satan.

In psychiatric terms, lycanthropy refers to the *belief* of the patient that he or she assumes the form and characteristics of a wolf or other beast. This belief often translates itself into violent and in the extreme, even cannibalistic acts. While it was never in my mind (I do not think) that I should become a beast and eat the flesh of the living (or the dead), I do believe that the acts which I was contemplating were of a potentially bestial nature.

When John first brought his theory to me, I was reminded of the case of the soldier Bertrand, who in 1849 in France began his horrific career by strolling through cemeteries at night just as I had. Bertrand took to digging up and mutilating the bodies of young women and girls. It took a spring gun trap set into a freshly buried coffin to end his diabolical career at last. I did not want my ailment to progress so far as had Bertrand's.

But these things are behind me now. The nightmares have ceased, and once barely controlled instincts have abated.

It is most ironic however, to have written this and now to have to tell that I am on a passenger steamer with only the remains of poor Quincey Morris for company.

But I must explain.

Having borne the body of our dear Mr. Morris back to London after the end of our travails, it was mutually agreed that as our American friend had made no preparations for his sudden and regrettable departure from this earth, we should let Arthur Holmwood also known as Lord Godalming, who was his eldest and closest friend, decide what should be done with him.

"He was a man at home in so many places, and yet...it seems to me that he should want to rest at home, in Texas. He spoke very fondly of his family's ranch there. Yes. Texas, I should think."

This was the proclamation I heard Lord Godalming give prior to my illness, and so far as I knew, it was carried out when I entered John's care.

Yet when I emerged again, Mr. Morris was still in London, reposing in an urn on Lord Godalming's mantle.

During my recuperation much had occurred in the life of Arthur Holmwood that did not allow sufficient time for a voyage to America. There were many decisions to be made regarding his late father's estate. Not only were there a good deal of unforeseen settlements to be arranged with his father's creditors, but there was also the managing of the will and the mediation of rival inheritors who were not at all disposed, in their shameful avarice, to allot to the executor and chief heir time enough to mourn for both a fiancé and a best friend. A miser's patience is as short as his compassion.

With John's encouragement (he seemed to see in the hiatus some therapeutic value), I offered and was then granted the task of bearing the remains and worldly remembrances of Quincey P. Morris home to his native land, which lay in the Callahan County of Texas, United States American.

CHAPTER
2

Dead Man Found at the Q and M, by A.N. Crooker (all articles reproduced with the permission of The Sorefoot Picayune)
August 15th, 1891 edition

Sheriff G.B. Turlough and Deputy Rufus Shetland rode into town yesterday with several men of the Q&M ranch in tow. Among them was Mr. Coleman R. Morris himself, who inherited the Q&M spread from his late father, Captain Quentin Morris, some years back. It seems that the lifeless body of an unidentified Mexican was found in the immediate vicinity of Mr. Morris' house. Sources advise that the deceased was discovered by Mr. Early Searls, foreman at the Q&M, sometime early yesterday morning upon the return of Mr. Morris and his hands from pursuing the mountain lion which has been making a nuisance of itself among most of the local ranches of late. The unidentified Mexican had been shot four times, and is reported to have been found in a state of undress. There is no word as to the fate of the mountain lion, but reportedly it has added two of Mr. Morris' new hounds to its growing roll of victims.

* * *

Early Searls Arrested, by A.N. Crooker (Sorefoot Picayune, August 19th, 1891)

Early Searls, foreman of the Q&M Ranch, checked into Sorefoot Jail today following an altercation in the street with Mr. Ivar Vulmere, attorney at law. The disagreement came about over the unidentified body erroneously reported to have been Mexican, which was discovered not by Searls, who had accompanied Mr. Morris on the hunt, but by Moises 'Pepperbelly' Vargas, the Mexican housekeeper on Morris' property last Monday the 15th. The corpse turned out to be one 'Thorsen,' an employee of Sig Skoll, the gentleman of Nordic descent who assumed the management of the Judson spread following the passing of old B.D. Judson one month ago. Our more oblivious readers will take note that the Q&M outfit has had several boundary disputes in the time since Skoll took over. Lawyer Vulmere, who is on retainer to S. Skoll, identified the body of 'Thorsen' at Undertaker Cashman's parlor this morning, after having come into town to report his disappearance. Mr. Vulmere then proceeded to publicly accuse Mr. Morris of having murdered and robbed Thorsen. Mr. Searls gave a manly and most appropriate answer to the wild slander against the character of his employer, which left the boisterous red haired foreigner sprawling with a broken nose. Mr. Searls surrendered himself to Sheriff Turlough in the manner of a forthright and dutiful citizen, and now sits in his cell awaiting arbitration from Judge Maximillian Krumholtz, who as of yet has not returned from the hearings in Bastrop in the case of Red Bill Beck. Sheriff Turlough has assured this reporter that his confinement of Mr. Searls is in no way related to the baseless charge of murder put forth by Mr. Vulmere. No representative of the Skoll faction was available for comment.

* * *

Telegram from Professor Arminius Vambry, University of Budapest, to Professor Abraham Van Helsing, Adelphi Hotel, Liverpool, Merseyside, England
31 JULY

HAVE FORWARDED THE VOLUME YOU REQUESTED TO NEW YORK CITY IN ANTICIPATION OF YOUR STEAMER'S

ARRIVAL THERE. STOP. SEE MR. PROCHNOW AT THE PUBLIC LIBRARY. STOP. SEND ME AUTHENTIC INDIAN ARTIFACT FROM TEXAS. STOP. REGARDS, ARMINIUS.

* * *

Telegraph from Professor Van Helsing to Professor Vambry
8 AUGUST

MANY THANKS FOR THE BOOK. STOP. WILL ARRIVE IN TEXAS THE 19th AUGUST. STOP. WILL BRING BACK SOMETHING WORTHY OF YOUR KINDNESS. STOP. DEFERENTIALLY, VAN HELSING.

* * *

Recovered from the Journal of Madame Callisto Terovolas (translated from Greek)
21st August

I am at last unpacked and ready for sleep in what is to be my new home...*our* new home. These Texas plains are lonely and too open. There are no trees in sight of the house. The wind blows hard, and the smell of the cattle is noisome. Yet Sigmund assures me that I will grow to love this land. I am sure that I must.

The conclusion of the train journey from St. Louis was ridiculously uncomfortable, and only made bearable by the company of a peculiar old gentleman whom I came to know as Abraham Van Helsing.

My first impression of him as I saw him clamber aboard was that of a doddering old fool, jostling people in the aisles with his arms full of luggage, and pausing at each one to tip his hat and excuse himself in a thick, broken accent. His large American hat seemed to be some effort on his part to assimilate, but when taken in consideration with his other attire looked positively ludicrous. The cut of his suit suggested it had been bought long ago, with the intent that it would last. He wore a great cloak typical of the English gentleman of several years ago, yet by his speech and incessant grinning he was no

Englishman. This habit of constant smiling, considered rude in certain circles, is an eccentricity commonplace among foreigners in any alien land. It seems those without command of the native tongue think that if they show their teeth they will be given the same sort of social pardon reserved for simpletons. Among beasts of course, it has quite the opposite effect.

I was already put out by the prolonged stopover in St. Louis, and was not inclined to spend the remainder of my tedious journey with a leering and stuttering old man beside me. I took the bag of the sleeping passenger across from me and placed it on the seat beside mine, thinking to ward him off. He would not be denied.

I pretended I did not notice him standing over me, until the force of his gaze made it impossible to ignore him further. I looked up, and saw his eyes flutter. They were very blue. Very dark. He tipped his hat and, smiling as always, requested my pardon and gestured to the bag.

I made as if I didn't understand him, and when he repeated himself, I purposefully made my excuses in Greek, thinking that would be the end of it.

To my surprise, he answered fluently in my mother tongue;

"Ah...I ask your pardon again madame, the car is quite full up. May I?"

I suppose the sound of my own language, so long absent in my ears, moved me to take pity on him. I put aside the bag, and he bowed in a courtly manner and settled into the seat.

"The Moerae, they smile upon me for the first time since this trip began," he said in Greek, as he stowed the greater of his baggage. "That I should be able to share the remainder of my trip with a lady whose courtesy is matched only by her charms."

I allowed him a thin smile. I had thus far found manners decidedly lacking in America.

"You will pardon me again, I hope," he said, as he straightened from his labors, one brown paper parcel and a single book still clutched in his lap. "But your accent seems familiar to me. Are you Arcadian?"

I was delighted.

"I am indeed. But *you* do not sound Arcadian..."

"I am Dutch, Madame. But my wife is from Patrai. I am Abraham Van Helsing."

I was thankful that he did not seize my hand and try to slobber on it. I told him my name and asked him his business in Texas.

"A gloomy errand, I am afraid," he said, drumming the parcel in his lap with his fingers lightly as he watched me. "And not the sort of business I should bother you with."

Ironically, I found I wanted to know, and persisted.

"If you insist, Madame. But please stop me if I should offend your sensibilities. You see, I am returning the remains of a close friend to his ancestral lands."

I think he must have seen my eyes fall to the parcel in his lap, because he shifted it to the side of the seat farthest from me. I giggled in spite of myself, and assured him that he need not worry. I had no superstitious fear of his late friend. He grinned in reply, but his eyes were not smiling. They were staring at me with some intensity. I do not know if it was lust I detected there. I have seen *that* sort of look in the eyes of many men since my journey began, and should think that I would recognize it straight off. But there was something else in Abraham's eyes. A kind of...furtive distress. Perhaps sadness.

I let my attention fall to the book in his lap - not out of my own discomfort, but out of respect for whatever lay behind his gaze. The title of the book elicited a chuckle from me before I could restrain it. It was Reverend Sabine Baring-Gould's nefarious *The Book of Werewolves.*

"Pardon me, madame," Abraham said, tucking the book beside his friend's remains, his cheeks reddening almost to match the fading rusty tint of his hair.

I asked him not to apologize, and then, out of curiosity, what he thought about the book and its subject matter.

He proceeded to give a fascinating and knowledgeable critique, speaking rapidly and fondly, as though he were a misfit with but one talent, who had been asked at last to give discourse on his favorite subject. He acknowledged the folkloric value of the work, and explained to me the ways in which social and regional beliefs of the past affected modern psychological perceptions. He was obviously a learned man. When he began to speak of mental aberrations, I interrupted him, asking him pointedly;

"Yes, but do you believe that a human being may become a wolf?"

"Madame," he said. "I do not discount anything I have not disproved myself."

"That is a laudable attitude for a man of science," I said. "I've always thought such men to be rather limited in their perceptions."

"On the contrary. The most important trait of a scientist is a mind open to infinite possibility. Well, but I am no scientist. Not in the proper sense of the word. I am just a schoolteacher."

Our conversation made the rest of the trip seem short. We spoke well into the night, our talk touching on science and faith and finally marriage. I learned that his wife had let slip her reason long ago and was cared for in an asylum in Holland. They had lost their young son to some calamity many years ago and the poor woman had never overcome her grief. I suppose this was the source of the deep sadness which I perceived in him. Perhaps I am being romantic, but I am quite sure that I reminded him of someone - perhaps the wife he spoke of.

I told him at last of my own reason for coming to Texas, and I invited him to visit Sigmund's ranch when he had concluded his errand, and to stay for the wedding celebration if it was within in his power. I do not know for certain why I did this. Whatever the reason, it was a happy coincidence that Sigmund's ranch and the ranch of Abraham's late friend both lay in the vicinity of Sorefoot.

When we arrived at the last stop, Abraham very gallantly carried my meager luggage to the platform before going back for his own.

Sigmund's man, Helgi, was there waiting, as promised in his last letter. He spoke but a few words of English, and I had a difficult time asking him to wait for my newfound friend. At last Abraham (being fluent in Norwegian too) translated my desire to have him ride with us, at least to town. Helgi was hesitant, but acquiesced.

There was some trouble with the horse team. I have never been fond of horses. At last Helgi managed to calm them, and we rode for the better part of the morning, speaking very little. Abraham had grown distant somehow. Perhaps our rapport lasted only as long as our mutual journey.

Helgi stopped the buggy at the edge of the miserable little town and we parted ways, each promising to see the other again before Abraham returned to Amsterdam. Whether or not these were just words I cannot now say.

I spoke not a word with Helgi on the ride to the ranch. As I have said, it is quite a desolate place, in the midst of a great expanse of brown, empty grazing land. I find the lack of trees disconcerting, but Sigmund's letter spoke true. It will be a fine place for children to run. I can see fat cows from my window.

The ranch house is large but not palatial, and decorated with many remembrances of Sigmund's. There is an impressive assemblage of antiquities and Nordic art. One of the effigies I find striking. It is a fanciful woodcut of a bearded fellow holding his hand in the maw of a wolf. I do not know the story behind it. I must remember to ask Sigmund about it when he returns. There is precious little that I do know about the culture into which I am marrying.

My betrothed was not there to welcome me. He left a note saying that there had been some sort of trouble in town with his attorney, which he must see about, and that he would return tomorrow.

In the great foyer Helgi presented me to the other men. I was embarrassed by what happened next. They all prostrated themselves before me and touched their foreheads to the hardwood floor. It was foolish, these huge blond men making such a fuss. But I decided, rather than offend their strange customs by spurning their flattery, to wait for Sigmund and speak to him about it.

So I am left alone with silent Helgi and Sigmund's other men, a dozen or so, I should say (though they are hard to count. With their beards they tend to resemble one another and they are always going in and out.) I have no fear, but the boredom is nearly unbearable. There is an oppressive feeling to this room that I do not like. Perhaps it is only this damnable girdle.

I wonder how Abraham is faring.

* * *

From the Journal of Prof. Van Helsing

21st August

I think that I am not well. John's craft has not saved me from infection of the mind as it once did the infection of the flesh I developed from that Zulu spear in Natal so many years ago. The psychic wound I was given by Dracula's wives I think has been laced with a more cunning poison. I am sure that like a cancer, my *lycanthropia* has returned.

On the train from St. Louis I became acquainted with a young Greek lady called Madame Callisto Terovolas - a charming woman of Arcadian descent traveling by curious chance very near to my own destination of Sorefoot, Texas, to be wed to a Danish cattleman.

At first our conversation was of the most benign sort, but when she took notice of my copy of Baring-Gould , my thoughts began to take once more a sinister turn. The book had been presented to me by the late Madame Blavatsky on a brief trip I had taken to New York City some years ago. I'd had it sent to me on a whim by Arminius. The Bertrand story was related in one of the later chapters, and I had wanted to reconsider it.

Maybe it is the subject matter of the book that has somehow rekindled my delusions, but there was something in this woman which fanned the flames.

Her singular features were of the handsome Mediterranean type; her long neck traced with slight hairs, and the dark eyebrows arched over her deep eyes faded to wisps as they nearly met over the bridge of her sensuous nose in a faint 'v' that lent her whole appearance an imperious air. Her lustrous hair, thick and dark as black wool was not entirely contained by her lady's hat and green silk ribbon. Indeed, there was some element of constraint about her whole person—something which made me feel as if I were looking at a bottled sprite barely contained in a delicate crystal prison.

And there was something else. Her soft eyes, so like a young fawn's, the heavy red lips of her broad mouth, pursed together in that oddly disappointed expression, her voluptuous form; she reminds me so much of *her*. Of Dracula's wife. His favorite. The feeling was so strong that I was short of breath. My mind wandered everywhere as my mouth spoke I knew not what. And in my mind's wanderings, I fear it traveled back to the dark place from which I have strived these many months to depart.

The notion that this woman was that undead creature somehow returned from the final death to which I had delivered her grew and festered in my brain. I began to imagine that all her idle talk was to distract me from the moment when she would lunge at my throat. I think that I endeavored to remain unconcerned, but the idea and the thoughts that naturally accompanied this wildness would not be denied within me. I began to think that I should take some preemptive action against her. In the back of my mind the old bloody images began to take shape again, and in desperation, I realized I was without mallet, stake, or consecrated vial. My only defense against the darkness had become to me as the trappings of madness. Yet I found myself wishing I had not put them away.

As our conversation went on, I grew more and more distracted. First I thought of what weapons I could improvise. The hatpin of a sleeping woman. The walking stick of a gentleman across the aisle. Then I began to believe that if she truly was trying to lull my suspicions, I might be able to do the same. I would be charming, I thought, perhaps even seductive. I would use the very wiles she was turning against me. And then, while she was under my power...I thought of things I am ashamed now to recall.

In the end I fell to silence.

It was all foolishness. The poor woman had her husband's manservant (a hulk of a man who could speak only Norwegian) drive me most of the way to my destination, and all the while I could provide no conversation whatsoever. I struggled with my own inner troubles, and only mumbled my thanks and a promise to see her again, even after she was kind enough to invite me to her impending wedding celebration.

Foolishness. In the walk into town I regained my composure. I found my way first to an eatery, thinking to curb my distracted mind with victuals. My steak arrived very bloody. I had not realized my hunger until I was sopping the red juices from the plate with a hard biscuit.

Now I must set about finding Mr. Coleman Morris, Quincey's younger brother. Lord Godalming told me all that he knew of the man;

his name, and that he was administering the family cattle ranch, somewhere outside the town of Sorefoot, Texas.

I fear I have much to bring beside Mr. Quincey's ashes, Bowie knife, revolver and Winchester rifle (which I have noticed a few gentlemen of dubious intent eyeing since my arrival). For what if Mr. Coleman Morris should ask how his brother died? I have noted in the past that there seems to be a certain willingness to believe in the supernatural prevalent among Americans. Some have said it is the inherent primitiveness of the people, but I believe it has something to do with all the mysterious, unsettled space. Our imaginations are not challenged by an empty room until the lights are dimmed and the corners fill with shadows.

On my walk into town, I noticed two bravos had taken an interest in me and my luggage. I can see them now through the picture window facing the street. They seem to be waiting for me. I have kept Quincey's revolver loaded in the bottom of my bag, having heard much talk of the propensity for western American passenger trains to be waylaid by bandits. I expect I am about to be initiated into the cult of the 'Wild West' as it were. It should prove an exhilarating distraction, and a good prospect for cultural observation.

CHAPTER
3

Excerpt From The Personal Papers Of A.N. Crooker, Esq.
Aug 21

The sun sets at last on August the 21st, and Alvin Nathaniel Crooker bids it good riddance.

I am now laid up at the Morris place with my arm swaddled in bandages like the baby Jesus. Yes, it has been rendered quite hole-y thanks to the infamous Harley Crenshaw's *pistola*. Harley consecrated this reporter's flesh quite nicely when he attempted to intervene in the manhandling of what turned out to be another damned foreign immigrant.

My tribulations began whilst I was chewing the saddle leather that passes for steak over at Gridley's. I was staring out the window mulling over the whole affair between Early Searls and that Norgie lawyer Vulmere, and getting in a bit of lunch before I rode out to Cole Morris' place to talk to him about it. It was the biggest bit of news we'd had in Sorefoot since that mountain lion started in on the cows. The biggest news that is, until yours truly spied Harley and Two-Step Crenshaw sizing up some poor old man just into town by the looks of his bags.

Indeed I do mean the very same Crenshaw brothers who made life so interesting for the employees of the Denison Stage some years back. Harley Crenshaw had a knack for getting mean drunk and blowing holes in things. Though the circuit court never got wind of it, it was generally accepted that one of the last things he'd vandalized with his .44 prior to lighting out with his little brother for Arizona land was a Jewish sheepherder named Levitz. Last I'd heard, the brothers had been snagged holding up the Fort Apache payroll and hauled off to Yuma.

I didn't need my spectacles to recognize that crazy shuffle of Two-Step Crenshaw as he and Harley came out from under the shade of the tonsorial parlor's awning. I had seen him get that shuffle, back when Old Alkali Firebaugh blasted his knee with a Whitney rifle in front of the Sunup Saloon a number of years back.

As I said, it was the old fellow with the bags that got them twitching. I should have spotted him as a foreigner straight off, with that old greatcoat and that John Bull suit. But he had a Texas hat on, and the stock of a handsome Winchester '76 poking out of a fine, tooled scabbard. I took him for a game hunter; probably some easy come swell from back East that got sold on a buffalo hunting holiday and failed to meet his contact at the train station. Joe Furrows had done a good business through the mail for a couple years pulling that very same scheme, never bothering in his glowing letters to tell any of his customers that the buffalo had gone the way of the dodo in this part of Texas years ago.

This old fool didn't seem to take any notice of those two as they came down off the porch of the barbershop. They followed him right down the boulevard, nudging each other the whole way like a couple of scheming truants, each one with a hand shading their pistols. Of course no one was allowed to sport sidearms in Sorefoot anymore; not even this reporter, who has necessarily fended off many a rival of free speech in his years as founding editor and top journalist for the Picayune. Sheriff Turlough and his lackwit deputy were not to be found, and thus it fell upon me to see to it this pitiable rube came to no harm.

The would-be victim came into Gridley's and sat down and ordered a steak, extra rare. Harley and Two-Step leaned against the post outside and shared a stub of a Contestogie between them, apparently deciding in some flash of gutter gallantry to allow the old man a last supper before they robbed him blind (and possibly made worms'-meat of him). As for the old man, he propped his rifle against the empty chair and opened up his bag. He took out a pen and a ledger and set to scribbling. Marking expenses, no doubt.

I watched the Crenshaws through the window for a bit, hoping Turlough might show his stupid face by the time the oblivious mark at the next table finished his raw meat. But good fortune was not with me. The old man ate like it was him that had been in Yuma for the past four years, and was soon gathering up his things and heading for the door, a solid dollar on the table for Gridley's Mexican waitress.

Well, in all my deliberating I had not got to warning him, and I saw that it was too late for talk.

I rose from my own half-eaten repast and caught the door as the old gent was letting it fall shut.

"What say, old timer?" I heard Harley say.

"Hallo," the old man said thickly, around a mouthful of lukewarm steer he was still chewing. He licked his fingertips, apparently ignorant to the danger.

"You new here?" Two-Step leered, one hand resting on the horse pistol in his pocket. The cigar end was tucked into the corner of his mouth and his yellow and black teeth showed like kernels of Indian corn.

"Quite," was the old man's reply. "As a matter of fact, I wonder if you might help me, my friends..."

Had I heard his guttural German intonations correctly, I might not have done what I then did, but being behind him, and with the blood thundering in me, I did not. Fool that I am, I actually stepped between the old fellow and the Crenshaw brothers, and struck a heroic pose.

"Leave the old fellow be, you devils," I said.

"I know you," said Harley, straight off.

I began to sweat and for all my talk, I was way down in my boots. I had written several unfavorable editorials about the Crenshaw clan back when they had made their home in Sorefoot, but I had assumed that, being illiterate, they had never had the opportunity to read them. Either they were not so uneducated as I had thought, or some friend of theirs' had read the paper to them, for Harley next said:

"Yes. I know you. You're that son of a bitch with a pen."

And he took out his pistol as easily as most men will take out a hankie or a pocket knife.

Then I was shot. I deduced this, having seen the smoke burp out of his ugly little gun, and heard the crack in my ears, and moreso, because I felt my arm break just below the elbow, as though I were some fool Philistine that had crept up on Goliath and caught a stray one from the jawbone of the ass.

I fell back swearing against the old man, and he caught me. And I'll be damned if when he dropped his bag to the boards there wasn't a revolver in his hand. In a half a second he was firing under my arm, so close I could feel the heat of the muzzle flash singeing my underarm hairs.

The old man was not Wild Bill Hickok, but with all the shooting he did, one of the bullets did manage to find a home in Harley's nose. He yelped and fell back, spitting blood and septum.

Two-Step had stood quite still during all this, bewildered as a wolf that had seen a rabbit turn and kick. As soon as he saw his brother fall, he forgot to be stupefied and pulled his six gun, the cigar dropping from his lips, an indication that real business was about to be done.

I was sure that our game was played out, as the click of his revolver told me the old man's wheel had run dry of beans. But by then I didn't care much anyways, as my legs gave way and I struck my head on the edge of the porch and lay flat like a good newspaperman at last. As a final indignity, I lay my hand right on Two-Step's discarded cigar, burning myself.

I lay there staring up at the old wasp's nest clinging to the roof over Gridley's porch and thinking what a shame it was the old man was going to get rubbed out, when I heard a yell from across the street followed directly by a couple more shots. When I was through feeling sorry for my arm (and my burnt palm), I sat up and saw Two-Step Crenshaw lying dead in the street with Old Alkali Firebaugh hobbling up, his trusty Whitney rifle (possibly the same one that had given Two-Step his limp) swinging in his hand.

As for that old Dutchman, he was kneeling over me as unconcerned by the bullet show and dead man as Daniel was with the lions.

"My friend, you are alright?" he said to me.

Bad enough to have a damn foreigner pluck my fat from the flames, but then to my intense embarrassment, my only answer was to faint dead away.

When I came to, I was spread out like a plate of steak and eggs on one of Gridley's tables, and the Dutchman was leaning over me in his shirtsleeves, smiling like a fox with a mouthful of hen.

Behind him stood the ever-punctual Sheriff Turlough, his patented confused expression worn low on his fat face. Old Alkali was standing beside him with his big lumpy fist on his hip, grinning from behind his huge, drooping silver mustache.

"Yessir, I'd say that was hands down the fastest patchin' up job I ever did see. Faster'n any American doctor I been subjected to yet, that is."

Old Alkali knew what he was talking about of course. He had been in as many scrapes and taken as many wounds as there were states in the Union. Some said he was only held together by scar, scab, and baling wire. He had one eye, one ear, one leg, and one hand, but he liked to say that he had purposefully gotten rid of one of every pair (except his balls) on his body because he'd found each loss had given his enemies less to shoot at. Despite his questionable past, he is one of the most prominent horse traders in the county, so maybe all these sacrifices on the altar of luck had paid off.

"You better think twice about playin' lawman again, Mr. Crooker," Turlough said to me, as though he was offended we had gotten so much done without his help.

Alkali cackled and said, in his gravelly snarl;

"Yeah! This Dutchman might not be there to save you next time!"

"On the contrary," said the Dutchman. "This man sought only to keep an old tenderfoot from harm. He is much to be commended for his bravery." He touched a hand to his chest. "I am Professor Abraham Van Helsing."

"Alvin Crooker," I muttered, thankful that he didn't insist on shaking hands, as my own was freshly sensitive from grabbing the lit end of Two-Step's cigar.

"A professor, no less!" Alkali laughed.

Alkali stuck out his paw to the Dutchman, while I sat up easy on the table and poked at my swollen arm.

"Aurelius Firebaugh. Friends call me Alkali. Horses are my game. Whereabouts you from, Professor?"

"Amsterdam," he answered, squeezing Alkali's good hand.

"Sounds like a long way..."

"It's in Europe," I said.

"Say, that *is* a long way," Alkali whistled. "Well, Professor, I can respect a surgeon that's as good at makin' holes as he is pluggin' 'em up. Even if he *is* from Amsterdam. Meanin' no offence, but what in hell's name are you doin' in Sorefoot?"

"It is not in hell's name that I come, but in the name of sorrow. I bring ill tidings to Mr. Coleman Morris."

Alkali looked perplexed.

"Ill tidings, you say? Well, I don't know that he'll be wantin' anything like that...Cole's a self-sufficient sort. You some kinda medicine peddler?"

"He means he's got bad news for Cole," I clarified.

"He's had enough bad news, I'd say," said Sheriff Turlough. "Lost a brand new hound and his foreman in as many days."

"You still here, Sheriff?" I asked bitterly.

"I got to take the Professor's statement. He *did* shoot Harley Crenshaw in the nose with a pistol he ain't supposed to have inside city limits."

"If you'd been out on the street, it never would've gone down the way it did."

"*Ja*," said the Professor. "I forget. Is the poor man I shot alive?"

"He'll live, I guess," Turlough said.

"Lucky he won't be able to smell your cooking down in the jailhouse, Sheriff," I muttered. "He'd be likely to try and break out."

"Please, you take me to him, Sheriff," said Van Helsing. "I want to make sure. I should hate to think he might bleed to death for want of proper medical care."

It took some doing to convince the Professor that Doc Ravell would be better off treating Crenshaw's wound. For a man so game under fire, he is a real dutiful sort when it comes to sticking to the letter of the Hippocratic Oath. As for Turlough's need for an official statement, I told him to read about it in the next day's edition. He made a half-hearted attempt to detain Alkali for the killing of Two-Step, but Alkali just laughed it off. Turlough went off looking steamed and ineffectual as always.

So it was that I found myself indebted to a Dutchman (and a proper Dutchman, not a German) - not something I cared to leave alone. I offered, with the help of Alkali, to whom the both of us were indebted, thanks to his timely intervention in the whole affair, to take the Professor to Cole Morris' place. I had been planning a visit anyway, to get a statement for the Picayune on Early's arrest and the troubles with the Skoll outfit. Alkali agreed to cart us over in his buggy. It was on his way.

I didn't inquire further as to the Professor's 'ill tidings,' as I figured it would all play out before my eyes anyway when we got to the ranch. Instead, I conducted an impromptu interview with my intrepid companions, taking notes and wondering how I would find time to set the type for an article on the shooting.

Van Helsing told us he was a Professor at the University of Amsterdam, where he taught biological science. A pretty weighty claim, if there is any truth to it. I still don't comprehend how a doddering old schoolmaster comes to carry a revolver in his book bag; nor do I understand how he handles it, if not expertly, at least with the alacrity of one not unaccustomed to handling firearms (and having them handled back at him). I suspect in my guts that he is on the run from something. It will make for good copy if he is.

When we got to the Morris place, it was nearly dusk. The Mexican cook, Pepperbelly, was sitting on the porch cutting up potatoes. He stood when Alkali drove his buggy up the road, and called into the house.

Cole stepped out to meet us. He had a hound limping at his heels, and the beast looked out of sorts. I wondered if it was one of the ones that had been reported killed by the lion. If it had tangled with that cat, it was lucky. Three other farm dogs had gotten torn wide open for their trouble. This one looked to have traded its left eye for a brand new limp. It hobbled toward us, growling uncertainly till Cole hushed it.

I have never thought of Cole Morris as a pleasant fellow. Surely the charm in his family dwelled in his late mother and his elder brother Quincey, who left for parts unknown in pursuit of a South American girl years ago. Cole is no dandy the way Quincey was. He takes after his daddy, Captain Morris. Quincey always favored silk shirts and fancy clothes, whereas his little brother was content to sport hide *chapaderos* and trail dust.

Captain Quentin Morris came to Texas fresh out of the War Between the States about the same time Alkali did, though they had served on opposing sides. It took awhile for both men to figure out that all they wanted from life was to raise livestock. Alkali had to shoot his way through both sides of the law before it dawned on him to breed horses, and by that time Captain Morris (who was always a sight quicker on the uptake) had already had his fill of fighting Comanches and had left the Army to begin staking out what eventually became the Q&M. And hereabouts, only the Judson - now the Skoll - spread is bigger.

Captain Morris and Alkali were of the same mold, and Cole comes from the run-off of that mold. Even as a boy, he could punch beeves all day long. Every night, if he doesn't sleep the sleep of the bone-tired and the saddle sore, I believe he doesn't feel as though he's had a productive day and will get up two hours earlier the next morning to make up for it. He runs the Q&M like an old hand. His boys say that if a twister were to carry off the ranch house and their boss was left only with a mule and a milk cow he'd still bring a herd to market come winter. Not that Cole would ever allow such a thing to happen.

After Captain Morris died, Cole came to look more and more like his daddy. He's not as handsome as Quincey, nor as soft. Not to say Quincey was soft; it is well known that he is not the sort to have his hair mussed, but that was only because Quincey was prettier and more refined. When you see him, Cole looks like a man made out of braided rawhide. The sun has cracked his skin and jerked his lean arms the way it does all working cattlemen. If you see him with his hat off, everything above his eyebrows is fish-belly white but for his thinning dark hair. He has got the same brassy blue eyes as all his kin, but he doesn't wear them as proud as Quincey - you have got to look under the shadow of his hat, and look hard, to notice them. There is something more honest about Cole too. He speaks his mind when he speaks at all, and he doesn't play the crowd the way Quincey always did. I suspect that's why I always liked Quincey better.

But then, everybody liked Quincey better.

Quincey had been a shoe-in for the run of the Q&M, even though Cole put in more time and had more practical experience. You couldn't help wanting Quincey to get it. He was just that likable. I think when he up and left for Titicaca after that South American woman, he broke the heart of everybody in Sorefoot, not just the local gals. I know for a fact he did break his daddy's. After Quincey left the old Captain's legacy sitting like an Indian treaty, the Captain just sort of lost interest and Cole took over so gradually that no one gave it much thought, until his father passed.

Quincey never even came home for the funeral. I asked Cole about him once, and Cole admitted the last letter he'd got, Quincey was sparking some English gal overseas. There was a sore spot between the brothers, and I don't think it was only the ranch and their daddy.

So it was sure a shock to hear what the old Professor had to say, with his hat in his hand.

"It is with intense sorrow that I inform you, Mr. Morris, of the passing of your dear brother Quincey."

Quincey P. Morris, dead!

But it was Cole's reaction to the news that struck me dumb. He just stood there for all the time it took a frog to fart and then turned his head and spat his chaw on the ground.

"Well," he said. "Y'all come on in the house, I guess we'll put you up. Gettin' late. Think I'll see if Pepperbelly's through carvin' them taters."

When he went back to the house with that sorry looking dog trailing behind, Van Helsing turned to me, a look of grave concern on his face.

"Mr. Crooker, has there been some mistake? Is this not Coleman Morris?"

"It sure is, and there ain't no mistake about it," Alkali answered, low.

"They weren't exactly close the last couple of years, Professor," I explained.

"Ah? Then what will he say when I tell him that I have brought his brother's remains here with me?" And he patted a wrapped up box he had been carrying with his baggage.

I just shook my head.

"I can't even imagine."

CHAPTER
4

I do not understand the sort of man Coleman Morris is. He is not at all like Quincey.

My new friend Alvin had not prepared me in the least for the coldness with which my news was received. I suppose had I shared with him the nature of my visit to begin with, I might have thus saved myself the embarrassment of being caught in the center of a delicate familial situation. But what could I do? Do I not owe Quincey Morris my very life?

I carried my bags into the house, feeling as welcome as the cholera. Mr. Coleman Morris did not even greet me properly, but loudly instructed his Spaniard to show us to our 'bunks' and took his place in the kitchen.

Alkali deferred at this point, and said he would continue on to his residence, which was only a few miles down the road, despite the gathering dusk. He was wise to have done so. I gripped his hand (his left hand—the other is nothing but a wooden cap with a barbed gaff affixed to it), and bid him farewell. He is a most interesting man, and I hope the opportunity will present itself during my stay to hear something of his past adventures, for like a well-worn book with binding creased and jacket torn, I think his story must be quite enthralling.

The Spanish manservant, Pepperbelly, had apparently learned all his manners from our stoic host. He led us up the carved wooden stair to the upper rooms without a word, the potato knife still in his brown hand as if he meant to murder us. I think that he must not speak English, as Alvin began speaking frankly to me as though Pepperbelly were not even present.

"You old fool," said he, "you should've told me about Quincey. I'd've saved you the buggy ride."

"From whence comes this ill feeling between them?" I asked.

"I'll tell you, if you tell me how Quincey got dealt out. If I can borrow a horse from Cole, maybe I can still reset the obituary page before morning. This is real news, old man!"

But I deferred, saying that it was surely not appropriate to relate the manner of Quincey's passing to him in preference to Quincey's own brother.

"In case you ain't noticed, the two of them got along about as well as Custer and Sitting Bull."

"But why? What can drive a wedge between two brothers like so?"

But like a disappointed child, Alvin would say no more. Only;

"Get it from the horse's mouth, Professor."

I sensed that my friend was only playing at his bitterness. His deepest passion is journalism, but I sense that it is of the sensationalist variety. By his intervention in the matter with the would-be robbers in town I know him to be a true soul, else I would not bother with him. And anyway, he is quite correct. It is only right that anything I learn about Quincey's past should come from his brother and not the secondhand suppositions of strangers.

Pepperbelly showed us to our separate rooms, and I wasted little time unpacking my things and changing out of my travel attire. My ablutions, though I thought them to be negligible and in haste, were apparently still too time consuming for Texas.

When I came down to dinner, Alvin was standing in the foyer looking annoyed. Seeing me in my dinner jacket, he wore a face of amusement. When I enquired as to the wellspring of his expression, he only shook his head and led me into the dining room.

The dining room was a spectacular example of rural American ingenuity. Being short of wood, the imported long table was surrounded by chairs constructed entirely from cattle bone, horn, and tanned hide. The décor was gauche, yet did not strike me as inappropriate given the setting. Lord Godalming might have cocked an eyebrow, but I, who have dined with Zulus in their *iqhugwane* in Natal, found it charming. An officer's saber hung on a prominent place on the back stone wall, beneath a painted portrait of an elder gentleman who bore a striking resemblance to Coleman himself. The gentleman in the picture was gallant in a blue uniform of the American Army with two strapping youths standing upright on either side.

I admit that I suffered from a bit of cultural disenfranchisement at the sight of my host. After all, the last dinner I shared with savages was in my younger days and I have since been gentrified by European life. Mister Coleman was already seated at the head of the table, and was halfway finished with his meal, being in the midst of sopping at the drippings of his steak with a torn hunk of bread. Beside him was Pepperbelly, supping loudly from a bowl of red beans. They were both of them in the same dusty denim clothes they had been wearing when I saw them. I was quite overdressed.

Coleman looked up from his ironware at me. His blue eyes (so much like Quincey's) regarded me dispassionately, as did the Spaniard's, who did not give pause in his eating, but stared in open admiration of (or was it disbelief at) my formal attire over the rim of his bowl. Even the mangy, miserable looking hound feebly cracking a soup bone in his jowls stared at me from the corner with his one eye.

"Take a plate, and get it while it's hot," Coleman said through his food.

I did so, dishing out mashed potatoes, gravy, and forking a piece of blackened beef onto my dish. I helped Alvin do the same, and we took our seats across from Coleman and his man.

"Why aren't you eating too?" I asked Alvin under my breath.

"I should be. You were taking so damn long I thought something was the matter with you," he whispered back.

"What happened to your arm, Alvin?" Coleman asked. "Get it caught in the press?"

"Not quite," replied Alvin. "This is a genuine battle wound."

"A battle wound?" Coleman repeated, just the hint of interest in his flat voice.

"Harley Crenshaw..." Alvin began.

"Thought the Crenshaws were both in Yuma," Coleman interrupted.

"Not anymore. Thanks to the Professor here, Harley is now cooling in the Sorefoot jailhouse. And his nose is for once being picked over by chickens instead of his own finger."

Pepperbelly looked up from his dinner.

"His *nose?*"

He spoke English after all.

"That's right, Pepperbelly," Alvin said. "The Professor took it off with a bullet."

Coleman's eyes flitted lightly on me for an instant, then back to Alvin.

"What's Two-Step going to say to that?"

"Not much, I'd wager," Alvin said, smiling as he fumbled one handed with his fork and tried to steady his knife with his wounded appendage.

"Let me, please," I said, moving to help him.

But Alvin waved me off.

"Get out. The day I let a Dutchman nursemaid me is the day I go back to the bottle."

Pepperbelly snickered into his bowl, brushing red juice from his black mustache.

I took it upon myself to finish Alvin's story, and related to them all the fateful encounter with the Crenshaw brothers, and the end that Mr. Two-Step had met at the hand of Alkali.

It seemed to me that Coleman, at least, was impressed.

"Well, now. That *is* something," he admitted. "Funny too."

"How funny, sir, if you will excuse me?" I asked.

"Funny 'cause the last two bullets Two-Step ever took were both from Alkali's gun." He produced a blue and white checkered towel from his lap and swabbed it across his lips, leaving it in a crumpled heap on the table.

"Old Alkali gave Two-Step his shuffle back before they lit out for Arizona. Some say he was the very reason they went."

Alvin concurred.

"Yes indeed. He told them if he ever slapped eyes on them again it'd be on the last day of their lives. Prophetic."

I wanted very much to speak of Quincey, but felt it imprudent considering the presence of Alvin and the Spaniard. I was interested in Mr. Firebaugh.

"Gentlemen, tell me about Mr. Firebaugh. Is he a desperado?"

Alvin smirked.

"Where'd you get that big word, Professor?"

I felt abashed. Indeed, my usage of the word seemed alien even to my own ears. I suppose I was picking up the vernacular I'd read in a particularly lurid Beadle dime novel on the train from New York.

"Old Alkali has been just about everything, I guess," Coleman muttered, sipping at his coffee.

"Yes sir," Alvin said. "The further down the road you get, the tougher they are, and Alkali hangs his hat in the last house."

My eyes passed to the portrait on the back wall.

"Who is the artist?"

Coleman looked at me, knowing well what I meant without having to turn around.

"My mother."

"She has captured your likeness perfectly. But who are the two boys? Your children?"

Coleman smirked.

"That's my father."

"Oh?" I said innocently. "Then the boys are you and...?"

Coleman's eyes flashed. The subtlety with which I had trapped him was neither lost nor appreciated.

Alvin cleared his throat.

Coleman pushed back his chair and stood. Like a wary lion he had smelled my snare and backed away.

"Guess I'll be headin' up. Pepperbelly'll get your plates."

Pepperbelly grunted.

"Cole," Alvin said. "I wonder if you might lend me one of your horses. I'll need to get to town early tomorrow if I'm to reset the print."

"You can ride with me. I've got to see the judge about Early."

"Ah yes, Early. I'd like to talk to you about that, in fact."

"In the morning," Coleman said curtly. Without another word he left the room.

I pushed back my chair and stood to follow.

"You don't know when it's better to sit down and eat, do you, Professor?" said Alvin.

I left him at the table with Pepperbelly and the dog cracking bones.

I found Coleman ascending the stair, and called up to him. He paused on the steps, but did not turn.

"I've a lot to do tomorrow, and little time to do it in, mister," his voice was low. "So..."

"I would like to know why you have not asked me how your brother died," I replied, thinking straightforwardness my only venture in this instance. "I have traveled a very long way."

Coleman half turned on the stair and looked down at me. "Look here. I appreciate the trouble you took, and as a friend of my brother's I won't turn you out. But now's just not the time. I've got a man in jail, I've got a killer wildcat takin' its pick of my beef, I've got troubles with..."

"When, then?" I asked promptly.

Coleman stared, his face barely perceptible to my eyes in the gloom of the lamplight. He opened his mouth to speak.

"When?" I said again, and not as a query. I suppose the travails of my journey combined with my aggravated state of mind and the violence of the afternoon had shaved my patience short. He looked on me for a moment, and in the space between us I could feel the slightest reduction in distance.

"I'll let you know," he said.

He turned and went up the stair. I heard his door shut.

I did not return to dinner, nor did I bid Alvin goodnight. Instead I went to the room I had been assigned.

I have not yet gotten used to the smell of the cattle outside, but I find the gentle lowing of their deep voices soothing in the dark stillness. It eases my mind of the disturbing thoughts I have had of late. As I write this, my lamp grows dim and I think now sleep may finally come.

I had planned to remain only a few days in Texas, thinking I might continue on, possibly to visit a colleague of mine in San Francisco. But Mr. Coleman's (I cannot yet bring myself to write of him as Mr. Morris, for did I not always refer to his brother as such?) words lead me to believe I may be here a bit longer. For Quincey's sake I will remain as long as is required of me.

I will tell Mr. Coleman the truth about Quincey's passing, and thus it is my hope, reinstate in him by the singing of his deeds some modicum of the love and respect for his brother which he has somehow lost.

But again it occurs to me...how to tell it, when at last the time for telling comes? How to make a man believe that the brother he remembers with ill favor died in heroic combat with the darkest enemy of all of humanity?

* * *

From The Personal Papers Of A.N. Crooker
Aug 22

Early Searls and Sheriff Turlough are dead.

I have seen a great deal of things in my years of reporting, but even now as I write these words I abhors to think on the way we found them, and worse, it makes me thirsty...and not for water. But I'm getting ahead of myself.

I didn't wake up nearly as early as I had promised myself. I suppose my wound and the events of the day had me sleeping the sleep of stones a half second before my head hit the pillow.

I had a nightmare in which the action in front of Gridley's was repeated, but in this version, the Professor, instead of a revolver, pulled a lady's shoe (of all things) from his bag. In this version Alkali did not appear and we were both gunned down by the Crenshaws.

As though to capitalize on the strangeness of the dream, it was Professor Van Helsing that shook me awake this morning, looking as spry as a goat in the springtime. He had his bag in hand, and I heard him talking about breakfast and 'Mr. Coleman's' saddling up, and the printing press.

That got me up and out of my grave. I had forgot all about the damned daily edition, and how I had to reset the type for the Crenshaw story and Quincey's obituary, and somehow pry open Cole's jaw about the Skolls on the trip back to town.

Well, that proved as easy as parting an Irishman with the last jug of his departed mother's home brewed whiskey. Cole didn't have much good to say about Sig Skoll and his Norgies, but he didn't have near enough bad to say about them either. All he said on the matter was;

"Them Norgies ain't played me fair nor false yet."

"But how can you say that? Skoll's lawyer called you a thief and a bushwhacker...well, he may as well have," I said, as he shot me a glance.

"The man can't be blamed for what his lawyer says or what a reporter writes. Unless he said it to 'em first." He looked at me, and his look was plain as dry bread. "As for me, I got no way of knowin' if that law dog got the idea from Skoll or not. All I know is somebody shot a man on my land and skinned out."

This got the Professor's attention, and he asked who had been killed. I advised him to read yesterday's paper, but somehow through the night the old man had grown on Cole, 'cause he said;

"You'll be hard pressed to find yesterday's edition, Professor. I hear tell Sheriff Turlough hoards every stack he can find. Half go to patching the holes in his boots."

"And the other half?" I demanded.

Cole smiled.

"The other half I see go with him into the shithouse. I can't say what happens to 'em then. He never carries 'em back out."

The old Dutchman got a good bellyache out of that one. I think from the way he let loose he must've been holdin' back a good long time.

"Oh my friends!" he said in between snorts. "Old King Laugh, I have thought him long gone from his throne, but you have called him back, and it is good to see his face again!"

He went on for a quite awhile in this light, and in a way that got me wanting to check his teaching credentials if I could. *King Laugh?*

To bring him back to some kind of state we could relate to, I told him about the troubles that had started when old man Judson passed on and the county auctioned off his land. Sig Skoll and his bunch of blonde behemoths had appeared right out of nowhere and put up a helluva sum of money to beat down all the bidders. They'd got that land, sure. Not soon after, trouble had started between them and their nearest neighbor, being Cole's outfit.

The Norgies had been caught once or twice on the wrong side of Busted Elbow Creek, bringing cattle to water that was by law Cole's own. Cole didn't see much of a problem with sharing the water seeing as how it nearly runs between their property, but his cowboys started complaining to him that the blondes were turning up on their side with less and less cattle each time. Nobody can quite figure out what they were up to, cause it seems none of them can speak a word of American. This has rubbed a lot of the Q&M boys wrong, and Early Searls has had to break up a lot of fights between them and the Norgies. More and more of them keep showing up among the Morris cattle.

Speculation as to just what the Skoll bunch is up to on Morris land has run the gamut from rustling to sexual deviance. The Q&M boys started a rumor that the big blondes were always being found among the cows (and sometimes on foot, no less) because they had not seen females so much like the ones they'd left back home since they'd got off the boat in New York City.

Add to all that the fact that the high speaking redheaded Lawyer Vulmere (the only one among those Norgies that can talk a lick of King's English, it seems) has been seen rooting around in the county land records office in Albany, and then drop a handful of cartridges into the mix, and you've got a pretty good recipe for a range war.

To my relief the Professor listened to all this quietly and didn't bring up King Laugh or the murdered man again. He did, however, ask several questions about the location of the Skoll spread, and then, whether or not Sig Skoll was married.

"Why, Professor?" I asked. "You got a daughter you wanna marry off?"

"No," he muttered. "Never mind. It is nothing."

You didn't need field glasses to see something was the matter when we got to Sorefoot. There were a whole lot people in the streets for so early in the morning. In my head I actually thought they were crowded around my office wondering where their papers were.

It turned out they were across the street at the jailhouse. When we rode up, that ghoul of an undertaker, Cashman, was standing on the porch of the jail with his long bony arm around Deputy Shetland. It looked like some sort of picture of death consoling a departing soul, with Cashman's pasty face passing easily for the grim reaper's, and Shetland's expression being just the sort you'd expect to see on a man faced with his own mortality. Shetland looked scared. His eyes were wide, and he was talking low to Cashman. His fleshy lips were quivering and his hand was trembling in the Irish way I knew too well, needing a bottle to weight it down.

Doc Ravell was there too, standing in the doorway of the jailhouse with his hands in his pockets, looking in.

"Whatever is the matter here?" asked Van Helsing, as though we would know.

Cole didn't answer, and I just shrugged. Whatever it was, it was news.

We reined in at the paper office and then ambled across the street to see just what was the matter. I led the way, smelling gossip and wanting bad to ink up my palms with whatever was going on.

It's a silly sort of thing, now that I think about it, being so damned anxious about the news when Sorefoot is small enough for word of mouth to pass it on faster than some two-penny copy of cheap, smudged paper. It's not as though I do it for posterity. Like Cole mentioned, people find all sorts of uses for my paper after I'm through pressing it. Nobody outside of Sorefoot gets a look at it, if they ever cared to in the first place.

Well, I pushed my way through the crowd like I was going to take charge of whatever the situation was. I demanded of Shetland and Cashman to know just what was going on. Where was Sheriff Turlough? Had Crenshaw escaped or something?

Shetland shook his head, and his lips were wet.

"I...I...don't know."

Well, I pushed past Doc Ravell and went right inside, hollering for Turlough. I don't remember just what I said. Something about the right of the people's free press, the usual noise I spout when I want attention. But that noise took one look at what my eyes saw and curled up at the back of my throat and cowered, begging for me to shut my slack jaw and hide the sight.

The thing that keeps coming back to me is the blood. How much of it there was. How it was everywhere. On everything. Dripping, like from a leaky pump. Dripping from where? I don't even know. All I remember was hearing the sound, and seeing it. Dripping in the center of the stone floor, making little concentric circles like a bull's eye being endlessly repeated. Hypnotic.

"Watch it, you fool!" Ravell snarled behind me.

I'd stepped in it. When I'd seen what it was I was stepping in, I'd jumped back, back on the shore of a lake of blood. Then I saw the bodies. Or rather, just bits of them. More than I'd ever wanted to see. More than I hope I will ever see of such a thing again.

The smell hit me harder than Harley Crenshaw's bullet ever could. It was like a punch between my eyes from a necrotic fist that exploded wet and heavy across my whole face, drenching me in its reek. I swam out of the room, clawed for daylight and fresh air, desperate to be out of that slaughterhouse. And when the fresh air hit me, I popped the remains of yesterday's steak dinner at Ravell's feet.

Ever the humanitarian, he shoved me aside with disgust.

I found myself grabbing the lapels of Van Helsing's coat, wiping the bile from my lips with the back of my good hand and staring up at him.

But he was looking past me – and his eyes! Lord, his eyes! They were cold as a whore's heart. That funny little Dutchman with the broken accent and the spectacles was gone, and I could see for certain what I'd missed from my vantage point yesterday, what Harley Crenshaw had seen head on when the Professor had blasted him in the nose. I don't know what it was, but it was as different as what I'd pegged him to be as night was from day. This man had shed blood in his day.

He reached into his vest pocket and took out something that sparkled when the morning light hit it. It was a little cross. He kissed it once, then passed it over his face and chest like a Catholic, never taking his eyes from the doorway.

He muttered something in his own language.

"Well that's a fine thing!" Ravell said, mopping at his shoes with a handkerchief. "A fine thing!"

I looked at him, and when I could summon my voice, I asked him what had happened.

"What's it look like?" Ravell said testily. He'd been a field surgeon in the War, and I guess he'd seen so much gore that it only annoyed him now. "Crenshaw's busted out. He killed Turlough, and Early too."

Behind me, a boot scraped on the walk. I didn't need to turn around to know it was Cole. He and Early had been friends since they were both kids.

"What're you tellin' me?" he hissed.

* * *

From Dr. Riley Ravell's Diary:
August the 22nd

Cole Morris, Deputy Shetland, and Alvin Crooker (who vomited nicely over my shoes, cuss him) rounded up a posse to head out after Harley Crenshaw, so I expect soon his brother Two-Step will have company in the dirt. Good business for Bill Cashman. Three corpses, soon to be four, in almost as many days. He won't have much trouble planting them; what was left of Early Searls could be ladled into his grave.

Of course I had to wade into that mess and declare them both dead, just to make it official. Not that I couldn't have done that from the door. Haven't seen such a slaughter since that little stone canyon near Gettysburg. Devil's something or other, I think it was called. I remember how the balls would come in there and just bounce around; grind the boys to meat, and blast their eardrums if they survived. Blood all over the rocks.

Jailhouse was just as bad. If it were up to me, I would've let Cashman do his job straight off, but that uppity Dutch Professor had other plans. He is the same one that shot Harley Crenshaw in the nose in front of Gridley's yesterday. Van Halsing. I had to clean up that mess too. Somewhere that crazy killer is running around with my stitches in him. I should've let him bleed to death. Maybe Early and Turlough would still be alive. Funny to think that they're not.

I didn't want to argue with the old Dutchman, even though he looked about as dangerous as a bottle of sarsaparilla. I guess the really mean ones never look the part. This one thought he was Allan Pinkerton, though.

He insisted we go in and have a look at the place, and do an autopsy, of all things.

"What in hell for?" I said. "We know who killed 'em, do we gotta know how?"

"I think, sir," he said, all proper like, "that in this case we do. For what sort of man is it that can murder two able men and effect his escape from an iron cage all without alerting anyone?"

'Harley Crenshaw, I guess,' is what I wanted to say, but I just mumbled and went and got my bag.

When I came back Van Halsing had his coat off and his sleeves rolled up.

Poor Turlough was face down on his desk with his throat cut, and the blood had pooled and run all down the front of the desk onto the floor. But it was Early got it worse. He was gutted and mangled with a knife so bad you could hardly recognize him. It was as though a wild Comanche had been at him.

I had been thinking about what the Dutchman said about not alerting anybody.

When I came back he was standing in Crenshaw's empty cell. It was the only place that looked the same as it had yesterday when I'd sewn up Harley's nose.

I told him how it wasn't hard to see how Harley had killed them without anybody hearing. The walls in the jail are necessarily pretty thick, and besides the Picayune office, there are no other buildings situated here on the edge of town. The only person who would've had a chance of hearing anything was Alvin, and he wasn't in last night.

"But how could Mr. Crenshaw have gotten out of his cell to do this much damage?" the Dutchman said.

"Well his brother sure didn't come and get him," I said.

"Ah but you see, my good man, someone must have."

"The Crenshaws haven't got any friends in Sorefoot, or anywhere else. Look. However Harley got out, he cut Turlough's throat and carved up Early."

"Why?"

"Early must've tried to stop him."

"Then he must have been out of his cell also."

"Aw, Turlough probably didn't lock Early's cell. He knew Early wasn't a criminal."

"Yes, but look at the manner in which Early died, as compared to the Sheriff. Surely even you must see the difference."

I wasn't sure how to take that, but I just shrugged and said what I'd been thinking – that for whatever reason, Early had gotten the worst of it.

"Precisely! The hand which killed Early was driven by a most malicious, wrathful will. That which slew the Sheriff, merely...efficient."

"So what? You think somebody sprung Harley? I'm telling you, he's got no friends in these parts. Bill Cashman was the only man at his brother's funeral, and he was only there 'cause he's paid to be."

Van Halsing just paced around, tapping his teeth.

"And yet..." was all he would say.

We got Turlough's body down on the floor, and laid it beside what was left of Early Searls. It was stuffy in the jailhouse, as we had the door and the shutters closed for decency's sake. We got out clothespins to keep out the smell, and then, like a couple of kids, knelt down on the floor and opened up our bags.

I must admit, this Professor had a good deal of fine instruments in his kit. Nicer than any I had seen even back in school. I asked him if he was really a professor.

"I have taught university for seventeen years."

"What kind of schooling have you got?" I asked.

Well, that old Dutchman rattled off such a row of letters, I knew he had to be a fraud. A man would have to be in school from the time he was four years old to have gotten so many degrees and doctorates. Yet he held his instruments like he knew what they were for.

As he set to work clearing Early's clothes from his wounds, and I, Turlough's from his, he asked me what my own credentials were.

To humor him, I admitted they weren't nearly as impressive. I told him I was only a country doctor.

"But you are not a Texas man?"

"No, I'm from Maryland, originally."

He nodded to himself, then a little later looked over and asked me if I had found anything. By the dimensions of the gash in the Sheriff's neck, and considering he had been sitting at his desk, so the cut had come from behind, it looked like a left handed cut. That made sense, as Harley was known to be a left hander. I told the Professor.

"Look at the angle of the cut. Are you certain it was made from the back?"

I probed the jagged rip in Turlough's throat some more. It was true that on closer inspection it looked more like it had come from the front. At that angle, it also looked like it could have been a right handed cut, crosswise, like a backhand. I asked how that could be, seeing as the Sheriff was seated with his back to the cell.

"But if there was another man, would he not have come in by the only door, the front? And wouldn't the Sheriff have been the first obstacle to remove? Look. What sort of weapon would you say?"

I looked. Something sharp, but not a razor. The wound was too big. Plus, it had scored the vertebrae. Nearly knocked his head off. I suggested a Bowie knife.

"Ah...the weapon of choice for Americans, is it not? Such a knife could have mutilated Mr. Searls. But where is it?"

I knew Turlough carried a knife like that on his hip, but when I checked, it was still there in the scabbard. His pistol was gone, though. I bet that pistol has been naked about as many times as my old Auntie Delia. Turlough was known to have a certain dread of guns, having blown his own little toe off once. I heard he kept the wheel entirely empty for safety. Crenshaw better have checked the loads before he took it, or he'll be cussing himself later. I made the suggestion that Crenshaw had stowed a knife in his boot, or hung it between his shoulder blades where it could be missed, as I have heard some cardsharps do.

"Or his accomplice provided him with it, after killing Sheriff Turlough."

I shook my head. He couldn't convince me somebody had sprung Harley Crenshaw from jail. Who would do that? Turlough probably just left the cell unlocked when he gave Harley his supper. Early was asleep in his bunk, and Crenshaw snuck out with his own contraband knife and got the Sheriff. Then he went back and finished Early.

"But why would the Sheriff open the cell?" Van Helsing asked. "Would he not slide the food through the space in the bottom of the prison door? Is that not its purpose?"

I looked. I'd never noticed the serving slot in the cell before. The Professor was starting to irk me. As the only physician for miles around, I'm not used to being wrong.

"Look here," he said then, wiping the blood from Early's face. "See? Beside these terrible cuts, his head is smashed. His cheeks are crushed. There are bruises all about him. He has been badly beaten."

I remarked only that he was indeed an eyesore.

"So!"

He clapped his hands together, and I'll admit I was startled. He was staring at me strangely all of a sudden.

"Lunch," he said.

I was flabbergasted. He said he was hungry. That we ought to go to Gridley's and come back after lunch.

He ordered his steak extra rare.

CHAPTER
5

From Buckner Tyree's Papers
Aug 22, 1891

Lord, I am scared.

I ain't seen Picker for days. I don't know how many...let me check. Four days. Picker ain't never been gone so long, not even when he's gone to visit his uncle. I think they have got him. I think Picker has got kilt. I wish I had his gun.

Lord, I am so scared I don't even leave my shack. Especially not at night. At night they move around. I hear them.

Last night was the worst. They were all out last night.

It was like a fandango. I seen it from the rim, down in the arroyo. They lit a fire, and I seen 'em pretty good. They had a couple of cows and somethin' else, but I don't know what. I think maybe it might could have been Picker. If it was Picker, than Picker is sure dead.

They played music, and they danced, and there were drums. They weren't like Tonk drums. They weren't like no Injun drums I ever heard, in fact. But they was dancin' to it like Injuns.

And I seen 'em good, and I know now what they are, 'cause Picker told me once about 'em. About the people that come before the Tonks, and about how...

Here the narrative is interrupted, but picks up again later in a steadier hand. There is evidence that Mr. Tyree's state of mind was such that his train of thought was very easily distracted, and when his stream of consciousness was diverted, he did not often return to his original course easily. The 'they' hereafter referred to, is evidently not the same party which he had been describing earlier. - JS

They just killed a man right out in front of my shack. I didn't know the one that got kilt. He was an ugly son of a b----- with only half a nose. But I knew most of the others. Cole Morris was there, and Mr. Gridley, and the newspaperman, the one Picker don't like. A man with a blond beard shot the ugly man. I seen it.

I heard the man they shot (this was before they shot him) running outside, and I blowed out my light and sat in the corner and watched through the boards. He was tired, like he'd been running a good long while. I seen right off he had a pistol, so I didn't make no noise. I figured he might be a murderer come a'killin.'

Then I heard the horses, and I knew right away he really was a murderer and that a posse must be comin' for him. He seen my shack then, and come a'runnin' at it, fixin' to bust in and hide, I guess. As soon as I seen what he meant to do, I got up and pushed hard on my front door, like with all my weight so when he come against it, the man that was about to be killed bounced back and fell. I think he lost his gun, 'cause he went down to his hands and knees, and the way he was cussing was fearsome to hear. But it was too late.

The horses come up the road, and they was spreadin' out, and I could hear the men's voices. Then the man with the blond beard on the big yellow horse come towards my shack, and when he seen the man he was about to shoot, he come over. He already had his rifle out.

Then something happened that I don't get. If I was that ugly man that was about to be shot, I would've got up and run, but when he seen the blond man come up, he just got to his feet real slow, and then he done somethin' real dumb.

He waved at the blond man like they were friends.

Well, then the blond man, instead of waving back, he put up his rifle and shot that ugly man right through the head. The ugly man bucked up against my door again when he fell, and since I wasn't tryin' to keep the door shut no more, he knocked it right open and fell half in my shack.

The blond man seen me, and when I seen him, I waved, just like the ugly man done. And then, for just a minute, I got the idea the blond man was gonna shoot me down too. Maybe he didn't like bein' waved at.

But then Cole and the others rode up, and they seen the dead man, and they seen me, and they seen the blond man pointing his rifle at me. And Cole told the blond man who I was, and not to worry 'cause I was harmless. He said hey to me then, and asked me if I was doin' alright. I just said sure I was, even though I felt like there was somethin' I needed to tell him, or somethin' I had to ask. I didn't say nothin' about it though, because something told me I had sworn not to say nothin' about it. I think I swore to Picker...

Picker! I shoulda asked him if he's seen Picker... It is dark now. I don't wanna go out. I think there's something out there. That mountain lion. I can hear it howling down in the arroyo, just like that one night...

Dear Lord I am scared.

* * *

From the Journal of Prof. Abraham Van Helsing
23rd August

My fears are doubled and I do doubt my own senses. How I wish John were here to confirm or to disprove the theory that is forming in my brain. I am not sure if it springs from the empirical evidence I have discovered or from the dementia that I have struggled against these past months.

The sight of that jail rendered a slaughterhouse almost struck me inert. I tried to plunge into clinical work, thinking orderly thoughts to keep the random perversities from re-entering my consciousness, but I should have known better. Old fool! When a man seeks to abstain from alcohol he does not do so by submersing himself in a tub of spirits. If he does, then he must trust his will so implicitly that he believes he will emerge a teetotaler and a hater of libations and not succumb to drunken gluttony. Once I believe I commanded such a will. I do not think I do any longer.

I am no master detective, but I suppose the time I once spent with my colleague Hamish and his famous friend have impressed upon me a great deal of respect for the deductive sciences. I gathered my evidence from the torn body of Mr. Coleman's foreman Early Searls, so badly disfigured as to be hardly recognizable as human. I dare not share what I believe with anyone, not even Dr. Ravell, who I think already suspects that I am unhinged. If I do, I fear I shall forthwith be committed in anonymity to some American institution from which I shall never emerge. That, or I shall find myself subject to whatever barbarities these Texans visit upon their deranged. If it is anything like the treatment they reserve for their criminals, I should think it cruel indeed. The body of Crenshaw is to be displayed in his coffin in front of the funerary parlor where children can gather to stare at it!

No, I dare not even write of it. Not yet. I pale to think that Alvin should go snooping among my papers. They would see print as fast as he could manage it.

We are to return to the ranch after the funeral. Alvin is working hard printing his paper while I smoke my pipe on the front stoop of his office, going in to assist him when he calls. I spent the night on a cot in the back. There are two broad Spanish matrons with pail and mop, laughing and talking in their quick tongue across the street. They have been hired to clean the blood from the sheriff's office. Even the women of this country are hard.

I am told by a glowing Alvin that Mr. Skoll, whom I have decided is the rancher to whom my friend Mdme. Terovolas is betrothed, is the one who killed the fugitive Crenshaw. Though his popularity has surged, and will only increase if Alvin prints half of the good will he suddenly feels towards the man, he did not remain long in town to share in the vigilantes' triumph. Surely he is anxious to return to his new bride.

But I must not think of her.

In my idle time I read through the archived editions of the Sorefoot Picayune, and learned a great deal in regards to both the Skoll situation and the strained relationship that must have existed between Quincey and Coleman. It seems clear as day to me now what the source of ill will between the brothers must be. I thank the unabashedly candid method of Alvin's reporting for making it obvious even to an outsider.

Quincey seems to have been the favorite son of Sorefoot. He is regaled as a living hero in a great many articles, as is his father. Coleman is hardly mentioned anywhere. Even his ascension to master of the ranch is only a footnote in the obituary of his father. Yet his father seems to have surrendered administration to Coleman a full year before he died, around the same time that Quincey departed for South America, to pursue a South American woman he met on a business trip to Austin. The editorial describing the event actually closes wishing him luck! But did his departure not break the heart of his father, who had been until then grooming him as his heir apparent? What then, did it do to Coleman?

That Quincey should have been so self-centered is disappointing to learn. But I think that I now understand Coleman a little better.

That is, if Alvin's reporting is to be trusted. I have found it to be inconsistent at times...initially referring to the dead man on Coleman's property as being Mexican, stating that both his hounds were killed when we have seen living proof they were not. His archives are filled with retracted statements and amended reports.

* * *

Fugitive Murderer Shot, by A.N. Crooker (reproduced from the Sorefoot Picayune, August 23rd, 1891)

Harley Crenshaw, the notorious bandit and murderer of Sorefoot's beloved Sheriff G.B. Turlough and respected Q&M foreman Early Searls, was gunned down by a member of Deputy Rufus Shetland's posse last night on the old northwest road just south of Misstep Canyon.

Credited with the deed, and deserving of this reporter's sincere apology for many past insults directed against him and his employees in this very paper, as well as the gratitude of our entire community for the justice he has meted out, is Mr. Sigmund Skoll Esq., proprietor of the former Judson ranch.

The posse of citizens, organized primarily by Deputy Shetland and Mr. Coleman Morris of the Q&M, set out yesterday afternoon. This reporter here must make humble mention of his own presence among the stalwart riders only to assure his faithful readers of the veracity of this account. Other members of the posse included Joseph Gridley, proprietor of Gridley's Eatery, and one Professor Abe Van Helsing, late of Amsterdam.

Despite some initial confusion over conflicting trails, the endeavor was soon brought in hand by the timely arrival of Mr. Skoll, who along with one of his men, met the posse on his way into town to pick up supplies. Upon learning of the vile deed perpetrated by our quarry, Mr. Skoll, in a well-spoken and righteous mode, declared his intent to join the punitive force and see that justice was duly served.

With decisiveness worthy of Solomon, Mr. Skoll soon regained the fugitive's trail, and by nightfall led the group to within a few minutes' ride of Misstep Canyon.

It was mutually decided that we hunters should spread out so as to better the chances of ensnaring the cowardly manslayer. Near seven o' clock, Mr. Skoll spotted Harley Crenshaw attempting to force his way into the shack of Buckner Tyree, a resident hermit who keeps a shack near the rim of the Misstep.

It is reported that Crenshaw turned on Mr. Skoll like the cornered coyote that he was, and fired upon him without any word of warning other than a curse as the shot from the weapon he had pilfered from his victim flew wide—perhaps aided in some preternatural manner by the ghostly hand of his poor victim, our lamented Sheriff.

If it was so, that vengeful spirit may well find his eternal rest now, for without further hesitation Mr. Skoll took up his rifle and blew the craven villain straight to the abyss of eternal torment prepared for him and his ilk.

The body of the murderer was borne back as a prize antelope, and may now be seen on display in front of Undertaker William Cashman's Embalmery and Funeral Parlor, where it is to remain for the next two days prior to being interred beside its closest relative, Jack 'Two-Step' Cashman, lately gunned down in the act of robbery by Aurelius Firebaugh. Let it be a lesson of the most direct sort to any who would enter Sorefoot fostering malice and villainous intent in their assassin's breast.

In closing, this reporter, at the risk of sounding idolatrous, would like to give special praise to the man responsible for ending the reign of terror of one of the worst killers and malefactors ever to plague this county. Moreso, I would draw attention to the sterling character that Mr. Skoll has displayed. He has taken his place unbidden on the side of law and order, even though it meant standing elbow to elbow with his rival and those who have in the past most reprehensibly and undeservedly maligned his reputation. There are many besides myself who if they but look into their hearts, will realize that if they consider themselves of any honor at all, they should upon setting this article aside, proceed forthwith to Mr. Skoll and bid him and his countrymen welcome with the firm hand of friendship and the admittance of any past wrongs and the full abolition of all supposed grievances. If they do not, then shame on them.

Funeral services for Sheriff Turlough and Mr. Searls will be held at two o'clock today at the aforementioned Cashman's Embalmery and Funeral Parlor. The inauguration of Rufus Shetland as Sorefoot's new sheriff is expected to follow soon after.

CHAPTER
6

Professor Van Helsing
23rd, August (Later)

The funeral of Mr. Searls and Sheriff Turlough is ended. Deputy Shetland is now Sheriff Shetland. The somberness of the ceremony was alleviated somewhat by the attendance of Mr. Skoll.

His is a commanding presence. He is quite tall, with broad shoulders and a severe Nordic face. Like the ideal of his race, he has shining blue eyes and hair like threaded gold. His ample beard with its long sweeping mustache completes the image of an earthbound Thor clad in the mundane trappings of civilization. Though he wore a stylish suit for the occasion, he seemed to me more suited to skins and horned helm. His man Helgi, who met Mdme. Terovolas and I at the train platform, was with him, as silent as ever, yet his bride did not appear.

The gathered mourners were much diverted from their grief by the appearance of the rarely seen Norwegians, all except Mr. Coleman, whose gaze remained riveted to the plain wood coffin of his friend. His regret at the loss of his foreman was plainly inscribed upon his face. I wondered if perhaps he was doubly burdened by the knowledge of the death of his brother, or if the rift between them was too great. Maybe in his grief over Early Searls, he has found the expression of that which his pride will not allow him to give in the name of his estranged brother.

The memorial service was conducted by Judge Krumholtz, who had arrived too late to dispense justice in the civilized manner and could now only preside over the leavings of vigilantism like a cur late to his master's table. He is an elderly, frightening looking gentleman, and throughout his vague and meandering eulogy his shaking hand kept going to his breast pocket, where a squarish bulge showed that he kept the cure for his ailment close to his heart.

When it had ended, we retired to the eatery for a brief lunch before we would return to the ranch. We found Mr. Firebaugh there at a table, eating ham (which he speared on his hook and nibbled) and reading the day's edition of the Picayune, which was so fresh that the ink had rubbed off on his fingers.

"Well," he said. "I can't say I'm too put out over that jackass Turlough, but I am sorry about Early. He was a good old boy. I guess I'm sorry for Crenshaw even. Sorry it wasn't me that took him out. Feel sorta like I owed the son of a bitch. Sorry I wasn't there. Cole."

Mr. Coleman dismissed his apology and we joined him and ordered 'vittles.'

Alvin fell immediately to praising Mr. Skoll for appearing at the funeral, and seemed to be trying to get Coleman to agree with him. Coleman would have none of it. He drank his coffee when it came, and brooded.

Alvin went on about Skoll. It amuses me that a man who so professes his dislike of foreigners can take so strongly to one of that very stock, apparently because he exhibited skill with a firearm. I wonder if the bitterness that seems to curl Alvin's lips whenever he refers to me as a Dutchman would have been quenched had I killed Harley Crenshaw with my first shot, instead of merely clipping his nose. I wonder too if this is a Texan trait or something peculiar to his system of values.

I do not mean to downplay Mr. Skoll's attributes. He has done all the things for which Alvin has vociferously praised him of late. Yet I cannot help but wonder. When I spoke to Mdme. Terovolas on the train from St. Louis, I detected no flutter of excitement in her tone when she spoke (and only in passing mention) of her fiancé. But, perhaps I am only an envious old man.

"I wish your golden boy'd try his hand at flushin' out that goddamned mountain lion," said Alkali. "He ripped up a coyote on my property pretty good. I worry about my horses."

"I'll be out there to help you just as soon as I can get the ranch straightened out," Mr. Coleman said. "I expect I'll have to choose a new foreman."

The talk turned to livestock and the merits and failures of Coleman's various ranch hands and a foaling mare of Alkali's who was due to give birth soon. My own thoughts lingered on Early Searls, now buried, and the foreign object I had taken from his body, which now rests in a fold of paper in my coat pocket.

On the ride back to the ranch alone with Mr. Coleman, I gave a great deal of thought to Mdme. Terovolas and her husband. Too much, really. Partly to relieve myself of the burden of my thoughts, I spoke to Mr. Coleman.

"Your foreman, he was a good friend?" I asked him, though I knew well the answer.

"He was," said Mr. Coleman. "We grew up together. His pa was my daddy's cook. Beef made an orphan of him when the chuck wagon rolled over his pa during a stampede. I wouldn't say daddy adopted him, but he was a brother to me anyway."

"And did Quincey feel the same towards him?"

Mr. Coleman did not answer at first, but then said;

"Quincey never had time for that sorta thing. Time to drink, time to go gallavantin' all over hell's half acre, time to dally with women, but no time for that sorta thing."

By 'that sorta thing,' I wondered if he also meant brotherhood.

Later at the ranch, I remarked off-handedly about the condition of the one-eyed hound, who looked as mournful as ever when it greeted our return. I asked whatever had happened to the poor animal.

"He had a tussle with that damn wildcat," Coleman said. "It killed the other one I had. I found this one huddled up under the porch same day Early found the Norgie lying out back. Damn thing's no good as a watchdog anymore. Scared of his own shadow. Useless. That's what Pepperbelly's been calling him. It fits."

I asked about the dead man found on his property.

"Other than the fact he was naked and full of bulletholes, there's not much to tell."

"And it was never discovered, who did this thing?" I asked him.

"I guess most people figure it was the Crenshaws. They might've been in the area at the time."

"But why would the Crenshaws steal his clothes?" I asked.

"Why would the Crenshaws do anything they did?" He shrugged.

Why indeed.

After dinner, I gathered together Quincey's personal effects. His rifle, the Bowie knife that had rested in the breast of Dracula, a gold watch, revolver, and the parcel containing his ashes. I still didn't think it prudent to speak of how he had died, but I presented Mr. Coleman with these things half hoping that he would ask.

There was a plaque bearing Quincey's name on the stock of the rifle, and faded etchings mentioning a shooting contest with the year 1883. Coleman's eyes passed with disinterest over this, the pistol, and the knife. He paused briefly when I handed him the parcel. He seemed to weigh it with his hands, and I half expected him to fix me with a wary look and demand to know if Quincey was 'all there.'

But when his gaze fell upon the watch, he set aside Quincey with little fanfare and scooped it into his hands eagerly, turning it over with a look of disbelief.

"I thought this was lost," he explained, catching my eyes and looking abashed at his display. "It was Daddy's. He carried it through the War."

He opened it, and inside, to my heartache, was a picture of the departed Miss Lucy Westenra.

"Who's this?" he asked. "Quincey's sweetheart?"

"No," I admitted. "Though he did love her."

"Somebody else's wife, then?" Coleman remarked astutely.

"Yes." Lord Godalming's, I wanted to say. For all of a day, before she was visited by the vampire in her bed and then...but I did not want to dwell on what we had done to her after that.

"That's like Quincey, alright," Coleman went on, not noticing my distraction. "Never let a little thing like a wedding band stand between him and what he wanted."

"You are wrong in this instance," I said, feeling a twinge of irritation. Although he may well have run from his responsibilities, he was no Lothario. I would not sit by and hear him so named. "Quincey loved this woman, yes. But her husband was his dearest friend, and he did not dishonor himself or her."

"That's a switch." He snapped the watch shut and tucked it into his shirt pocket.

"Many things happened in the time between when he left this place and when I came to know him," I said. "Perhaps he was not the same man. By what you say, he was a rogue – shiftless and reprehensible. And yet the Quincey I knew was a gentleman of grace and infallible loyalty. He was as true a soul to his friends as any I have ever encountered."

"Never said he wasn't loyal to his friends," Coleman said. "It's his family he walked out on. Right when he was needed the most. Quincey always took the good of the world and left the rest for the rest of us. He was a fella liked to live it high on the hog. A lot of folks around here loved him for that. But the view of the man's different when you're the hog."

A thought occurred to me, then.

"Perhaps," I ventured, "he did not think he *was* needed. Perhaps he believed that you were more deserving of your father's estate than he was. You do seem to have gotten along fine without him..." I stopped myself, and saw him staring at me intently.

"But, it is only a theory," I said awkwardly.

Coleman shook his head, blinking as though to rid himself of some spell. He made an excuse about having to rise early to inspect his cattle. Then he went upstairs to bed.

The candle in my room is sputtering now, and the sky outside my window is turning blue. I have not slept, for fear of what awaits me behind my eyelids. I have turned again to Baring-Gould , in spite of my apprehension.

I thought of Mr. Coleman's simple statement as to the motive behind Harley Crenshaw's murders. 'Why would they do anything?' Mr. Coleman said. In that, does he mean to say that there is no reason for murder?

Baring-Gould writes of the seven accounts that drive a wolf to devour a man or a child. The first is Hunger; that is, necessity. The second is Savageness.

'Because they are savage,' he writes. *'And that is proper.'*

The third, Age. Either they have young needing to be fed (for when the wolves have young, they are more savage than when they have not), or else they are old and feeble, and can no longer pursue the stag, and thus prey upon men and children, who are easier to catch and mash with their brittle teeth.

The fourth account is Experience. When a wolf tastes human flesh, it will settle for no other. The fifth is ignorance born of Madness, says the Reverend.

'A mad dog will bite its master, not recognizing him – and what is a wolf but a wild, mad dog that knows nothing of sanity and tameness?'

With the sixth comes the influence of the Devil, who it is said transforms himself into the shape of the wolf and makes himself a scourge of man. And the seventh?

The seventh is the ordinance of God, who sends the wolves as punishment on the sinful and the infidel.

1. *Esuriem* - Hunger.
2. *Rabiem* - Savageness.
3. *Senectutem* - Old Age.
4. *Experientiam* - Experience.
5. *Insanieum* - Madness.
6. *Diabolum* - The Devil.
7. *Deum* - God.

I wonder how true these accounts ring when applied to man. Which account is to blame for my own murderous impulses, and Crenshaw's...or whomever perpetrated the murders of Sheriff Turlough and Early Searls? It is very late. Or rather early. I will think no more on these things.

CHAPTER 7

Letter from Mr. Ivar Vulmere to Mr. Coleman Morris, dated August 24th, 1891.

Mr. C. Morris,

It is with cordiality that you are invited to attend a reception at the ranch of Mr. Sigmund S. Skoll, Callahan County, Texas, this Saturday, 26th of August, to celebrate the occasion of his matrimony to Madame Callisto Terovolas. Please extend the welcome of Mr. Skoll towards those of your men who would be of a mind to accompany you.

With Deference,
I. Vulmere
R.S.V.P.

* * *

Skoll to Celebrate Nuptials – by A.N. Crooker (Sorefoot Picayune, August 24th, 1891 Edition)

Local rancher and hero Sigmund Skoll has married.

Sources advise that the new Mrs. Skoll arrived in Dension from St. Louis four days ago and proceeded unannounced to the Skoll Ranch. The ceremony was held in private on their property on the 21st. Details on who the officiator was, are unknown at this time. This reporter had the opportunity to interview Mr. Skoll on the occasion of his latest foray into Sorefoot for supplies (his last was interrupted yesterday by the pursuit of a certain notorious murderer whose name is not worth mentioning here), and he spoke about his new bride, his career thus far, and the trials and tribulations of being the only Nordic landowner of note in this county.

Skoll is of old Norse stock. His family has long been in the import shipping business overseas. When asked what decided him on trying his hand at Texas cattle, he replied that he had been keen to see the American West after having sat in at a Wild West show while on a trip with his father to London as a boy. He learned of the auctioning of the Judson spread after having spent a great deal of time observing the market from Austin, where he has lived for the past year, awaiting just such a chance to put both feet into a stock raising venture.

The gentlemen who work for Mr. Skoll are all of Scandinavian origin, and not exclusively Norwegian as has been erroneously assumed by most of the community. Many of them are the children of the same men who worked for years for his father's company, the Stavanger Shipping Corporation. The Scandinavians are a very familial group, and thus, says Skoll, their working relationship is both affable and productive, being that even the least among them sees himself as working towards the betterment of the collective and thus the improvement of his own standing as well.

But, he wishes to assure the readers of this paper and his neighbors, he is not running any sort of crackpot utopian cult. If they seem secretive, he believes it is the barrier of language which walls them in and he assures that if there have been confrontations in the past, they have almost always stemmed from these Babellian misunderstandings.

The strained relations between his men and his neighbors is a condition which Mr. Skoll hopes to change this Saturday with a fandango at his ranch, to which all citizens of Sorefoot and the folks of the surrounding ranches and farms are invited to attend.

Of Mr. Skoll's new bride, the fresh-faced groom spoke with passionate eloquence and love-born regard. He describes her as a Greek woman of surpassing beauty and grace, whom he met and courted during his initial tour of the American continent, she being the daughter of an olive oil merchant. He says she is an educated woman of culture and refinement, whose wit is the match of any man's. She is also of the most industrious sort, and besides purging the main house of dust and grime (all the product of his own masculine disregard for domestic chores, he freely admits), she has approached him with the idea of teaching his men how to speak English. Now if only Mrs. Skoll would hold classes for some of the less articulate of this community!

The celebration is scheduled to begin at twelve noon this Saturday the 26th, rain or shine. The editor of this paper wholeheartedly encourages our loyal readership to attend and judge for themselves the inborn cordiality of Mr. Skoll as this writer has come to know it.

* * *

From the Journal of Professor Van Helsing
24th August

Today I was awakened not by the shining sun, but by Pepperbelly, who told me in broken English there was *un hombre alto,* 'a tall man,' at the door asking for either Mr. Coleman or myself. Coleman had arisen before dawn and rode out with his employees ostensibly to survey the lands and round up stock. Really he has set about the task of finding among his men a new foreman to replace his friend Mr. Searls.

I rose quickly and came downstairs. There was an immense man waiting in the foyer, whom I knew by his fair hair and grim countenance could only be one of the Scandinavians in the employ of Mr. Skoll. The tall man introduced himself tersely in a thick accent as Hrolf, and thrust a pair of sealed envelopes into my hands. One was addressed to Mr. Coleman, and the other to myself.

It was an invitation to the Skoll ranch this Saturday. Apparently a party is to be held commemorating the wedding of Skoll to Mdme. Terovolas. The invitation was written in the broad masculine hand of Ivar Vulmere, the attorney whose off-color comment and subsequent broken nose placed Early Searls in the last jail cell he would ever inhabit. Beneath, in a small feminine hand, I found this inscription in Greek:

Do say you will attend. I should like to have someone to talk to—C.

I blushed as I read this, for I had no doubt it was written personally by Mdme. Terovolas. Had she written this independently, or had Vulmere seen? The man Hrolf stood before me, eyes dull and expressionless like a great ox waiting to bear back my reply. I procured a stub of a pencil and a sheet of paper from Mr. Coleman's writing desk and scrawled a reply saying that I would be present at the party. I hesitated, then added that although Mr. Coleman was unable to reply as of yet, I was certain he would accompany me. I folded the note and handed it to the giant, nonchalantly slipping the invitation into my shirt pocket.

Hrolf seemed to take neither notice nor care. He bobbed his chin and was out the door and rumbling down the road in a surrey without further pause.

Like a boy, I have read and reread the letter with its personal note. What a fool I am! I am wondering what I should wear already. Perhaps a trip to town is warranted. I have asked Pepperbelly if he will take me, and he has agreed, providing I lend him drinking money. I intend to be back before nightfall, hopefully in time to meet with Mr. Coleman and discuss the matter of the party with him.

* * *

Aurelius Firebaugh's Journal, August 24th

Horses were spooky last night. Think that damned lion has found his way over. Found tracks over by the creek, north of where Cole said he and Early looked. Damn thing has found its way up to my place. Probably down in Misstep. Tracks funny. Big. Not like a cat's. Claws are on the outside. Pads...all wrong. Might ride over to Buckner's and see what's what, if he has heard or seen anything. Haven't seen him or that Picker around.

Came back from the creek, found invitation to Skoll's fandango. That'll be the day. Colt is coming. Maybe today or tonight - will have to sit with that mare and see. Head to Buckner's tomorrow or Saturday.

* * *

From the Pen of Alvin Crooker
24th Aug

Van Helsing's acting strange.

Saw him at the dry goods store fishing for a clean white shirt of all things. It seems he was personally invited to Skoll's on Saturday, though the two of them have never met, so far as I know. Come to find out there is more to the Professor than it seems.

I bought the man breakfast at Gridley's and wrung out of him that he met the new Mrs. Skoll on the train from St. Louis and apparently hit it off fairly well.

But I said:

"How could you have met her on the train? Skoll told me she arrived four days ago, and you only got here three days ago."

Van Helsing only shrugged and offered, "Perhaps the excitement of the past few days has made him muddled. A man does not often go from the town pariah to its most respected citizen in so short a time."

But can a man get the date of his own wedding wrong before the first year is up?

Van Helsing had the gall to chide me on the editorials I'd been writing about Mr. Skoll. Do they really read so worshipful? Shetland and Doc Ravell both took me to town on it as well on separate occasions. I just think that after all the man has done for this town in ridding it of that murdering son of a bitch Crenshaw, we could all stand to blow a little smoke up his ass.

Partially to change the subject, I asked the Professor how things were progressing with Coleman, and if he had told him all that had happened to Quincey yet. I have had to hold off on his obituary until I can learn the right date and circumstances.

"No," he said, around his red steak, "but I shall not leave Sorefoot until I have."

Thinking I could weasel the news out of him, I remarked that Quincey must have made quite an end to impress upon him such a sense of loyalty.

But that slick old badger just smiled at me faintly and said;

"Your obituary will have to wait, my friend. But I promise you, it will be a worthy story indeed, if you have courage enough to print it."

All through breakfast he kept putting his hand in his coat pocket...

* * *

From the Journal of Professor Van Helsing
24th August (Later)

Never again will I allow Pepperbelly to so take advantage of me. After my meal with Alvin, the Spaniard was nowhere to be found. I at last discovered him at the edge of town where he was passed out in a house of ill repute, fleeced of the sum I lent him for drink. I had to bodily carry the man back to the wagon and drive back to the ranch myself. He is most intemperate, and I had to stop the journey home twice to allow for his sickness.

Of course when we reached the ranch, Mr. Coleman had already retired early. I do not know if he saw his invitation or not. It is gone from the bureau. Some of his men were still awake and speaking in front of the row of quarters (called the 'bunkhouse') to the side of the main house, where they sleep. I decided to visit with them.

The 'top hand,' or, the most able bodied man, is a handsome young fellow called Ranny Brogan, not more than nineteen years old. He has a pleasant manner, and there is a competent ease about him which the other cattlemen seem to respect. Some of the older men knew who I was by word of mouth, and had known Quincey. They tried to encourage me to speak of his end, but again I demurred.

I asked them if they had heard about the party being given by Mr. Skoll on Saturday. I had brought the daily edition of the Picyaune, and showed them the article Alvin had written about it.

Several of them were noticeably agitated, and I pressed them to learn the source of their ill feeling towards Skoll and his men. They repeated what I had heard from Alvin, that there had been a good many altercations over their constant trespasses and other minor violations of range etiquette. There is a general distrust of the 'Norgies' by the Texans.

Ranny at least was reasonable, and suggested that perhaps in inviting everyone to meet his bride, Skoll was in effect promoting better relations. To support him, I mentioned Skoll's own theory that a good deal of their troubles stemmed from their inability to communicate. With Ranny's help, I managed to convince some of the men to attend, if Coleman would allow it.

I like this young man immensely.

I retire early tonight, exhausted from my travails with Pepperbelly. I will not even pick up Baring-Gould . I will see Mdme. Terovolas again soon. I wonder if she is happy in her new home.

It will be good to see her.

Will it be good to see her?

Still the mystery of the object I recovered from Early Searl's chest cavity haunts me. Several times I have checked my coat pocket today to assure myself of its reality. When my fingers close on it, I am more afraid then if it had been all some phantasm in my mind.

* * *

Letter to S. Skoll from Coleman Morris, dated August 25th
Skoll,
I accept your invitation, and will bring along some of my men. -C.
Morris

CHAPTER
8

From the Pen of Alvin Crooker
26th Aug

Well, the chips were certainly stacked against poor Mr. Skoll. Not only did the weather prove a miserable deterrent to his proposed fandango, some of his guests that did show up made utter jackasses of themselves. Of course I'm speaking of Cole and his boys, but Van Helsing too. What has gotten into that old man?

Temperamental Mother Nature and her fickle sister Lady Luck whipped up a frogchoker of a storm, which lasted the whole day. This kept a good deal of people from attending, but I wasn't one of them, even though the weather had put a deep-down ache in my arm. Van Helsing somehow badgered Cole into making the trek along with some of his cowboys, including Ranny Brogan, whom I expect Cole will make foreman when he's tried him out on the idea a little. Doc Ravell and Cashman and their wives showed, as did that whey-bellied misfit Rufus Shetland, who drove Judge Krumholtz and his wife in their buggy.

I was the first to arrive. The rain was coming down steady, but I missed the worst of it. The old Judson place has a quiet look to it. The big house is as close to a castle as you can get on the Texas plains. Two stories, and sturdy as a fort with a real stone foundation and chimney. I think all the rock in the county must have gone into that house. The old storm cellar can be seen behind the place; it looks as though Skoll has fixed it up some. No trees as far as the eye can see, but plenty of old stumps left by Judson and his sons. The cattle were roaming around as though they owned the place. You would've thought they'd been rounded up, it being the season. The horses in the corral were big. They're not any kind of Texas horse I'd ever seen. It was like they'd been specially built for the men who rode them. I spied a couple of crows shuffling around under the eaves. There was probably a nest in there somewhere.

I wouldn't say I'm any sort of judge of decor, but the queer assortment of foofaraw Skoll has in his house is a sight to see. He has the whole place decked out in Viking junk, of all things. There are bright round shields, horned helmets, paintings, and the odd woodcarving. Quite a collection.

Mrs. Skoll was still upstairs getting painted up when I showed, and one of Skoll's men, a blonde Goliath that has got to be well over six and a half feet and solid as a roll of double eagles, got me a big glass of gold beer (which I had to lay aside when I had the chance, though it was supremely tempting). This tall one's name I forget exactly (something like Rolf or Holf), but Skoll told me around the place they all called him Walker, on account of there wasn't a horse they had big enough to carry him (which I found hard to believe having seen the size of the horses out in the corral). As he handed it to me, he made a kind of half-sign of the cross over it, and mumbled something in his own language.

Skoll is a charming fellow once he gets to know you, and he can talk English enough for you to understand it without having to sift through his accent.

Seeing an odd expression on my face after the tall fellow's benediction over my beer, he chuckled and said to me;

"Walker was raised in the country. It's an old folk blessing. 'Odin bring inspiration to this drink.'"

"Who's Odin?" I asked.

"A god," he said. Then he smiled. "Of wisdom."

"Well now that's a rare thing...a god that approves of libations," I mused. "Wise indeed, if you ask me."

"Alcohol excites the senses, and moves the mind in new directions. Even Christ drank wine at Canaan, Mr. Crooker."

"Hm. Leave it up to the Christians to misinterpret."

"They usually do, don't they?" Skoll said, and laughed.

I smiled back.

He was pointing out a weathered looking rowing oar hanging on a wall and telling me a family legend about how it had come from an actual Viking ship some ancestor of his had captained, when Shetland arrived with the Judge and his wife.

Shetland had gotten the buggy stuck in the ditch right by the turnoff to the ranch, and they'd all gotten soaked as Injuns in a whiskey barrel unhitching the horse and running for the house. Mrs. Krumholtz was nigh on hysterical, and the Judge himself kept giving Rufus a look like Pharaohs must've given Moses after all the damned frogs. I knew it wouldn't be long before old Krum discovered that home brewed beer and took to it like a calf to the teat.

I was left on my own for a while as Skoll made arrangements for the Judge (he was already asking if there was anything to drink in the place, so he could 'get warm') and his wife and Shetland to get some dry clothes, so I wandered about the big house, peering at the ugly faces on the figurines and wood carvings. There were weapons on one of the walls - iron headed spears, old green bladed swords, that kind of thing, but no sign anywhere of a gun. I finally found a case situated in a corner. The few shotguns inside were hard to see through the dust. I guess Mrs. Skoll has an aversion to guns.

Others started to arrive, and Skoll greeted each one like they were the guest of honor. He forgot about me, so I chewed the rag with Shetland, who had hustled up an oversized coat and shirt, but had kept his muddy trousers as though in penance for having ditched the Judge's buggy. Rufus has always been just about as interesting as a bowl of headcheese, though, and I was glad when Van Helsing showed up with Cole and four of his boys.

When the round of introductions was made, I saw that if Cole had been strong-armed into coming, he was putting on a rare grin for the boys at least. He thanked Skoll for the invitation.

"Ah," said Skoll, "and thank *you* for accepting. Welcome, to you and your men. I should like to speak to you Mr. Morris."

"Oh? What about?" muttered Cole, as though the two of them had never had anything to do with one another (and who knows? Maybe in Cole's way of thinking, they hadn't—not directly, anyway).

"Business matters," said Skoll. "We have much to discuss. But later."

I figured straight off that there was a ceasefire in the works.

Van Helsing introduced himself to Skoll, but the old man's eyes were roving about the room. Whether he was taking in the artifacts as I had, or keeping an eye out for Mrs. Skoll, I couldn't tell.

Then Skoll said something to the Dutchman that could've passed for German in my ears. I figured it must be his native tongue (or else Van Helsing's). The Professor replied in kind, and they went on for a little while. The rest of us all just sort of stood around until Van Helsing seemed to notice us, and said;

"Your command of Dutch is admirable, sir. But I think we are alienating the others."

Skoll laughed.

"You must forgive us. My wife told me you gave her much pleasure in speaking to her in Greek. I only wished to return the favor. And now, please allow me to introduce you to my men."

There were a passel of tall fellows in starched shirts and coats hanging around that none of us had taken much notice of, and Skoll called them over. They were his ranch hands and cook, a little more than a dozen in all, and every one of them as big as a bull ox. I was relieved as a turkey on the last Friday in November when the Q&M boys shook hands. There was some hesitation when a little later, the lawyer walked up.

This was Vulmere, the man Early had dusted his knuckles on and gone to the calaboose for. He is a redhead and not particularly likable. The swelling in his mashed nose has gone down a bit, but it stares at you like a great yellow potato, and has left him with two dark purple rings under his angry eyes. He speaks good English, but with his snout packed full of cotton, comes off sounding nasal and irritating.

He shook hands with Cole first, and expressed (I think) his condolences. Cole took it in stride, but I saw the hackles rise on the Q&M boys, and I wished they'd refused their beers.

Then Skoll turned and glanced up the stair, as though he had heard something, or it was a cue. A minute later Mrs. Skoll appeared on the landing.

To say that she is a beautiful creature would be an understatement. I don't think a prettier woman has ever set foot in this county. Out here a man gets used to the sort of raw skinned female with tough hands and body that are fashioned by the hard plains, wind and sun. Texas weather and Texas life will carve a woman just like it will sweep the rocks on the Llano and comb the grass in tangled waves. If you don't want that, then you've got to go elsewhere, or pay for it, and the ones you have to pay for are somehow never as good as the ones you don't. That's not to say Texas women aren't good looking. I've known a great deal that were and still are, though they are all spoken for, like plots of land with their own water.

She's like something woven out of that black silk that gets stretched across the sky at night. They left two stars in her eyes when they made her, and filled her corners out with that stuff that twists a man's insides into triple knots. Her skin is buttermilk and crushed strawberries, and she breezes along like one of those naked angels you sometimes see on the wall behind bars, lounging on a fancy pillow, or a cloud.

In the time it took her to come down those stairs, I think everybody's respect for Sig Skoll doubled. She was dressed in a fine tailored dress the hue of an April thunderhead, with handsome gray gloves to match.

I expected her to hold out her hand like some queen, but instead she went right to Van Helsing and kissed his cheek, smiling in a way that made you want to shoot the old Dutchman a few times. She said something in a language unlike the Dutch that Skoll and the Professor had used, and Van Helsing answered right back, smiling. The old fellow speaks more languages than the Apostles.

Skoll kissed her cheek and introduced her to the rest of us.

"My wife, Callisto."

"Hello," she said. She could have said 'damn all your eyes' and it would've sounded just as sweet.

Every man there stumbled over their fellows to introduce themselves, including myself. All but Cole and Van Helsing. When she was hit with all of us talking at once, she giggled, and the sound was like a silver bell ringing.

Skoll made introductions one at a time (he let Cole present his boys himself), and when it was my turn, I took her hand and kissed it, thinking it was what she was used to. She gave me a polite smile for my trouble. I found that her glove was not material, but a kind of fur, slightly coarse. When I came away, there was a bit of it tickling my lips. I tried not to make a show of it, but the sensation was intolerable, and I found myself brushing at my lips with a knuckle.

I excused myself, embarrassed.

"I'm sorry. It's your gloves, Mrs. Skoll. The...fur." I licked my lips, blowing slightly. This sent some of it up my left blowhole, and in a minute I was snuffling.

Beside her, Skoll smirked   .

"They're antiques, Mr. Crooker," she answered, swapping an amused glance with her husband. "A gift from my husband's family."

"Mink?" I asked, wishing I had a pocket handkerchief and eyeing one of the cowboy's bandannas with envy.

"Ah no...," Skoll said. "Cat."

Everyone had a good long chuckle at that one.

It turns out I am as allergic to cat skin gloves as I am to cats.

Judge Krumholtz was showing no sign of slowing down, though his wife Ettie was whispering to him that he ought to. He put on a dignified air for Mrs. Skoll when the lady introduced herself, but the second she was gone to greet Doc Ravell and his wife Sarah, he was signaling Walker for another glass.

I found myself standing next to Van Helsing, who was pretending to look at a big woodcarving on one wall, while his eyes kept going to Mrs. Skoll across the room.

I decided to have some fun with him.

"You're old enough to be her grandpappy, Professor," I whispered in his ear.

He sipped his glass of beer while he thought of a reply and his eyes flashed on me.

"I don't know of what you are speaking," he said thickly.

"Sure," I said. "She's quite a sight, though."

"Your article yesterday," Van Helsing said, staring down at his beer glass and changing the subject quick as you please.

"Which one?"

"The one with your interview of Mr. Skoll."

"Like it?"

"It had a few errors."

I was getting plumb tired of him pointing out 'errors.'

"Besides the discrepancy in dates? I thought we had that worked out."

"What means 'Babellian?'" said Van Helsing.

"Of or pertaining to the Tower Of Babel," I replied. "A journalist is permitted certain flourishments of the language now and then, Professor."

"Flourishments?"

"You teach science, right? Not English."

Van Helsing raised his eyebrows.

"Words interest me. Especially their regional evolution. And spellings."

I shook my head.

"I won't be blamed for any spelling errors. It's the typesetter's fault."

The old man smiled.

"I see. And who, please, is your typesetter?"

I just swirled my beer a bit, and watched the bubbles a little longingly.

There was a sudden smell of lilacs in bloom. I looked into the two most bewitching eyes any man has ever looked into. I'd previously wondered before why Skoll had sent all the way to Greece for a wife when he could've just picked up any big blonde Danish gal he wanted off his back porch. I didn't wonder anymore.

"You're not drinking, Mr. Crook?" Mrs. Skoll asked.

Standing there with the lilacs in bloom, I would've almost been Mr. Crook for her. Almost.

"Crooker, ma'am."

"Forgive me," she said. I would have forgiven her the crucifixion. "The beer is not to your liking? Our man Hrolf brews it himself."

I was very tempted to take a drink, just to have a taste of what a man like Hrolf might call beer, but I excused myself, and said I didn't drink.

"Oh, I see," she said. Then she tactfully glanced at the woodcarving we'd been standing in front of. "You have found my favorite piece."

"Tyr and Fenris, is it not?" Van Helsing commented.

She seemed delighted.

"Yes, that is what I was told...is there nothing you haven't studied, Abraham?"

Abraham! My name is Alvin, I wanted to say.

"I read a good deal of the old sagas for a discourse I did on Northern European folklore," Van Helsing said.

I looked at the carving for the first time. A dwarfish, ill-proportioned looking character with bug eyes and a beard had his hand jammed in the mouth of some nasty looking man-sized critter with rows of sharp teeth and a chain linked around its neck.

"Biting the hand that feeds him?" I wondered aloud.

"He is not feeding him intentionally."

This came from Skoll, who walked up and put his hands on his wife's shoulders.

"No," agreed Van Helsing.

"So which one's Tear and which one's Fen...fen..." I struggled to remember the pronunciation.

"Fenris," said Skoll. He pointed to that nasty looking creature. "That one. Son of Loki the god of mischief, and Angrboda, the giantess."

"Does he have his father's looks, or his mother's?" I quipped.

No one smiled except Van Helsing, and him only faintly.

"When Fenris was born, he was taken by Odin, the chief of the gods, to Asgard. Odin hoped to befriend the wolf," said Van Helsing. "But Fenris grew."

I peered at the carving.

"That's a *wolf?*" I remarked.

"He became so large the gods grew uneasy," said Van Helsing.

"Ain't hard to see why," I said. "What in blazes were they feedin' him?"

Van Helsing went on;

"They decided it best to bind the wolf lest he turn on them. They forged two magic chains to fix about his neck, but he broke each one."

Skoll smiled and took up the story.

"And then the master smiths of the dwarves created Gleipnir. A rope as fine and thin as silk, made from the spittle of birds, the footsteps of cats, the whispers of fish, and the anguish of bears—woven with the hair of a dwarf maiden's beard and threaded with the roots of a mountain."

I grinned and opened my mouth to speak, but Van Helsing cut me off;

"Gleipnir would not break, but only grow stronger the more the wolf struggled."

Then Mrs. Skoll said: "But the wolf was smarter."

Van Helsing looked at her, his eyes all of a sudden strange.

"Yes. Fenris would not allow the rope to be put upon him, unless Tyr agreed to place his hand into the wolf's mouth."

I chuckled, a little out of nervousness. This talk had suddenly taken a peculiar turn, but for the life of me, I couldn't put my finger on what was so odd.

"Poor old Tear," I said.

"You pity him, Mr. Crooker?" Skoll asked.

"Sure. I pity fools."

"Pity Odin, then. He was the greater fool," Van Helsing said.

Skoll turned to Van Helsing, and I could swear he had puffed up a little like a game rooster.

"What do you mean?"

"He already had many wolf companions," said Van Helsing. "He didn't need to bring Fenris to Asgard. For his folly, he lost his life. Fenris devoured him too in the end. Tyr only lost a hand. That is a small price to pay for wisdom."

"Why do you think he brought the wolf home, Abraham?" Mrs. Skoll asked.

Van Helsing shrugged.

"Perhaps he thought he had found something he could use, but then it grew too large."

"And what would you have done, Professor Van Helsing?" Skoll asked, his voice low.

I was bored of this odd talk. Without thinking, I said;

"He shoulda drowned it when it was a pup."

The Skolls were looking at me strangely. At my side, Van Helsing nodded his agreement.

"Precisely."

This seemed to put a damper on the conversation if it was ever very lively, which for my taste it was not.

"You are well versed in the old stories, Professor," said Skoll, after they all had sipped their beers in quiet, listening to the low talk around the house and the patter of the rain outside.

"I like the way you tell them better, husband," Mrs. Skoll said, resting a hand lightly on Sig's shoulder.

Van Helsing looked stung.

"If I have given some offence..."

"Of course not," Skoll said. "What offence can there be in old stories? We must talk of these things again sometime before you return to Amsterdam. Please excuse us."

And they went off across the room to mix with the Ravells.

"What in hell was all that about?" I asked, when they were both gone, arm in arm.

But Van Helsing had nothing else to say. He just stared at that woodcarving.

The day went on in much the same way. Food was served. Beef stew with fresh baked bread for sopping. Mr. and Mrs. Skoll did a lot to avoid us for the rest of the day. A few more people from town arrived in time to eat, but not many.

Judge Krumholtz and his wife departed early. Ettie made the excuse that the judge was feeling under the weather, though everyone knew what she really meant was 'under the table.' The Q&M boys and a couple of the big Scandinavians went out into the rain in a spirit of brotherly love to help Rufus drag their buggy out of the mud and they were underway, Ettie emphatically promising Skoll they would return the borrowed clothes.

That was when the trouble started. The boys failed to return from outside.

At first no one noticed. I was jawing with the Ravells and Cole had retired with Mr. Skoll to the back porch to smoke and talk business. With a pang of jealousy I noticed Van Helsing speaking with Mrs. Skoll in what I figured must be Greek in a corner of the den. I wasn't the only one who noticed. Vulmere was leaning on the mantle preserving a beer and letting his stew cool. If his eyes had been .44's they would have blown Van Helsing to little pieces. The lawyer was talking in angry tones to one of the men, who was on his haunches stoking the spluttering fire. I couldn't hear if it was English he was speaking or not.

Then one of the Q&M boys burst in like a bull in a china shop, knocking over a little wood statue with the front door. He was hatless, covered in mud, and leaking blood from the corner of his lips.

"Where's Mister Morris?" he yelled, shattering the peace of the party once and for all.

Those that were seated stood up and those that had been facing the south turned a hundred and eighty degrees on their heels. Mrs. Ravell dropped her teacup and it thumped on the throw rug.

I set my warm beer down on a table, kicking into action. I was never much for parties anyhow.

"He's in the back. What's up, son?"

The wrung looking cowboy jabbed his thumb over his shoulder, spattering the white robe of a gold-locked woman in a painting on the wall with mud, and stomped towards the back door, leaving a trail of grimy footprints.

The Scandinavian poking at the fire stood up and at a look from Vulmere went to intercept the determined looking lad. But the boy would not be dissuaded, and shoved the taller man to one side.

The Northman didn't take kindly to that at all. He caught the filthy fellow by the sleeve and jerked him right into his waiting fist.

The waddie's nose crunched and he slid to the floor.

The back door flew open and Cole stalked in with Skoll right behind.

"What the hell is this?" Cole roared, the most animate I'd ever seen him in all my days. Why, the back of his neck was scarlet!

Skoll took in the scene, then barked sternly at the man that had just laid the cowboy out. The fellow looked like a kid brought to heel, and actually dipped his head as he spoke back rapidly in his guttural tongue.

Cole was standing over his man, and helping him to his feet. I inched closer so as to hear better. Van Helsing got on one knee beside the boy and peered at his lump of a nose, ever the dutiful healer.

"Jack, what happened?"

"It ain't our fault, Mr. Morris," said the cowboy. "You got to believe me!"

"What ain't your fault?"

"Them damn Norgies started it. That big son of a bitch is gonna kill Ranny if somebody don't do something!'"

I think I led the pack that headed for the open door.

What awaited us outside was a pitched battle of the sort Attila the Hun might have been right proud to participate in. Two Q&M boys were trying to punch and claw their way into a ring of Scandinavians. The cowboys were on the smallish side and the bigger men were responding to their ferocious little dog attacks with derisive backhands and shoves that sent them splashing down in the mud, only resorting to the occasional pulled punch when one of the Americans managed to do something particularly annoying. The rain had drenched the whole lot of them, and the blood from those that had lost any was washed away in the downpour.

Whatever the enraged Q&M boys were trying to get at, it was in the center of that ring of giants. That treetop son of a bitch called Walker was looming over the heads of even his fellows, sprouting up in the center of that circle of mud-splashed bodies like a big organ pipe cactus in a tangle of chaparral. Walker was engaged with something we couldn't see, something that seemed to be giving him quite a lot of trouble by his crushed and bloody lips. Seeing as how Ranny Brogan was the only Q&M man not accounted for, it wasn't hard to figure out where he was.

Cole yelled as before;

"What the hell is going on here?"

The cowboys looked over at the sound of their master's voice, and one of the Scandinavians took the opportunity to punch one of them in the ear.

Skoll's deep voice boomed its disapproval. The Scandinavians all stopped and turned to him in unison.

Skoll barked an order and they moved aside, revealing a battered and muddy Ranny Brogan picking himself off the soppy ground at Walker's tremendous feet.

Skoll was already apologizing, but Cole acted like he didn't hear, and cut him off.

"Ranny? You alright?"

Ranny Brogan squinted against the rain and wobbled on his feet. His shirt was untucked and torn and there was a steady flood of red running from his nose.

"Yassir!"

"Get over here!" he called.

Ranny spared Walker a hard glance and shoved past the other blondes. The two other cowboys took their places beside him. When all three were on the porch, the Scandinavians were still standing in the rain, dominated by Walker, whose long blonde hair was plastered to his broad shoulders. They all stared, not at Cole and his men, but at Skoll, as if waiting. Skoll paid no attention to them. He watched as Ranny stood in front of Cole.

"What happened?" Cole asked.

One of the other cowboys began to splutter anxiously.

"We got the Judge's buggy outta the mud, and..."

Cole glanced at the cowboy.

"I'd like to get it from Ranny."

Cole turned back to Ranny. Ranny's right eye was swelling shut.

"Like Ray said, we got the Judge out of the ditch and were headed back to the house when that big sumbitch slipped in the road. Paul just laughed, and the big one went crazy. He picked up Paul and tossed him like a piece of paper." Ranny rubbed the back of his neck a little shyly, and shrugged. It made him look all of twelve years old. "Well, I hated to see that, Mr. Morris, so I...I hit him. Next thing I knew, they went and made a ring around me, and well...I guess you seen the end result."

"We tried to stop it, Mr. Morris! Honest!" Ray broke in.

Cole looked at Ray, and then at Paul, the other cowboy. Paul just nodded his agreement.

Skoll called to Walker. The lumbering man came over. Still the others remained out in the rain. It made me nervous to see them standing out there so quiet, as if it was just dandelions falling on them. I shivered. It was a cold rain, and I wasn't even under it.

Skoll and Walker traded thick words in Danish or Norwegian or whatever.

Skoll turned to Cole.

"It is as your man says."

"So what's his beef?" Cole growled, gesturing to Walker.

"He thought your man was insulting him."

"So he goes and does that to a man?" Cole pointed to Ranny's swollen, bloody face. Cole was hot now, and that was plain. You didn't hurt his cattle or his boys.

Skoll spoke curtly to Walker and the large man went sulking into the house.

"You must forgive him. He didn't understand," said Skoll. But he didn't sound too apologetic. I guess it's his accent.

"Hell with him! What about the rest of 'em?" Cole glanced at the men still standing out in the rain. He paused momentarily, and I could see he was as confused by the way they were standing there all quiet in the downpour as I was. But he didn't let it stop him. "What kinda men are they?"

This seemed to irk Skoll. His blue eyes flickered.

"They are *mine*," he said, in a voice to match Cole's.

"Well, it seems to me like you might could teach them not to beat on a bunch of poor dumb cowboys for a giggle."

"You would do well not to tell me how to run my affairs, Mr. Morris," Skoll said icily.

"Don't you worry about that," Cole said. "I think we've said all there is to say to each other."

"Yes, I think you are right!" Skoll hissed.

"Well adios, then!" Cole said, and walked off the porch toward the corral, not even stopping for his hat and coat.

I called after him, but he wouldn't listen. Ranny and the other cowboys scrambled off the porch after him.

Helluva way for things to go at a man's wedding party. Helluva way.

* * *

From the Journal of Professor Van Helsing
26th August

I must change my writing habits. To have to squint under the flicker of the candlelight so late at night is painful to my old eyes. Much to write of.

The Skolls' party fell to disaster as members of the opposing factions could not sufficiently pretend to honor the unsteady peace their leaders had orchestrated. Coleman left not long into the day with Ranny and the other cowboys, after the employees of both sides participated in an unruly brawl. I was left quite to my own devices, but thankfully Alvin had brought his buggy.

We did not remain long after Coleman and his employees departed. Mr. Skoll was not in the end the charming host he had begun the evening as (earlier he had even been so congenial as to have welcomed me into his home in fluent Dutch). But even before the fight I had noticed a certain coldness in him towards me after the talk of Tyr and Fenris.

Perhaps he thought mine and Alvin's comments in some way disrespectful to his heritage. I had thought we were only speaking about stories. Certain men will not hear criticisms towards the histories they have been weaned on. I suppose it so, too, with our favorite tales. Men will share appreciation, but they will not readily hear criticism. Yet his reaction was so strong...it has planted the seed of suspicion in me about something else, which has been germinating in my mind since the autopsies of Early Searls and Sheriff Turlough.

I felt that I had offended Callisto too, and I managed to speak to her alone after escaping Alvin. She was not really angry, but she admitted she had found Alvin's comments a bit boorish. I apologized profusely on his behalf, and we were friends again.

Friends, indeed, for she shared with me much that she has most assuredly not shared with anyone else. Quite possibly even Skoll himself. Certainly not the other men of his household.

She confided in me that she was unhappy in her new home. She was not fond of the emptiness and quiet, and spoke particularly of the lack of trees.

"There are no trees anywhere! And no green. It is like a wasteland. And the stink of the cows, it gives me a headache. There is no one to talk to, Abraham. Not for miles. And Sigmund's men, they are like dumb brutes. All but my husband's attorney Ivar, and I do not like him."

"Why?" I asked.

"I don't know. He's...like some...red-headed fox, lurking about. He smiles that ugly smile of his, but he stares as if he were plotting something all the time. I suppose he is like all attorneys, is he not?"

"What is really the matter?"

She was silent for a moment, and she bit her lower lip as she looked at me. It was an unthinking gesture, but it flooded me with emotion. What are these strange feelings I have when she is near? They are disturbing. When I look into her eyes, I see something that I feel I must destroy and protect all at once. It is the same feeling I had in Dracula's tomb...

"I'm going to have babies, Abraham."

She said it as simply as that, and it was then that I realized I had known all along, somehow. The flush in her cheeks. The strained look. She had hid it quite well, but when I looked at her, it was suddenly obvious. I wonder if Dr. Ravell knows.

"When are you expecting?"

"Within the next month."

But this did not seem like it could be true. She could hardly be full term, by the look of her.

Yet, she assured me that she was.

"Have you been examined?"

"Not here."

"Perhaps...perhaps I could...perhaps I should..."

She actually giggled.

"Oh no, Abraham. I don't need another opinion. If anyone is certain, I am." Then her face became serious once again. "But you mustn't speak of this to anyone. You won't, will you?"

How could I refuse? I quite understood the scandal of bearing a child a scant month after being legally wed, and how it might affect the Skolls' already precarious favor in this community. Americans like to pride themselves on their casual attitudes, but they are as prim as the stodgiest English dame when it concerns sex. I swore myself to silence.

I noticed Vulmere then. He was standing across the room from us with his arm draped on the mantle. If his master is a golden Vidar, then Vulmere with his shock of red hair, redder even than mine had been in its youth, is a plotting Loki. I can see how Callisto dislikes him. He has the face of a schemer, narrow and vermin-eyed. He is not like the other men in Mr. Skoll's employ. The others all seem to exude strength, whereas Vulmere...I cannot say what it is Vulmere projects. *Cunning.*

Nevertheless, he had fixed his eyes on me, and I could read right away what was in them. A disapproval, born of...envy? Or was it that he found my familiarity with Callisto inappropriate? Had he seen the inscription she had made on my invitation? Did he suspect my intentions less than honorable?

I thought to speak to him, but at that moment Mr. Coleman's young cowboy burst into the room with news of the altercation outside (followed immediately by an altercation inside), and soon after Coleman and his faction departed forthwith.

After the incident, Skoll roared at his men out on the front porch, perhaps forgetting I could understand his Danish.

"Idiots! Are you children that you allow yourselves to be bandied into brawls with lesser men?"

One of the men replied;

"Are we women, that we should bear with the insults of these camp dogs?"

"No, you are not women....you are men of the Sleipnir! And these shit farmers are not worth staining your hands with! Or am I mistaken?"

There were muttered oaths of assent from the men outside.

The Sleipnir. I remembered Sleipnir as the eight-legged horse that bore the god Odin into battle. But what does it mean, *men of the Sleipnir?* It struck me odd. There was something I felt I was missing, something itching at the back of my brain. It was his next admonition that I shall not forget.

"Our time will come yet," Skoll said. "Do not slake your thirst on water when wine is in your reach."

Callisto touched my arm.

"I'm sorry for this. I will speak to him."

I opened my mouth to speak, but she had left my side and gone out on the porch.

Dr. Ravell and his wife approached me then, interrupting my eavesdropping. Ravell introduced his wife, and commented dryly as to the sour turn the whole affair had taken.

I remarked distractedly that it was unfortunate.

"When you put the red ants and the black ants together, there's bound to be a fight," Ravell remarked.

Indeed.

Alvin appeared at my side, and anxiously wanted to know if I could understand what was being said outside. I thought it prudent to deny the truth.

Mrs. Ravell made a comment about the weapons strung about the walls. It was just idle talk, a polite way to distract our attention from the argument between Callisto and Skoll on the front porch. I could not hear the particulars, but Skoll seemed outraged that she was questioning him in front of his men.

"Yes," said Alvin loudly, pointing at one of the swords on the wall as he sipped his beer. "Some nice long knives. How old d'you think that one is, Professor?"

It was a Norse long sword with an etched pommel and cross guard. I am no archaeologist, but it did seem very old. Possibly, the hilt was bronze. It was sheathed in a leather scabbard, and I felt compelled to examine it. I went to the wall and taking it in my hands, eased it off the hooks from which it hung.

The relief on the cross guard depicted a Thor's hammer. Once a pagan emblem representing power and fertility, with the coming of Christianity it had been fused with the sign of the cross somewhere around the 9th century or later. But this did not appear to be one of those cleverly disguised crosses. The head of a beast capped the pommel — a sharp-eared wolf. There were faded runes on the crossguard, but without reference material, I had no hope of reading them. The blade was heavy. I could feel the strain in my arms when its weight left the wall. As I grasped the scabbard and began to draw it out, a heavy hand clamped on my shoulder. I almost dropped it.

"Don't touch that!" hissed Vulmere. The violence of his words caused froth to leak into his red beard. I noticed dimly that the knuckles of the hand with which he had gripped me were red and raw.

"Ivar!"

This came from Skoll. He stood in the doorway with Callisto at his side, lips pursed in silent anger.

"He meant no harm," Skoll said tersely. Then, to me, "But it is an antique, Professor. I'll thank you not to handle it."

I acquiesced and offered my apology, but I placed it back on the wall rather than hand it to the spluttering Vulmere.

"My friends and neighbors, I am heartily sorry," Skoll announced to the room. "I think, considering recent events, that it would be better to draw the party to an early close."

Lightning crashed outside. I could not believe that he meant to expel his guests into the storm, but it was exactly so.

"My men are bringing your buggies around. Please take whatever food and drink you will. Good day."

Without another word, his arm locked securely around Callisto, he marched past his speechless guests and up the stairs. Callisto stole a glance at me before she was hurried off.

"How do you like that?" Alvin remarked to me as he drove us down the muddy lane later.

Doctor and Mrs. Ravell's coach lurched ahead of us, and I heard the doctor's whip crack as his miserable team slipped upon the mired ground.

My thoughts were in turmoil. I felt I was on the verge of something, but what was it? Purpose, or madness? It seemed like madness. Yet, there is such order to it. Such rationality. How readily I had accepted the reality of a vampire in modern London...why then, can I not come to terms with the idea that something far less unlikely is occurring here in Texas? Is it because my thought process is colored by my recent bouts with delusion? But delusion would suggest an inability on my part to discern what is real and what is not.

I put my hand in my pocket as we rumbled along the road. What lie there was certainly real.

The fact that Skoll's 'antique' sword had an edge as keen and clean as any modern surgeon's scalpel...that was real too. I knew, for Vulmere had so startled me as I inspected the blade, I had mistakenly passed its edge across my thumb, and the cut was not shallow.

But what does the thing I carry in my pocket have to do with the wedge I have sliced into my thumb?

Perhaps there really is some sort of puzzle here, and I am not weaving webs of gossamer in my poor, befuddled braincase. But am I the only one with the perception to see that things are awry?

I am not.

For good, beloved Alvin turned to me from the driver's seat of his leaky buggy, and said;

"Do you think something...a little off is going on at Skoll's?"

I could have embraced him, but having remained silent with my own thoughts, to have done so without preamble would surely have confirmed the suspicions I have read in his eyes from time to time. Namely, that I myself am 'a little off.'

And I do not think it would be advisable for anyone with lesser credentials than myself to come to that conclusion.

CHAPTER 9

From Aurelius Firebaugh's Diary
Aug 25th

Found Buckner Tyree dead in his shack today. Think the lion killed him. Never heard of a lion going for a man like this, especially not one that's fat on cattle and coyotes. But it couldn't be nothing else by the state Buckner is in. Busted right through his door. Never heard of a lion doing a thing like that. Never. Might be it has gone mad. Expect it made for the canyon. Wanted to try and track it, but that damned rain hit and hit hard. Put what was left of Buckner in the buckboard and made for Cole's place, but got bogged in the mud and will have to spend the night in the wagon. Too old for this. Keep hearing sounds out there, and the horses are skittish. Let that damn cat show its face and we'll see what's what.

* * *

From the Pen of Alvin Crooker
26th Aug

We got as far as Cole's before the rain started really pouring, and so spent the night once again. I expect he must be getting tired of having houseguests. The Ravells stayed as well. The damned weather slowed us to a crawl, so by the time we got to the Q&M I only had time to strip off my wet clothes and crawl into bed. Van Helsing stayed up talking to Cole. I suspect that old man knows a good deal about what was going on at Skoll's yesterday. At least he understood a whole lot more than he told me.

I woke up too late to catch the Ravells, and too late for breakfast again. When I came downstairs Cole, Ranny Brogan, and Van Helsing were having coffee and watching Useless lick the breakfast plates clean. Having the dog do the dirty breakfast crocks was a curious Morris family tradition first instated by Quincey, much to the Captain's annoyance. I was surprised to see Cole allowing it, and wonder if he remembers it was his elder brother who first started it.

Van Helsing seemed as preoccupied as ever. I still can't believe Cole hasn't asked him about his brother. It's as if he doesn't want the old Dutchman to leave, as though if he avoids the Professor's news he's somehow preventing Quincey's death in his mind. Why? Does he think he can reconcile himself with the man somehow, in between training a new foreman and getting the cattle ready for the winter drive? Maybe I'm just reading into things. I know for certain he is prolonging what Van Helsing has teasingly assured me must be a helluva good story. I'm certain if nothing else, Quincey must've made a game end to have induced this old coot to come halfway around the world to tell about it.

Cole has sure soured on Skoll though. His dislike of the man was never so keen as that of his men, but now he has been infected. I don't think it's entirely because of the big fight, either. I remember they had words on the back porch before that. I asked him what they'd talked about.

"Ain't no concern of yours, Alvin," was all he would say.

These are trying times for the free press.

A wagon rolled up midmorning. It was old Alkali, and he looked like something the cat had dragged in. His eye was red and cracked and there was a tremor in his voice I'd never heard before. He had us come over to his wagon and directed us to the buckboard, where a grey bundle stained red was piled in back. Hooking the edge of the cloth, he peeled it back, revealing the dead face of old Buckner Tyree.

"He's been mauled," said Alkali, "by that damned lion." His voice seemed strained like after a long night of whiskey and tobacco.

"Where did you find him, Mr. Firebaugh?" Van Helsing demanded, his eyes all alight at the sight of the corpse.

"In his shack over by Misstep Canyon," Alkali said, stifling a phlegmatic cough in his fist. "It busted in and got him."

"*What?*" That was from me.

"I spent all day with that foalin' mare, then when she finally dropped her colt, I went over to Buckner's to ask him if he'd seen any sign of that lion, on account of that coyote it brang down on my property. That's when I found him. It busted his front door right in. I wanted to track it straight off, but with that son of a bitchin' rain I didn't know how long it'd take me, so I tried to bring the body back here. The wagon got stuck. I had to spend the night out on the road."

That explained the cold he seemed to have developed.

"I never heard of a lion busting into a man's shack before," Ranny said.

"Think I have?" Alkali growled, making the boy cow slightly. "This ain't no ordinary critter. *I seen it.* Last night, out on the road. The son of a bitch is *huge.*"

"Hold on," said Coleman. "You *saw* it?"

"Mr. Firebaugh," Van Helsing said, "are you certain it was a cat you saw?"

"It was," Alkali nodded. "But it was huge. It had shoulders like a goddamned buffalo. I could hear it movin' around, and when I saw it snufflin' at the back of the wagon I took a shot at it. Don't know how I could've missed, but it run off."

"What kinda animal fills its belly on coyotes and beef and then still has room to go after a man?" Coleman wondered out loud.

"Maybe it's got the hydrophobia," I said. "Maybe its rabid."

"It sure acted crazy," Alkali admitted. "I scared it off more'n a couple times with the rifle and it kept comin' back all night. I didn't get a wink of sleep. And I ain't ashamed to admit it, boys. I was scared. I kept thinkin' how if it got at the team I might get stranded. And I knew I couldn't outrun the damn thing."

"You mean to say it was trying for your horse?" Ranny said.

"That's sure what it looked like," Alkali nodded.

"Strange," muttered Van Helsing.

He leaned forward and started to undo the bloody wrappings around Buckner's body, but I laid a hold of his wrist. That slaughter in the jailhouse has been the last thing I see before I fall asleep most nights. So far I'd resisted the bottle. I didn't need any new nightmares to bring me closer to falling off the wagon.

Coleman was set on going after the animal forthwith. It was agreed that by the lion's bizarre behavior it had surely gone loco. And if there's anything more dangerous than a mad lion, it's one that has had a taste of man. An animal that has killed a human being is no different from a murderer; once he gets the taste, you can bet the farm he'll be back for more.

We decided to let Alkali rest up for an hour before we headed out to Buckner's shotgun shack and the canyon. The old man made us promise not to leave without him. I guess the wildcat had struck at his pride by forcing him to sit up all night in the road and saddling him with a cold.

He dearly wants satisfaction.

So now we sit waiting. Cole and Ranny are cleaning their rifles. Ranny's boyish face is a mass of welts and yellowing bruises. He can see through both eyes today, at least. I noticed Cole has the Winchester that once belonged to his brother Quincey — the brass nameplate on the stock was there, as shiny as I remembered it. I guess Van Helsing must have brought it. I wonder if Cole elected to use it on purpose or if it's just because it was on hand.

Quincey won it in a shooting contest in Ft. Worth. I still remember the day he brought it home. He let all of us try it out just once, with the understanding that it would be the only chance we ever got to handle it, and that we need not ask again. It had the smoothest action of any gun I've ever fired. It's funny. Him coming home with that repeater—it was like all of us had won that contest. Everybody was proud of him that day. Captain Morris never bragged about anything in his life, but I can remember how he puffed his chest out as Quincey passed that rifle around. I can't remember Cole. I think he was away then.

Van Helsing has elected to spend the hour indulging in his usual ghoulish past time. He is outside by the wagon examining the corpse.

Poor old Buckner. He was just a harmless tramp, half crazy. He couldn't have picked a worse end. What to write in his obituary? I don't know much about him. Just that he had hunted buffalo way back, and when they'd played out, he had made a living as a wolfer, along with that Indian partner of his, Picker. Come to think of it, I haven't seen Picker in some time either.

Alkali is snoring like a hog in a sun patch.

* * *

From the Journal of Professor Van Helsing
26th August

With cursory examination, it would seem that Early Searls and this Mr. Tyree were both savaged by animals, but this is not so. I have ruled out the possibility that it was an animal that killed Searls, despite the foreign object I retrieved from his body, which I have not yet produced a plausible explanation for (my best guess would surely be grounds for my committal). There was no animal hair found on Searls. Buckner Tyree's wounds are rife with it.

Yet he was not killed by any indigenous cat. The copious hairs in the lacerations on the body are coarse and long, not the fur of a feline. Also, the patterns of the wounds do not suggest a cat. Feline predators are quite generous in the use of their claws in attack. They rend and tear their prey, knocking it senseless and bloody, or else they hook into it with their front claws and tear it apart with vigorous kicks of their back legs, only resorting to the bite as the *coup de grâce*. I would assume that a cat driven mad from sickness would be even more savage.

But the marks in the flesh and bone indicate bites, as of a canine. There are claw marks interspersed, to be sure, but they are less pronounced, more like the claws of a dog, which are intended for digging, not fighting. Those bones which are exposed have been thoroughly gnawed, and the plethora of jagged tears in the throat point also to teeth. There are several hemispherical puncture wounds suggesting the arrangement of an animal's maw in various places. But the immensity of those jaws! They certainly do not belong to any of the smallish, timid coyotes, or the feral domestic dogs I have seen.

I am told the wolves were hunted out of this region, but what else but a mad wolf — a very large mad wolf, and not the sort that would have existed here (or anywhere in modern times) — could have inflicted such bites with the precision of the born hunter?

Why should an animal of any sort engage in such odd behavior? Even a very hungry beast would hardly force its way into a man's home if it could summon the courage to approach it at all. This animal was not hungry by any means. Not if the reports that it has had the pick of the country for the past month may be believed. Yet if it did attack Buckner Tyree for food, which by the absence of several of his choice internal organs seems likely, why did it not attempt to drag the body back to its den? Mr. Firebaugh says he found the man dead lying in his shack.

There is the possibility that this is not a lone hunter, but a member of some communal pack. If this is so, it could be storing food to regurgitate later and share with less able members of its group, or perhaps with young. Such practices are not unheard of in the animal kingdom.

Then there is the odd behavior attributed to the animal by Mr. Firebaugh (if the animal he saw was the same one which attacked this man — but why would it follow his wagon, having freshly dined?). For it to actively seek to bring down the horse seems reasonable, if it were hungry enough. But to return after having been fired upon by a repeating rifle, it would have to be more than mad.

This land is sparse, but it supports a good deal of animal life of the lower orders. I have observed field mice, hunting birds, and deer in abundance. Why then, with such diversity of prey about, is this cat (if it be a cat, and alone) displaying the characteristics of a mad, starving animal? Beasts attacking men are but stories from the middle ages, and if they occur at all in present day, they are confined to the Dark Continent, where creatures more capable at killing than men still roam.

So while I am convinced that it was indeed an animal that killed this man, I am not convinced it was any kind of normal hunting cat; at least not one indigenous to this part of the world. I am also doubtful that it is diseased. This is the handiwork of a strong, vigorous beast, quite capable and possessing of all its predatory faculties, whatever they may be.

Baring-Gould works his black magic. Just now I took the object I kept from the wounds of Early Searls and tried to match it with the punctures in the body of Buckner Tyree. They are not the same. The wounds on Buckner are significantly larger. Is there any connection here?

Was this truly the work of an animal, or is it only meant to appear so?

I am quite bothered by the sight of all this blood.

But why? Have I not worked in blood and death all my career? Why are these dark visions haunting me now? Is it because suddenly I feel so near to the animal? Have I not carved and dissected men and women in the same manner all my life? Have I not in some way emulated the natural talents of the beast with my poor clumsy tools, my claws of surgical steel and my fangs of needle and bonesaws? What difference, if it be I or some wild beast which slices up the man before me? The end result is the same, a shapeless thing, barely recognizable as God's own image. What difference then?

There is a difference. I do not kill.

But that's not entirely true, is it? Have I not broken that commandment before? Dracula's brides were not the first to die at my hand. How many died in Natal by my will?

Yet I have never taken a life in vain.

Never in vain? Because it was in defense of my life? Who is to say my life is worth more than that of the men I killed in Africa? Who is to say that raving Zulu could not have thrown off the trappings of savagery in time and become a great humanitarian? Did he not have children and a wife? Isn't that for whom he was fighting? Where is my wife? She lingers like an earthbound ghost in a gray room, tended by strangers. Where is my progeny? Spitted long ago on a native spear. What have I added to the sum total of man's accomplishments, except the death and ruination of poor, damned women?

But I didn't kill those women. They were dead already. I freed their eternal souls.

It frightens me to read what I have just written. How many murderers have rationalized their crimes in the same way? 'I freed their souls from the prolonged torment of a sinful life (or un-life, in this case)?'

Who am I to judge whether their lives were a torment? Indeed, perhaps they reveled in their existence! They were after all, immortal. If I were granted immortality, wouldn't I...

But what would I, Abraham Van Helsing, do with immortality? Gather knowledge, like some shambling Faust, hoarding the dusty secrets of the universe, and forever frustrated in my pursuit of the one Great Secret which all mortal men are eventually privy to? There is the rub. An immortal like Dracula and his wives could fill their heads with all the secret lore of the earth, but it would be just that. The secrets of heaven (and yes, perhaps even of hell) are promised only to mortal man.

I see that I am at war with myself. The darkness seeks to bloom. May God grant me strength. I do not know the root of this evil inside of me, but I pray I can find the strength to conquer it.

CHAPTER 10

From the Pen of Alvin Crooker
26th Aug, Later

We set out a little after noon when Alkali woke up. Van Helsing was sitting on the porch writing in his notebook when we came out. Useless was licking the blood off of the Dutchman's fingers, and the Professor seemed not to notice. I gave the mangy hound a good kick. I should've spared one for the Professor too. The more I'm around him the more I begin to doubt he's got his hat on straight. There's something off about the old man.

I almost objected when Cole offered Van Helsing a rifle, but the old man demurred, saying Quincey's pistol ought to serve him well enough. The scattergun I was carrying was borrowed from Cole's cabinet anyway, so I had no right to say anything. With my busted wing I was lucky enough to be allowed to come along.

It will take us till about two 'o clock to get up to Buckner's shack. Cole sent Pepperbelly and one of his waddies into town with Alkali's wagon and Buckner's body. Cole sent Paul with money for the old wolfer's burial. That lush of a Mex would've surely drunk it down and dumped the body somewhere otherwise. Me calling Pepperbelly a drunk is something like the buzzard shouting 'ugly,' I expect. Had I not sworn off whiskey two months and eight days ago, we would have been bellying up to the bar together as we had so many times in the past. My arm itches, and I keep thinking a dram would do it good. I watched Paul and that dear old Mex depart with a fearful longing.

The ride has thus far been pretty uneventful. Around high noon we came across the spot in the road Alkali said he'd been laid up all last night. We found his shells, and a lot of odd tracks all over. Odd, because they don't look like much of anything. That is, they look like something, but not a lion or a dog either. Too big. It was a puzzle to Cole and Alkali and Greek to me. I can't tell a hoof print from a Michelangelo.

They are at this minute trying to figure out if the lion went off finally in the middle of the night, or if it bedded down somewhere around here. If it slept, they figure finding the spot it rested will tell them more about it. Cole seems bothered.

We broke to rest the horses and expect to start up again in a few. Nothing to eat but jerky. Wish I'd got up in time for breakfast.

* * *

From the Journal of Professor Van Helsing
26th Aug (Later)

We will be in Misstep Canyon soon.

The scene at Buckner's cabin was a testament to the strength and peculiar savagery of the animal we hunt. Its power is almost unthinkable.

Buckner's door, though constructed of poor wood, should have been ample protection against even a maddened animal, but we found it smashed to splinters as if a Brahma bull had charged in. The walls of his hovel were painted in his blood, the earthen floor dotted with animal prints, and his meager possessions were flung all about.

There is little to catalog. Some empty liquor bottles, a set of rusted old iron wolf traps, stacks of *The Sorefoot Picayune* whose dates rival even Alvin's archives, and a bottle of arsenic, half full.

I was amused by the peeling label on the poison; *Apollo Brand Arsenic, Cherry Hill, New Jersey.* I once read somewhere, I think it was in Pausanias, that it had been the god Apollo who taught the shepherds of ancient Greece to leave poisoned meat to kill wolves. Something I assume must still be practiced by wolf hunters today. I wonder if the name on the label is intentional. It's ironic to think that the owner of an apothecary in Cherry Hill, New Jersey would deliberately put such an obscure reference on his product, and that only I, a Dutch professor in a dead man's hovel in the middle of the Texas Plains should fully appreciate it.

Scattered among the shredded newspapers I did find a sheaf of scrawled, dated notes, which I think must be the dead man's diary. The documents are quite out of order and Buckner's penmanship is atrocious. It will take some time to decipher, but I gathered all that I could find together.

There was little else to be learned in the fly-ridden dank of that small house. There was no legacy, no testament, no penultimate clue left behind by the dead vagabond. Only congealing blood and wreckage.

It appeared the old beggar put up a gallant struggle by the torn condition of his hard packed floor, but there was no evidence that his killer tried to drag his body away. This does not entirely rule out my theory that it is some sort of communal creature however. It could have gorged itself in the shack and taken its food back to its brethren. That an animal should be so bold is unsettling, but not implausible. That a man did this is almost unthinkable. Almost.

It is certain that the killer (be it man-killer or killer-man) fled in the direction of Misstep Canyon, which Coleman and Mr. Firebaugh say is nearby. They tell me that the tracks indicate the animal doubled back across the wet ground after having left Mr. Firebaugh's wagon on the road sometime last night. Something about the animal's footprints seem to bother Coleman, but he says nothing.

So we rest the horses before beginning our trek to the canyon. I am endeavoring to sort Buckner's papers, but there are many dates missing.

* * *

From the Pen of Alvin Crooker
Aug 26ᵗʰ Later...

Well, there is an Indian in our camp now. A Tonkawa called Plenty Skins, of all things. He claims he's Picker's uncle. I've never known Picker to talk about any family, but the democracy of our little band has won out, thanks mostly to the Professor's campaigning. For my part I'm pretty confused and, I must admit, a little scared. I don't expect to get any sleep for fear of having my throat cut. Wish I had a drink.

Cole and Alkali tracked the lion into the canyon and we had a helluva time getting down. The varmint had chosen a particularly rocky and terrible descent; Van Helsing's horse stumbled and he damn near broke his neck. We all had to dismount and lead the animals the rest of the way, tying at least another half an hour on.

It was four 'o clock when we finally reached the canyon floor. The trail had disappeared somewhere in the rocks, and I was given a hard look by Cole for wondering aloud why we hadn't brought Useless along to sniff the wildcat out. The cur was better acquainted with the beast than any of us, after all. Then we spied the smoke from the campfire.

It was a wonder to all of us just who would be camping out at the bottom of the Misstep. Despite Alkali's misgivings, we opted to mount up and head out quick to meet the fire-builder. The reasoning in this was that it might be some lost saddle tramp who was ignorant of the presence of a dangerous animal, and that the cat might be attracted to a cooking fire.

Discretion got the better of us when we got to within a couple yards of the camp. We dismounted again and got real still. There was the sound of Indian singing careening off the canyon walls.

Well, needless to say that shocked the hell out of us one and all. There hadn't been wild Indians in this part of the country for ten years or more. Cole and Alkali crept ahead and around the rocks while the rest of us remained to keep the horses from bolting.

Ranny looked as nervous as a bride on her wedding night. He confided in me that all throughout his formative years he had heard a good deal of talk about Comanche depredations from his old buzzard of an uncle that had been a trader at Ft. Sill.

"My Uncle Kay said he once seen a drummer skinned from his ass to his eyelids with his balls stuffed in his mouth like an apple in a pig," he told me.

"That was all a long time ago," I said, trying to offer some comfort but finding none myself.

"So what's Indians doin' out here?" Ranny asked in a frightful hush.

For that I had no answer. I'd never even seen a wild Indian.

Then the signal came we had been waiting for. The singing stopped, and Cole's voice called for us to come out.

We picked our way through the heaps of stone and came out into a kind of natural amphitheater, a bowl-shaped formation all in rock. At the edge was Alkali and Cole, their rifles pointed at a lone figure standing in the center alongside a medium-sized bonfire.

He was an old Indian, the strangest looking Indian I'd ever seen. He was all done up in a robe of animal skin, coyote or wolf by the looks of the pointed ears and the grey dog-face over the hood. His lined face was tattooed with black swirling lines, and he looked every bit the cannibal. His long, iron-colored hair was shaved on the left side of his head and hung loose to his shoulder on the other. Strung about his neck was a necklace of animal teeth, and his wrists and ankles were draped with much the same kind of fare. He had a long belt of big green copper conches around his waist, and an ash handled knife shoved through his waistband. He wore greasy deerskin leggings and an overlong loincloth whose dull red fringe dusted the ground at his bare feet.

As we filed into his small camp, there was a look of firm disapproval about him, but no trace of fear. He had some kind of rattle in his knobby fist.

I heard Ranny suck in a breath beside me and gave him a reassuring wink, though I thumbed back the hammer of my rifle and propped its barrel across my bad arm.

"A remarkable looking fellow," Van Helsing said.

"What in hell's he doing way out here?" Ranny asked.

"When we came up, he was dancin' around the fire on all fours like a dog," Cole said, lowering his rifle and eyeing the wary old Indian.

"What sorta Indian is he?" Ranny wondered.

"Don't look like no Comanche," Alkali said.

"Well, somebody ask him if he's seen that lion," Ranny said.

"How?" Alkali asked.

Coleman tried his Spanish, but the old Indian said nothing. He just looked beyond us, like we weren't even there.

While they deliberated over what to do with the Indian, I walked around his camp, toeing over hide sacks, an old U.S. Army canteen, a buffalo blanket.

Then I spied a great circle scorched black on one of the large flat rocks, as if there'd been a big fire there. I ambled over, Ranny right behind. There was a lot of rubbish lying around, and some broken pottery. Half obscured by the rocks there was what looked to be a hand-built platform made of birch, like some Indian funeral scaffolds I'd seen, though a little smaller around, almost like a seat or chair that had been raised about six feet off the ground. I clambered up the side to have a look, but there was nothing up there, just a bare platform.

"There is another possibility, my friends," Van Helsing said. "Perhaps our 'lion,' he is standing right here before us."

Then Alkali whistled. Van Helsing had found something next to the Indian's fire, something he'd taken at first to be kindling. It was a pile of scorched bones, obviously human.

The Indian did not react to our curses. It was sure as a Chinaman in a laundry house that this Indian was some sort of crazy killer. But whose bones were these?

"What's this?" Cole asked, coming over.

"I would submit to you," Van Helsing began, putting on the airs of a twenty dollar law dog, "a theory I have been considering since the night the Sheriff and Mister Searls were murdered..."

"What's that got to do with anything?" Cole asked sharply.

"Permit me," Van Helsing answered, reaching into his pocket. "Harley Crenshaw was not the sole participant in the carnage enacted in your jail. There is significant evidence that he could not have made his escape without aide, let alone singlehandedly dispatched both men."

"In plain American?" Alkali said, furrowing his brows, and inclining his good ear toward the Dutchman.

"He's saying two men were in on the killin' of Early and Turlough," Cole said.

"Why didn't you say anything before?" I demanded.

"I *did* partially confide in Dr. Ravell, but the details of the evidence were such that I could not readily decipher them. In truth, until this moment my theory had taken such a fantastic turn that should I have confided it to all of you, my friends, you would have reviled me as a lunatic, and thus I have kept it mostly to myself."

Then he clapped his hands and gave a weird laugh, shaking his head as if at some joke you had to be Dutch to appreciate.

"Good thinking, Professor," I muttered.

Alkali looked at Cole for explanation, but Cole was no longer in a translating mood. The old man's talk had captured him for once. He kept the Indian covered, but addressed Van Helsing.

"So who do you think helped him?"

"Gentlemen," Van Helsing said, pulling something out of his pocket (that same pocket he had been fussing over for the past few days, I realized), "My evidence."

He held it out. Whatever it was, it was small enough to fit between his finger and thumb. He showed it to us one at a time, moving about our stunned circle with that same air of a lawyer in front of the jury box. When he finally got to me, I couldn't stop myself from exclaiming;

"Great God, man! Is that a tooth?"

Van Helsing nodded.

"It is indeed. I extracted it from a gash in Mr. Searls' chest."

At that moment I believed that old Dutchman had taken the big jump. I could only guess at what sort of crackpot theory this old fool had chucked in favor of this one.

"As I said," said Van Helsing, moving towards the quiet old Indian. "My mind developed all manner of reasons as to why this tooth should be in Mr. Searls' wound. It is not a human tooth, gentlemen. Note the dramatic curvature of its shape, the savage efficiency of its symmetry, its very length? *This* is a fang."

"A *what?*" Ranny exclaimed.

Van Helsing strode right up to the Indian.

"A *wolf's* fang."

Now I saw where he was headed. That Indian was done up in wolf's teeth like a lady with lace.

"I was unable to produce a likely suspect because I could not think of a logical reason for a wolf tooth to be found in the victim's body. Nor could I reason how a civilized man could so ravage another. But the answer is plain to me now," he went on, staring at the Indian as though he were addressing him. "A civilized man could never do such a thing."

That was enough for Alkali and Ranny, and hell and be damned if it didn't convince me. The three of us forgot all about the mountain lion. Maybe this crazy Indian *was* the mountain lion, at least where Buckner was concerned. It made sense that a renegade out on his own would do his murders while a lion was about to blame. That way he could write his crimes off on the animal and get away scot-free. Maybe he was even some crazy partner to the Crenshaws they'd brought back from Arizona. He sure looked like the sort of maniac those two might've found it amusing to keep company with. Well, we were set to lynch that Indian, and were hunting up for the means and the place to do it, when that Indian did an astounding thing.

He reached out and snatched Van Helsing's hat from his head just as quick and easy as you please.

And he said, in English as plain as day:

"Red hair."

That struck us all dumb for a minute. Even Van Helsing, who had the most to fear, didn't move out of the Indian's reach.

"Not red like fire," the Indian continued, "red like the rising east. You're from the east."

He offered Van Helsing his hat back.

Well, I hollered for the Professor to get back or get down, and I brung up my shotgun to draw a bead and cut that crazy killer Injun in two. But the Professor didn't move, and Cole held up his hand for me to rein it in.

"I ain't civilized. I ain't no mountain lion," said the Indian to all of us, "and I ain't killed no sheriff."

"Just who the hell are you, then?" Cole said, finding his voice where we couldn't.

"Bill Plenty Skins," said the Injun. "I come over from Bastrop. A week ago my nephew come to me. He said he thought he killed a white man, but he wasn't sure."

"What do you mean he wasn't sure?" I said.

"He said what he shot was a wolf. But when he went to skin it, the wolf was a man."

We all looked at each other, except Cole. He stared at the Injun. Van Helsing took a step back. I saw he was shaking his head, and had his hand over his mouth.

"You're certain of this?" he mumbled. His voice was very high, and it seemed to me, frightened.

"Picker brang me all the man had on him," the Injun said, pointing to a pile of skins lying beside his canteen and bedding. "Look."

It looked like Van Helsing couldn't get over to examine it fast enough. The Injun stopped him though, with his own hat.

Van Helsing took the hat.

"Thank you," he said, and went to the pile of skins.

The Injun lingered on the Dutchman for a minute, then turned back to the lot of us.

"I come to find my nephew's pardner, a man called Buckner."

"Well you met him alright, didn't you?" I said, hoping my meaning was clear.

The Injun looked at me, playing at bewilderment, I thought.

I could hardly believe it, but Cole stepped up and let the hammer of his rifle down, putting it over his shoulder.

"I'm Cole Morris," he said. "Last week I found a man on my property. He'd been shot six times and he was naked as a jaybird."

"Mr. Morris," said the Injun, "maybe you knew my nephew. He was called Picks For His Food."

"Picker," Cole nodded. "What do you mean 'knew?'"

"That's why I come," said the Injun. "Picker's dead."

"Killed?"

The Injun nodded, and gestured to the pile of bones beside his fire.

"Right here. About two or three days ago."

Alkali rumbled now, and came over, staring down at the rick.

"You trying to tell us that's Picker? There's no way a man ends up like that after only two or three days. Them bones is clean."

"Yassir," Plenty Skins agreed. "How 'bout Buckner?"

"We just come from his cabin," Cole said. "He's dead. Mauled by a lion."

"It weren't no lion," said the Injun.

"Damn straight it wasn't," I said, being unable to stomach the malarkey any longer. "Come on Cole, we know damn well it wasn't the lion got to Buckner."

"Then what'd we track here? It wasn't no man," Alkali said. "Surely not this man."

"Not you too!" I swore. "Look at this fella, boys! It's plain as the nose on my face he's a damned murderin' cannibal. Hell, didn't I read somewhere the Tonks used to be cannibals? It's like the Professor said. He sprung Harley and killed Early."

"Why would he do that?" Cole said.

"He's one of the Crenshaws' gang, I bet," I reasoned. "He probably killed Buckner too. Isn't that right, Professor?"

"No," said Van Helsing, his voice almost a whisper. He was staring at the ground, his back to us. "No, I was mistaken. Whoever killed Mr. Tyree did not kill Mr. Searls and the Sheriff. And I don't believe this man killed Searls."

Van Helsing stood, and he had something in his hands. It looked like a bracer, the kind those dime novel pistoleros always sport on the cover of *The Police Gazette*. It was sort of like a hold out contraption I'd seen once. A gadget that fitted to a sharp's wrist and allowed him to pass aces into his hand from his sleeve. But it wasn't that either. It had a fan-like protuberance on what would be the back of the forearm. This was shaped like a rake, and on the end of it were a series of small sharp stakes; like hooks, or...what?

"What the hell's that?" Ranny asked.

Van Helsing said nothing. It turned out he wasn't even looking at the bracer. He was fishing something else out of the bundle, and when he pulled it loose, it fit in his palm. It was a set of false teeth, but not like any I'd ever seen. Whatever orthodontist had whipped up these teeth must've been signed on by Lucifer. The teeth weren't meant to be human. They were like an animal's, sharp and carnivorous, with protruding canines.

Van Helsing put the fang he said he'd taken from Early Searls next to the wicked dentures for comparison. They may as well have come from the same wolf.

Absently, he handed the rest of the weird paraphernalia to me while he turned the false teeth over in his hands, inspecting them, and then stooped to regard the rest of the clutter.

The odd bracer was made from tough boiled leather. It was made to fit over a man's arm. The fan spread out over the back of his hand, the claws stretched over his knuckles. I could smell the sweat soaked deep into the leather, feel it.

"Lord what *is* this thing?" I mumbled.

"I seen 'em in a dream," Plenty Skins said.

Van Helsing looked at him.

"They pretend to the Power of the Wolf People," said Plenty Skins. "They imitate the Wolf People with tools. They gain Power, but not wisdom. They are warriors. Yellow-haired wolves."

I had to laugh. I threw down the thing Van Helsing had given me. Something about it, holding it, made me sick and thirsty for brandy. Ranny picked it up and wrinkled his nose, handing it to Alkali.

"Yellow-haired wolves, did you say?" Van Helsing repeated, rising to his feet with a bundle of fur in his arms.

The Indian nodded.

"How do you know these are Picker's bones?" Cole said.

"You ain't buyin' into this, are you Cole?" I exclaimed.

But he sure enough was. He waved me off again and repeated the question.

"They staked him out there on that big rock," the Indian said, gesturing to the scorched flat rock. "They danced around a big fire. They cut out his heart there and they put it in a bowl."

"What?"

"There were animal hearts too. A coyote, a rabbit, maybe a bull or a cow. I found 'em all lyin' in a heap back of them rocks over there. They didn't eat the meat, just took out the hearts. Somebody ate or drank from the bowl. The blood splashed over on the ground. The big bowl I found over there. Whoever drank from it was wasteful, or they didn't want it. They dropped it on the ground. It broke into pieces. Then they stripped the meat offa my nephew. They ate him. Not the animals, just him. They threw his bones on the fire."

Van Helsing finished unraveling the tangle of hide. Another of those wicked looking bracers fell to the stones. It wasn't just one wolf hide, but a couple stitched together in the unmistakable form of a shirt.

Van Helsing mumbled something. Some word that didn't sound a thing like English. It was like *oolf-hey-oh* something.

"Professor?" Cole said.

"The carvings in the house, the strange talk...all the signs," the Dutchman mumbled. His lips were quivering with excitement. "Who had a motive to kill Early Searls?"

"What do you mean? If the Injun didn't do it, then it was Harley, right?" I said.

"No, no, no, Alvin. Harley Crenshaw is incidental," he spat, and for a minute I felt like I was in a schoolhouse again, and I didn't know two and two. "His escape was but a ploy. I said I thought that someone else must have aided him. The one who helped him was there to enact his vendetta upon Mr. Searls. Sheriff Turlough, he was killed outright, but Early Searls was slaughtered, as though in a frenzy. As though...by an animal. Whom had he angered to such a degree only recently by your own reporting, Alvin?"

I was dumbfounded. Cole answered for me, and his voice was cold as the snow.

"Vulmere."

"Precisely. Lawyer Ivar Vulmere."

I was skeptical.

"You're sayin' Vulmere busted Crenshaw loose just to kill Early for mashin' his nose?"

"And direct attention to an escaped fugitive. A proven killer to whom anyone would by force of habit assign blame," Van Helsing said.

"But listen," I began, "Skoll killed Crenshaw himself. He..."

Then Van Helsing smiled, the wily old bastard, for as I trailed off he knew I could see it too. For a man who never went to town, Skoll had been in just the right place to meet us on the road and take command of the posse. He had led us right to Crenshaw, even if it seemed to us at the time like he hadn't. And Skoll had killed Crenshaw himself. Not because Crenshaw threw down on him, but because Crenshaw had seen Vulmere and he would have talked. It all looked like a cover for Vulmere. And now Buckner was dead, because maybe he'd seen something too.

"What I can't rightly get is all *this*," Alkali said, flinging the weird 'claws' down. "Professor, what in blue hell's this all about?"

"Skoll and all his men..." Van Helsing began, still looking at the fanged dentures in his hands. He looked at the Injun, as though for approval.

"You know. Say," said Plenty Skins. "They will not believe if it comes from me."

Van Helsing stared in wonder at the Injun, then looked at all of us. A minute ago he had accused the old savage of murder. Now he was standing next to him. To my disgust, he began idly snapping the fang-dentures open and closed like a hand puppet's mouth as he spoke.

"Yes. They are a murder cult, gentlemen. For all intents and purposes, they worship the wolf in its incarnation as a vehicle of Satan. And Sigmund Skoll...." he actually tilted back his head and *laughed*. He took off his glasses and wiped at his eyes. "Forgive me, forgive me. *Skoll*, if that is his real name, he is their leader. Their chief and high priest."

When he had his glasses back on his face, the fire seemed to double and dance in his eyes, and his tone was mean. "And they are keeping Madame Terovolas, Madame Skoll, as their hostage."

CHAPTER
11

From the Journal of Abraham Van Helsing
August 26th (Night)

In the Vatnsdoela Saga, they were called the *Ulfheonir*—the 'wolf coated.' And in Hrafnsmal, the poet writes:

> *Ulfheonir are they*
> *called,*
> *Those who bear*
> *swords*
> *stained with blood in*
> *the battle,*
> *They redden spears*
> *when they come to*
> *the slaughter,*
> *Acting together as one.*

Well known is the phenomenon of the old Norse *berserker*, those fierce solitary warriors who rushed into battle garbed only in bear skins, biting their shields and ignoring their wounds. Such men were *eigi einhamir* (not of one skin), and in their transfigured form, they took on the strength and ferocity of the bear.

But Baring-Gould writes of a subgroup of the *berserkir*, who traveled in the company of King Harald Hrafagr, and who wore wolf skins and howled in battle. Whereas the great *berserkir* fought individually, the *ulfeheonir* mimicked the pack, and fought each in cooperation with the other.

If Skoll (this cannot be his real name — *Skoll* is the wolf in the Northern myths who nips at the heels of the sun, seeking to devour it) and his men believe themselves to be modern day *ulfheonir*, which by the wealth of evidence we have amassed both physically and in observation of the artifacts of their home, I must beyond all rationality accept as truth, then the danger lies in striking against them. We will not face one, but all twelve, each with the supposed strength and assurance of his fellows. For, if their faith is total, as the faith of the fanatic most often is, they will fight like pack animals.

They are spoken of in the sagas as having the skill to behead men with a single blow, to dismember them and cleave through their helms. When I remember the sword I observed hanging on the wall during the party, that razor sharp 'heirloom' which Vulmere was so averse to me examining, and I connect that to the strange cut Dr. Ravell and I observed on the body of Sheriff Turlough which notched his vertebrae, then I am assured in my deduction that it was Vulmere who freed Crenshaw from his cell, after slaying Turlough with the very same blade. The cut he made was one that would have been celebrated in the sagas.

I assume that he then freed Crenshaw, instructing him to flee to a predetermined place. Buckner's shack, or someplace thereabouts, where Skoll would later lead the posse and silence him. It was probable that Vulmere waited for Crenshaw to make his escape before he unlocked Early Searl's cell and murdered him. I think that he did this act in the ecstatic mindset (and perhaps in the peculiar garb) of an *ulfheonir*. This explains the fang found in Early Searls' wound, which matches the curious apparatus Plenty Skins' nephew took from the body of the Scandinavian he killed on Cole's land. The very existence of the nightmarish costume proves everything. If the tooth matches the dentures from this man, than it must have come from another set. An identical set. Probably each of Skoll's men owns a matching pair.

I have no further need for speculation, but I can here recount the other warning signs, which I was loathe to relate before.

Besides the strange talk of the legend of Fenris and Tyr at the party, there was the mention of *The Sleipnir*. I think that Skoll and his men believe themselves to be a kind of Viking band or crew. All his talk of being descended from ancient seafarers explains the tight-knit bond that they seem to share. I should like to have an opportunity to further examine the wealth of artifacts in Skoll's house. What if *The Sleipnir* is the name of the ship whose oar hangs on his wall? What if he and his men believe themselves spiritual (or actual) descendants of the crew of *The Sleipnir*, much as the Rosecruitians trace themselves metaphysically back to the priests of Egypt? Of course these are only speculations.

The wolf is sacred to the Allfather Odin (or *Ooin)*, whose name in and of itself means furious, raging, and intoxicated. Odin had at his side two companion wolves and two ravens. The historical *ulfheonir* then, were probably champions dedicated to Odin. *Sleipnir* was Odin's eight-legged mount. Thus the crew of a ship christened *Sleipnir* might consider themselves the horsemen of Odin, and thereby, bearers of their God; as the practitioners of Vodoun believe themselves 'horses' who, in their religious ecstasy, are 'mounted' by their deities.

The possibilities are fascinating to ponder. But we do not deal with the supernatural here. There is no otherworldly evil to fear. These are but addled men. As a doctor I would treat them (or ship them to Purfleet for Jack to treat). But they are also criminals, and more, they have an innocent girl in their sway and are intent on indoctrinating her into their diabolic rites. There will be time for study when they have been defeated.

It is certain to me that Callisto knew nothing of her husband's alter ego, but she must know now, or she suspects. I have thought so since I first heard her speak with a hint of trepidation about her fiancé and his men, and I am confirmed in it after having seen the way in which Skoll dominates her. Skoll's madness knows no boundaries. I am certain he has deliberately conceived with Callisto to pull her further under his influence. She has admitted to her early pregnancy. Skoll must have beguiled her as a way to assure their wedlock.

As for the strange rites which Plenty Skins described, based solely on empirical evidence already three days cold, I am not certain as to their meaning. Precious little in the way of records exists to describe the rites of these ancient pagan cults. What the Romans did not flay from their subjects, the Christians burned away with fire.

I pray that Callisto was not exposed to the unholy practices that transpired here.

I am galvanized in my desire to save her from this barbaric fate. I do not think the others are entirely convinced. Of them all, only Coleman said nothing. Firebaugh shakes his head, while Ranny and Alvin call me an old fool to my face. Whether Coleman thinks me mad as the others do but is too polite to say, I do not know. That no longer matters. They will be convinced soon enough. For now I at least, am sure.

Of Plenty Skins, he only seeks revenge for his dead nephew. As the fire began to die and the snores of Mr. Firebaugh went on, only he and I were awake, staring into the fire.

From an anthropological viewpoint, this Red Indian is himself quite unique. As the others bedded down for sleep (for night is falling and though we are determined to return to Coleman's ranch and gather his men, we cannot get there in time to be of much use now), I interviewed this marvelous fellow. I have tried for posterity to record some of our talk. He claims he is the last of his tribe, and I feel much of what he has to say is of note.

I asked him first about his reference to Wolf People.

He claims his tribe was dug from the earth by wolves, and that it was they who taught his people to hunt and survive. It is a fascinating affirmation of a study I had been doing at the time I was called upon by John Seward to participate in the events in Transylvania, which have already been recounted elsewhere.

I was then studying archaeological artifacts left by primordial cultures. In the dawn of man, humans were naked, helpless things, quite unsuited to the harsh environs of the earth, where predators such as the wolf thrived. Surely men saw the natural abilities of the creatures around them — the strength of the bear, the cunning of the wolf, the speed of the rabbit. So it was that they came to observe and learn from the beasts how best to make their own way in the world. This began probably with the simple wearing of animal skins to insulate against the cold of night and winter. Man is not inherently savage, but primitive man had to subsist, and in the cold seasons there were no growing things to be had. He had to quench his vegetarian nature and learn to kill.

Even today, do not criminals go masked to hide their identity from the law and to disassociate themselves from their crimes? So too did early man don other disguises, to hide himself like guilty Cain from his Creator. Men could not kill, but animals did. So men became animals. This is most probably where the werewolf myth originated.

But I digress.

Plenty Skins claimed that all his tribe is dead but him, now that his nephew is gone.

It seems unbelievable to me that whole race of men with their own culture could be wiped away, and I said as much.

"It's not so hard," he said. "When the whites came, the Tonkawa worked for them against our old enemies. I was a scout, and I killed Horse People and Mexicans. When the fighting was done, soldiers could take off their blue coats like snakes. But a wolf can't shed his skin. We had lost our independence. We were infected by the white man's comforts. We begged for them: we drank, we forgot how to hunt. I moved away from the others. Once they respected me. I was a holy man. But they forgot their lessons, and all their ways. They went crazy and married Lipans. Those that were left got put on a train and went to Indian Land, where they put all the Goddamned Good Indians. I stayed. I'm not a Good Indian."

"We will avenge your nephew," I assured him, seeking to offer some sort of solace.

"Yes. My dream told me so."

When I asked him about his dream, which I assume he purports to be of a prophetic nature, he would say no more. My years in Africa taught me a deep dislike of a certain sort of witch doctor; the confidence-mediums and false 'spiritualists' who fleece the gullible in London are their civilized equivalent. In my experience I have seen shamanism at its worst, in the politicking and rabble rousing of a lot of charlatans who play with the deepest beliefs of their followers. I have also encountered men whose power could not be explained by prestidigitation and mere hypnotism. Still, I am wary when talk of dreams and visions is introduced. I know next to nothing of the Red Indian variety, so I will do my utmost to reserve judgment.

It is dark now, and very cool. I have not slept under the stars in some time. It reminds me of Natal, to hear the animals stirring nearby in the dark, and hear the wind, and feel the naked sky on my face. One almost expects to hear the roar of a lion out in the brush. It is quite refreshing.

Although this canyon seems to quiver from the memory of dark deeds, I am not afraid, for I am at last certain that despite the incredible truth of the diabolic society we have uncovered, at least my secret fears have been validated. I am unburdened.

Thank God I am sane.

CHAPTER 12

Aurelius Firebaugh's Diary
     Aug 27th

Woke up before the others and fed the horses. Slept bad. Nightmares. Something about the canyon all wrong today. Lay here this morning thinking last night was part of a dream, but this morning them burn marks and the bones and the carcasses are still here. Don't know that I trust that crazy Tonk. Lot of Indian bullshit if you ask me. Nobody asking though. Thought the Professor was alright, but now I ain't so sure. His story don't make sense. Cole worries me too. Does he believe this hash? I asked him, and he was the same as always, 'Don't know that I do or don't.' Well, that's genius. Feel like I should get back to my place, but don't want to break off alone. Old fool. Will ride with them as far as Cole's to get together the Q&M boys. Don't know what'll happen after that. Horses need looking to. Wonder how the new colt is doing?

Later

The Morris place has been burned out. We seen the smoke a few miles off. Nothing to do about it. Found that ragged hound Useless about a half mile up the road, hiding in a ditch. Some watchdog. It wasn't no accident either. Horse tracks all over the place and you could smell the oil. Whole house lost. Cole and Ranny picking through the rubble while the rest of us try to figure out what happened to all the boys. Want to get back to my place to see that it's alright. Indian says the Yellow Haired Wolves done it. Skoll and his boys? Hoof prints are deep and big around—like the kind them heavy Norgie horses might make. One thing's for sure. There's going to be a damn war

* * *

From the Pen of Alvin Crooker
27ᵗʰ Aug

I need to get back to the goddamn printing office.

The Q&M boys came in from the south forty, where they'd been rounding up the cattle all night. Somebody had cut the wire and stampeded the herd. It took them all night to rope them all back in. They said they saw the fire, but were too far out to do any good.

They were luckier than poor Pepperbelly. Ranny found the Mexican lying in the yard. He had been caught in the stampede and run over by so much beef he had to be pried out of the dirt.

All those hooves made it pretty impossible to tell for sure who did this, but everybody is hell-bent on riding straight for the Skoll place and getting answers. It looks like there's going to be a heap of trouble.

Van Helsing keeps going on about his murder cult. Can't believe he's serious. A hide shirt, some hoe gloves and a pair of pointed dentures isn't enough to make me believe in wolf men, especially when the best testimony comes from a fella we found howling around a campfire in the middle of a canyon at night. At least he has shucked his wolf getup into his war bag in favor of traveling clothes. As for his story about Picker...well, I don't know. I still think it was this Plenty Skins that killed Buckner. Hell, the tracks led right to him! And anyway, who's to say that wolf shirt and the teeth and the rest of that stuff he claims he got from Picker aren't his?

Cole wants to ride into town and get Shetland and the Judge to go with us to Skoll's, so as to keep a lid on things. He is one cool customer. If that were my place burned to match sticks, I'd be hollerin' for blood right about now.

* * *

From the Journal of Abraham Van Helsing
August 27ᵗʰ

My worst fear was that the receptacle containing Quincey's ashes had been lost in the fire, but when I made this regret known to Coleman, he told me candidly that he had dashed Quincey's ashes among the graves of his parents early yesterday morning without fanfare. This was a great relief, as much because Quincey's ashes had not been lost, as because they had not been disdained. Technically, my initial purpose is complete. Quincey Morris now rests with his family, even if his ancestral home has been destroyed.

But there is a greater task ahead now, and I believe that God has put me here in this place in this company and under these circumstances to once again mete out His will. I do not think of myself as a crusader, but I must admit it is rather strange that I should find myself again in such odd circumstances, facing such deliberate and naked evil. Perhaps I am being given an opportunity to make reparations for the sins I have committed in my younger days.

Before we rode out I asked Coleman what he intended to do. He is remarkably composed for one who has just lost all that he cherishes to the fire. Yet I fear that this composure is but a half-fixed stopper for some unguessed rage which may yet pour over into brash violence. We must not approach Skoll without a carefully devised plan of attack.

"I'm just going to ask the man some questions," was all Coleman would say. And in that instant I thought that I was hearing Quincey.

As I went to my horse, he called me back to him, and looking me in the eyes, asked me plainly if I believed in everything the Indian had said.

As he looked at me, I was struck by his resemblance to his brother. Although at a distance they are clearly not the same, when close they seem very much alike, especially in their eyes. Yet in looking at Coleman, I did not see in his gaze the angry denial I had seen in Quincey's the night I told them all the truth about Miss Lucy Westenra. In Coleman's face there was a more honest expression. Quiet, reasonable. I understood then that Coleman Morris was a man more honest than even Quincey had ever been. He did not raise his voice without good cause, and he never drew attention to his fear.

And why then, should I lie?

"Yes I do," I whispered to him. "Quite assuredly."

Coleman watched me for a moment, studying my face; then he leaned close from his saddle.

"So do I."

"And now, may I ask you something?"

Coleman paused. I could see he was anxious to go.

I asked him about the tracks of the lion around Buckner's shack — why they had bothered him so.

In answer, he held up one of his hands, pointing to it with the other.

"These lines on my hand..." he said.

"Papillary ridges?"

He shrugged. More of my 'flourishments,' as Alvin would call them. I had learned the term on my adventure with Hamish and the Great Detective.

"You ever heard of an animal havin' 'em?"

I have not, unless it was a great ape. And they are noticeably scarce on the Texas plains.

Later

Fool that I am! Why did I not have Alvin or Mr. Firebaugh accompany me to the telegraph office? It was very nearly a lasting regret.

I had thought to send a message to John, presuming that he must be worried as I had assured him I would do so upon my arrival. So, as Coleman and his men went to see Sheriff Shetland, and Mr. Firebaugh and Ranny went to purchase supplies for the trail (and ammunition, I am sure), Alvin hurried to his press and I to the telegraph office.

I paid for a short wire to London assuring John and Lord Godalming of my safe arrival, and that I had met with Coleman. I did not make mention of anything that is now afoot, for fear John would find a way to have me shipped back to Purfleet.

When I emerged from the telegraph office, I was confronted by none other than red-headed Ivar Vulmere, glaring at me from around his yellowing, misshapen nose, as he had at the party. Behind him was the tall one called Walker, and he was armed with a pistol. They both stood on the plank walk before the door, waiting for me as had the Crenshaw brothers.

My first instinct was to fly like a rabbit from those hateful eyes, but I fought my urge to cower and stood my ground, even going so far as to speak well before he had the chance.

"I know what you are," I said, clenching my fists at my side to keep them from shaking. Strange that I, who had faced an immortal and countless madmen and dangers both manmade and alien to this realm of being should be so unnerved by this one. "And I know what you've done."

Vulmere smiled, and with his grotesque nose and evil, purplish eyes it was like a grimace.

To further illustrate my point, I took from my pocket the curved canine tooth, and let it fall to the boardwalk between us. I watched Vulmere's eyes alight on it, and then flash up at me with naked hate. He cocked his head slightly, and the expression was distinctly bestial. All of this confirmed that it did indeed belong to him.

Walker stirred at his side, but I was not as frightened by the giant as I was by this little sharp-eyed man. There was a pent up fury about him. How had he ever become an attorney?

"Who are you, Van Helsing?" he hissed in Danish, sucking in spittle.

"What matters is I am coming for her," I answered back, in kind.

His shoulders shook slightly.

"Do you know what you're facing, old man?"

"I know what you think you are."

"You have no idea what we are," he said, and there was a fierce pride in his feverish eyes. "How can you?"

"You claim you are men of *The Sleipnir*. Wolf-Coats. Odin-Worshipers. Odin was a god of slaughter, but he also sought wisdom. There, I think you fall utterly short. You are lunatics at play, like children in their grandfather's clothes."

Vulmere took a step forward, his face turning to match the fading dark rings under his eyes.

"Take care, old moon. And be afraid. The wolves are at your heels."

"*You have shown you have the courage to kill. Do you have the courage to die?*" I said, savoring the irony of the words, for they were foretold as the words Tyr would say to Fenrir at the end of days. Of course Vulmere knew them too, and his nostrils flared at their intonation. "Tell your master if she is harmed, I will lay him lower than stones," I added.

I thought my taunt would induce him to strike at me. With no help, I feared I should not give much account of myself against a man younger and stronger and with the conviction of a lunatic.

But then a voice from nearby said:

"Red Hair!"

Vulmere and I both turned at that, and there stood Plenty Skins, leaning against the clapboards. The Indian had followed me without a word and waited outside. Only now had he made himself known. I wasn't certain which of us he had called. Beside Vulmere, my fading hair was a pale gloaming to his raging flame. Then I saw that Plenty Skins did not look at me.

Vulmere and Walker both seemed dumbstruck by the appearance of the Indian. He was not in his wolf skins anymore, and seemed comparatively tame in a plain blouse, jeans and blanket. He was unarmed but for the knife in his belt, and yet to my surprise, both brutish men seemed to shrink before the Indian's hard look.

"Not red like the east," said Plenty Skins, suddenly at my side. "Red like blood."

Nothing further was said. Vulmere and Walker backed away as from some unseen menace and went to their large horses, tied at the post. They mounted up and rode off without a word, though Vulmere spared the Indian a lingering stare.

Plenty Skins watched them go.

I breathed deeply and expressed to Plenty Skins my gladness at his arrival. I had thought I might be accosted or worse had the encounter been prolonged, and I had foolishly left my revolver in the saddlebags of my horse.

"I'm glad too," Plenty Skins said. "I thought I was here to kill you."

This took me quite by surprise, and after I had found my voice, I asked why.

"In my vision I seen Picker killed by a wolf with blood red hair, who came out of the east. When I saw you, I thought I found him. But your hair wasn't the right color red."

He smiled, and it was oddly disconcerting to see his teeth. He clapped me on the shoulder like a drunken crony.

"Walk with me, and we'll talk," he said.

Then, on the walk back to Alvin's printing office and the jail, the Indian disclosed to me through the recitation of his dream a great deal about what he believed to be his purpose.

"After Picker was et up by the red-haired wolf there was a big howling all about, as of many wolves. In my dream I killed Red Hair, but his pack rose up to tear me apart."

He must have mistaken my pursed lips for concern, as he smiled.

"Don't worry. The she-wolf took pity on me, and I was safe. But a great hunter saw her and wanted her pelt. I was wounded, and couldn't interfere. I wished I could've thanked her, but I couldn't. You thank her for me, Professor."

I could not fathom what he was talking about, nor what he wanted of me. Prophecy is often vague, sometimes by nature, other times by deliberation. Before I could determine which style Plenty Skins practiced, he went on.

"Things will be harder now that I've shown myself to Red Hair."

"What do you mean?"

He turned to me, and there was a gravity in his eyes that was superb if it was pretended and harrowing if it was not. I saw why Vulmere and his man had turned away.

"We've seen each other before, Van Helsing. In a dream. I dreamed him and he dreamed me. But now that we have seen each other in the real world, not even hell will keep us apart."

I asked for clarification again, but he only said;

"I can't tell you what you have to learn for yourself. Just quiet your thinking. That way when it does speak to you, you'll hear."

Then who should we see, gesticulating to us from the doorway of the very same pub in which the late Pepperbelly had debased himself on our last trip to town, but Alvin.

I saluted him, asking him why he was not at his press.

"Get over here, you dumb buzzards, and fast!"

Plenty Skins and I exchanged wary looks, but obeyed, ducking into the dim of the drinking house.

It was hardly after noon and the patrons were few. The paint was peeling off the only painted wall, and a thin man with a waxed mustache was seated on a stool behind the bar obscured behind a yellow copy of the Picayune. As we came in, he looked over the lip of the paper with mild interest.

There was a frightful air to Alvin's face, and his hands were shaking.

"They arrested Cole and Ranny!"

I couldn't believe what I heard.

"Listen to me, old man. Shetland arrested 'em both on Skoll's orders."

"Skoll's orders? But they burned his house to the ground! Did he not..."

"Skoll says he has proof Cole killed that man Thorsen. And that ain't the half of it. When Rufus tried to place Cole under arrest, that dumb pup Ranny took a swing at him, so Rufus had to buffalo him upside the head with his pistol. The Q&M boys went plumb loco, and there was nearly a shootout. Cole yelled for 'em all to skin out. Now Skoll says he's afraid they're going to head to his place and make a grab for his wife. Krumholtz has deputized most of Skoll's men, and they're headed out after 'em right now!"

Skoll's men had been empowered to legally hunt down what force we had mustered, and Coleman and Ranny, our field marshals, were imprisoned all in the space of half an hour.

"Where is Mr. Firebaugh?"

"Right here," said a gruff voice from the end of the bar.

Firebaugh stood coolly dispensing a glass of whiskey, his gaff hand hooked lazily on his broad belt, his one eye slightly glazed. I hadn't seen him there in the gloom.

I was at something of a loss. Could the law be so misconstrued and our situation made so irreparable so quickly?

"How can this be? Shetland..."

"Is scared," Firebaugh said. "And with good reason. Them damn Norgies outnumber him. They were heeled like a goddamn militia. Rifles, shotguns, and mounted on them monster horses. Rufus ain't got no choice."

"Then what shall we do?" I asked, suddenly wary.

"I been sittin' here thinkin' on that. I figure it won't be long before Skoll or that red headed son of a bitch figures out a way to get us in the calaboose."

"The what?"

"So we're getting out of town," he went on. "Now."

He slammed back his whiskey, smacked a dollar hard on the bar top, and went without a word to the rear exit.

One and all, we followed. What else was there?

CHAPTER
13

From the Journal of Alvin Crooker
27th Aug

I am drunk.

Gloriously, uproariously, stentoriously drunk.

Have to be. When the world is not what we have been taught to believe, it is best to be drunk. I would say it is a necessity.

Van Helsing was right about everything.

We got the hell out of Sorefoot quicker than a politician through the back door of a whorehouse. Just in time too. Two of Skoll's men came looking for us. Vulmere and that big son of a bitch Walker. They chased us for about three miles, but their big horses couldn't hold up against our quick Q&M ponies (which Cole had bought from Alkali). We ran those horses ragged though, and had to rest them flat on the ground like Alkali showed us.

If Alkali had not stopped into the Sunup for a snort of whiskey as soon as we got into town, he might've gotten himself arrested like Ranny and Cole. God Himself only knows where we'd have been then. That old sourdough has kept us safe and in our skin strictly by the lessons he learned on the owl-hoot trail.

We stayed off the road, but kept it in sight. Slow going. Had to ride and stop, ride and stop, ride and stop. Every time we heard a horse we flattened. Figured the only safe place to head was for Alkali's place, but it is way out past Cole's. We heard gunshots on the plain around four o'clock. It might've been the Scandinavians and the Q&M

boys swapping lead. We were in no condition to risk a gander, so there is no way of knowing.

As we lay there waiting for it to end so we could move, the Injun fished a sharp looking hatchet out of his war bag. It looked as old as he was. A lot of good a tomahawk was going to do us, I wanted to say. I'm glad now that the need for silence kept me from eating my words later.

Night came on quicker than I would've liked, but Alkali kept us moving. He had to stop us and get down on his belly to check our direction more than a few times, as the sky was overcast with no stars. It was like those Scandinavians had belched out black breath across the sky to mire us. We didn't get turned around, though. Old Alkali kept us going. He knew where he was headed at all times. At least, if he didn't, he never let on.

When we got to his spread it was near eight-thirty and black as a dog. I could just make out the roof of his stable.

"Hate to leave my horses in the dark so damn long," Alkali whispered. "'Specially with a new colt...I tell you Bernice dropped her colt, Alvin?"

I couldn't have cared less about Bernice's colt. I was dead tired and saddle sore, and the night had turned cold and my arm was hurting.

But it wasn't me that told him to hush, it was Plenty Skins.

Damn Injun hadn't said a word the whole long ride, and it sort of made me mad to hear him speak so to Alkali, even though I myself had been harboring the notion.

I could hardly see him in the dark, but I turned to the direction of his voice and whispered back;

"Hey, you red devil, don't you..."

But that was all I got out. There was a growl out in the dark somewhere, as low and mean sounding as a temperance woman's admonition. Something shuffled, and the horse underneath me started to fidget.

I heard Alkali and Van Helsing pulling out their guns. I had left the shotgun Cole had loaned me leaning against my desk at the Picayune. In my mind I thought it must be the mountain lion. Damn fool. I guess there never was a mountain lion.

None of us said a word. Alkali got down from his horse and crouched in the tall grass, listening, and pushed the reins of his horse into my hands. Then he went off into the dark, quiet as a rabbit, despite having to contend with a wood leg.

We waited there, listening hard and not being rewarded with anything for our effort other than the night breeze through the grass. Or was it? Maybe they moved when the breeze blew, and the sound they made was indistinguishable from the swaying weeds. Maybe that was why we didn't hear them. They moved like...wolves.

Then there was a hiss to my left and something came galumphing through the grass. I could hear it coming, but couldn't see a thing. Then my horse shook its head. It had had enough of the whole affair, and pitched me right over the rump and beat it for the stables and the smell of hay and others of its kind, I guess. I landed hard on my bad arm and let out a yelp involuntarily.

I don't know how well they could see in the dark, but with my caterwauling, if they hadn't known exactly where we were before, they knew it then.

As I rolled on the ground hugging my busted arm, something huge passed over me, and the night got darker, if that was possible, for just an instant. I couldn't clearly see what it was. I only got a hint of some big shadow, and the smell of animal musk thick in my nose. There was a peculiar howl as it bowled right into the side of Van Helsing's horse.

The pony screamed in surprise and crashed over on its side. Van Helsing's pistol went off, and I saw it flash from the corner of my eye. The sound was louder than anything out in all that empty, like a pair of Dutch ovens banging together on a winter night.

The one that had knocked over Van Helsing and his horse moved faster than a rabbit in springtime. It bobbed away from Van Helsing's gun and seemed to move in and out of the shadows at will, like a nightcrawler wriggling through the mud. The howl it had let out on the charge turned into a ferocious snarling bark that was deeper and more vicious than any dog I'd ever heard. Something went whistling through the air and connected with a wet sound.

Van Helsing yelled.

The thing's roar broke into a man's unmistakable shriek. Human, and yet somehow not.

The huge thing whirled, bringing one long, ape-like arm around, and I heard Plenty Skins grunt and saw him flung from his horse. He landed in a heap beside me. His horse took off after my own.

Van Helsing's pistol crashed over and over, and I managed to turn and look.

The sporadic glances from the muzzle of the Professor's revolver shed a flickering light on something I will take with me to my last day.

It looked like a huge grizzly reared up on its hind legs. Its monstrous forearms were outspread and the light played upon its hooked talons, which dripped red. Those huge furry arms led to a broad set of shoulders upon which sat a hairy head capped with pointed satanic ears. And sprouting out of the top of that head like a bloody sapling was the ash handle of the Indian's tomahawk.

How could it still be moving with that hatchet sticking out of the top of its skull?

As the last light from Van Helsing's gun burned itself on my eyes, the thing slumped over, kicking in the grass.

Although the skirmish in our little circle had ended, out in the dark Alkali's rifle blasted to pieces the short interim of relief. Another one was out there with him. We heard its howl, heard Alkali curse mightily, and then the sounds of a struggle out in the tall grass.

Van Helsing tried to induce his horse to stand, but it thrashed strangely on the ground, nearly dashing my skull with an errant hoof.

Plenty Skins got to his feet, shaking off the effects of his fall. He whipped the big knife from his belt and plunged toward the fight, fading into the dark.

Van Helsing's horse continued to screech, and the sound ground itself into my skull, which was already throbbing from the pain of my fall.

"Can't you shut that nag up?" I hissed.

Van Helsing said nothing. He was hard at work reloading his pistol.

Out in the dark the other one snarled and Alkali snarled back. The Injun let out some weird war-whoop that sounded almost like the howling of the thing that had jumped us. I heard another howl to match his. Alkali's rifle spoke no more.

I rose up on my knees and then light flooded the patch of ground I knelt in.

Beside me, Van Helsing had lit a bit of oily rag from his pack and was holding it up to see.

"Put that damn light out you old fool!" I said.

Or at least, I think I said. The words didn't come in time to beat the nightmare I saw not four feet away. Maybe they never left my throat at all.

Van Helsing's horse had been torn open at the shoulder. The cut was so deep I could see the leg bone, white in the firelight. The horse was kicking out frantically, tearing the wound wider.

Van Helsing was standing over it, his pistol in hand, and I thought he aimed to put the horse down. But he wasn't looking at the horse.

Lying on its side in the grass nearby was the thing that had attacked us. Except it wasn't a mountain lion or any other kind of critter. It was one of the Scandinavians. One of the big blonds. He was wearing the same sort of wolf-hide tunic and cape that the Indian had shown us in the canyon. His huge arms, crossed haphazardly in the grass, had those claw bracers strapped to them, and the nails on one were bright with horse blood. To complete his odd attire, there was a furred cowl over his face made to give his head the shape of a wolf, with pointed strips of stiffened hide as ears. Plenty skins had planted his axe right in between those two false ears, and blood flowed freely like red lightning down his face.

His face.

His eyes were wide and staring through the eye holes of the cowl, and right there in front of me I saw the pupils, which had been open and large enough to color his whole eye black, close slowly as death came over him, returning them to their nickel blue. His expression was one of leering, ecstatic surprise. His lips were pulled back and frosted with a bubbly foam that ran down his face, mixing with the blood, and I remembered seeing him at the party smiling and sipping brew. In his mouth, just as if they were his naturally, was a row of pointed carnivorous teeth. I knew it was just those damned false teeth, but the effect was fearful in the winking gloom; like some grinning thing straight out of hell. A parody of man and animal handcrafted by the devil to put terror and loathing into a man.

"You can put that light out, Professor!" Came Alkali's voice out of the dark. It was cheerful.

"Yeah," I said, fighting hard to keep the shaken, begging lilt out of my voice. "Put it out, Professor."

We sat there in the dark with that thing. I keep calling it a thing. I know it was just a man, but when I think of that face in the dark, and the way it kept on fighting even with an axe stuck in its head...I can't make myself call it a man. We sat there with it for a few minutes before we all decided there had only been two set to watch the place.

I didn't go and see the one Alkali and Plenty Skins killed.

Alkali remarked that he had put two bullets into his when he'd seen it coming and the son of a bitch had still managed to tackle him. Alkali treated it all as a matter of course. He let me have it for letting go of his horse when I fell from mine.

Van Helsing wanted to look my arm over, but I wouldn't let him. I knew there was only one thing to cure my ills, and Alkali always keeps a little around the place for chilly winter nights.

So I bid a fond farewell to sobriety and toasted the late and lamented Pepperbelly. The hell with teetotaling. Tonight I learned there are worse things in heaven and earth, Horatio, than a bottle of whiskey.

CHAPTER 14

From Aurelius Firebaugh's Diary
Aug 28th

I never seen a man in skins or cotton take two blue pills from a Whitney rifle and a gaff in the neck and keep on fightin'. The one the Professor done in took every cartridge in his wheel and a hatchet to the braincase besides. The one I danced with had my hook stuck up under his chin when Plenty Skins finally run up and cut his throat. The son of a bitch carved me up pretty good with those long nails (he knocked my Whitney away after the second shot), but Van Helsing sewed me up. I asked the Professor what we could expect from here on in. This old dawg don't need to get whupped twice with the same stick.

He told me the Norgies believe that they can't be kilt on account of their religion, and that the more of them there are together, the stronger they'll be. I guess it's sorta like them old mountain preachers that handle the snakes. If you can make yourself believe in somethin' like God grantin' you what it takes to ignore the bite of a copperhead, I 'spect you can disregard any sorta pain.

As to bein' together makin' you strong, I reckon that's like anything. Back when I rode with the Black Flaggers during the War a single bushwhacker was only as mean as the other fellers around him. Get one lone dawg out on his own and he might not put up much of a fight, but when there was a pack of us, lock your doors.

I almost envy them Norgies. Sure they're crazy as shithouse rats and murderous besides, but what the hell were us bushwhackers? Takes me back, to think on it that way. The boys. Heck and Petey Slidell, Zeke True, Cullen Baker, Black Jack, Thrailkill, they wouldn't even know me now. The South is gone and for all them Yankees we dusted you wouldn't even know we'd ever been around to look at the world today. 'Course we weren't no blood crazy madmen runnin' around in wolf skins like wild Injuns either. But I guess they must think whatever they're about is the way to go if they can just shake off bullets and keep comin.' Hell, I wish I still believed in somethin' just half as much.

The Professor, Alvin, and Plenty Skins is holed up in the house, whereas I am sitting in the barn with my horses. I'll be straight damned rather than let a buncha foreign savages fire the stable with all this prime horseflesh inside and Bernice with her new colt besides. Them two dead Norgies is damn lucky they didn't touch my horses, else I'd have dug 'em up and shot 'em again, then lit out directly for Skoll with dire intent.

What we ought to do next is anybody's guess. Can't sit here forever and that's a fact. Particularly with the way Alvin is draining my liquor. I hate to see the little scribbler tumble off the wagon, as I know he had a real problem for awhile, but a man goes his own way.

Going to get some shut-eye for now. Expect we will have a plan in the morning.

* * *

From the Journal of Professor Van Helsing
August 29th

A fitful night has given way to a clear and sunny day, and with it a plan on what course of action we shall take next.

Our cowboy army has been scattered in the face of Skoll and his deputized marauders, though two of them will pose no more threat.

Mr. Firebaugh's house is eminently defendable, though I confess that his insistence on remaining in the barn with his horses is infuriating and a liability. However we are not the ones in danger. I fear more for the safety of Coleman and young Ranny Brogan in the Sorefoot jail. They are prisoners and the law is not with them. Whether Sheriff Shetland and Judge Krumholtz are a party to Skoll's machinations or have been cowed by his superior numbers into neglecting their duties, I do not know. However, it is certain that we cannot proceed to liberate Madame Terovolas without first seeing to the safety of our fellows. Theirs' is the more immediate danger. At any moment Skoll's 'deputies' could elect to drag them from their cells and treat them to a dance on the gallows, or worse, such savage deaths as they inflicted upon Early Searls, Sheriff Turlough, Tyree and Picker.

We must engineer their escape.

Alvin, who has proven himself unable to effectively deal with the stress of our situation and has resorted to drink, said, in a surprisingly lucid tone:

"If it's a jailbreak you're looking to pull, Professor, then we ought to get Alkali back in here. He's dodged the law more than anybody I know."

It took the promise of breakfast from his own cupboard to entice Mr. Firebaugh into joining us in the main house. He is quite anxious about his horses, but when we brought up the notion of removing Coleman and Ranny from harm's way in the jail, he warmed to the idea.

"Well, you were right to ask me, Professor," he said, settling into a chair while Alvin poured hot coffee and Plenty Skins doled out ham and eggs. "Why I've busted the locks on more jailhouses than any man in this county from the inside and the out, and that's a fact. The Sorefoot calaboose ain't no better'n a rickety shithouse with a pair of busted bat wing doors for keepin' a man in. But the thing to consider is who'll be there watchin' it, and where to head when it's all said and done."

"I can find out who's standin' guard," said Plenty Skins. "I was a scout for twelve years. Nobody'll even see me."

I asked why we couldn't simply come back here.

"Soon as word gets out that Cole and Ranny busted out, they'll know right away who done it. My place won't be safe," Firebaugh said grimly. "Besides, you know what a long, hard ride it is to get here."

I suggested Misstep Canyon. It wasn't much closer than the Firebaugh ranch, but it was surely not equated with our group.

"Misstep ain't too bad," Alkali said. "I reckon it'll be a good place to hide out till we figure out what we ought to do. I guess…"

Something was bothering him, but he waved it off with his hook when questioned.

"What we'll need is a distraction. Now in the old days, we'd fire a wagon, or a building in the town. Half the deputies would nearly always head for the fire. You could lay money on it."

"Nobody's burning my press!" Alvin said.

"Don't worry, Scribbler. The Picayune's too close. Gettin' em to run just across the street wouldn't do us no damn good. No. It's got to be further off."

"The telegraph office?" Alvin offered. Now that he knew his beloved Picayune was not in danger, he was eager to participate. "Gridley's?"

"Dammit if I ain't getting' respectable in my old age, but I'd hate to do that to poor John Gridley. I do enjoy his steak and frijoles. I'd say the telegraph office, but it might not do to cut off the town from outside help. We might could get Marshal Ruddles down from Bastrop with some men. No, there's a storehouse out back of Sagramore's store, where he keeps his extra feed. I don't like to ruin good feed, but it's better than torchin' the place."

I asked when we should depart.

"Don't be too anxious to get shot, Professor. I figure we give it two hours and then head out. By the time we get there it'll be sundown, and Plenty Skins'll have cover to work under."

"What if it's just Rufus guardin' the jail?" Alvin asked. "You going to shoot him?"

"I ought to, on account of him givin' in to these damn foreigners without a fight…no offense meant, Professor. But no, I 'spect not. At least if it's just him things ought to come off without a hitch."

"And if it's not Rufus?" Alvin asked.

"Pack all the cartridges you can carry."

As breakfast ended and we made ready to enact Firebaugh's plan, there came a sound which very nearly sent us all into a panic. A frantic scrabbling came from the back door. For a moment only I feared that there was more to Skoll's fanatics than I had judged, and that the bloodied madmen whom had been dispatched by a full cylinder of my bullets and Plenty Skins' hatchet had dug his way out of the shallow grave we had heaped him in, and was now clawing feebly at the back porch.

But Mr. Firebaugh, fearless or perhaps careless, I do not know which, went nonchalantly to the door in question and opened it. A furry form came bounding in, but not the one my fear had placed there. It was Coleman's one-eyed hound, Useless. Apparently he had followed us at a leisurely pace. He came directly to the table and cast his mournful eye expectantly at Plenty Skins, ready to be given his chore of dirty crocks to clean.

Mr. Firebaugh kept a well-stocked cabinet of arms, and we divided every box of ammunition within between us. Plenty Skins and Alvin were both given a pair of revolvers, and I was handed a second, which I had to push through my belt. When I asked him about the wisdom of weighing ourselves down with so much firepower, Firebaugh replied, "Maybe all that iron'll keep you in the saddle this time, Professor."

As he shrugged into a shoulder holster-harness and pushed a long barreled pistol under his left arm, he went on.

"When I rode with Bloody Bill, we used to tote four, sometimes six pistols at a time. One under each arm, two in the belt, two more on the saddle. Always faster to grab and make ready a fresh weapon than to reload. 'Course I mostly make do with three nowadays. If I put one under my right arm I'd hook myself like a dern catfish grabbin' for it outta habit."

I am not familiar with this 'Bloody Bill' character to whom Firebaugh keeps referring, though by the unquestioning manner of my fellows he must be a man of some competency. Whether he is (or was) an outlaw or a soldier I cannot tell. But his lesson was passed down to me that day as I felt the heavy burden of two pistols on my hips.

When the time came for us to take our leave, Mr. Firebaugh asked for a moment of our patience and went off once more to his barn. We could see him plainly from the yard as he flung open the door and walked down the center of the stable, flipping up the latches on each of the stalls. He was speaking as he went, but we were too far away to hear. When he reached the last stall, the one in which the mare and her colt resided, he paused for a moment and seemed to speak to the animal. Then he swung the stall door open. He came back down the row, jerking each door open and giving a lusty shout to each of the animals within. With each stall he passed, a fine specimen of horse emerged, shook its mane, and bolted off to freedom. By the time he had traversed the length of the stable not a single horse was left under the roof.

Alvin was dumfounded by this.

"What in the hell's he doing?"

"What he's got to," said Plenty Skins.

When Alkali returned to us, Alvin asked him plainly what he meant by releasing such a crop of ponies.

"If them sons of bitches come back and we ain't here, they might fire the place. I'd hate to think of all them animals burnin' up."

"But that's your whole stock! I remember when you caught some of the mustangs that sired this bunch down in Misstep. You won't ever catch 'em all again!"

Alkali shrugged as he pulled himself up into his saddle. I noticed he had strapped a brace of huge pistols over the pommel.

"Let's get goin'," he said.

As though he had heard and understood, Useless came loping out of the house to trot behind us, having licked the dishes clean.

As we rode away I twisted in the saddle, unable to keep my eyes from the astounding sight. Thirty beautiful horses bounded off across the plain headed north, the sun in their wavy manes.

Later

We have stopped to rest our animals within sight of Sorefoot. As Alkali predicted, it is nearly nightfall. Soon Plenty Skins will go to his duty, and Alvin to his. Alvin is to break into the telegraph office and dash off a message to the federal Marshal in Bastrop asking for help, as he is the only one among us who is adept at its operation. I say a prayer for all of us, for our success and our survival.

CHAPTER 15

This town is going straight to hell.

John Gridley contracted syphilis. Told him to stay out of the cribs over at the Sunup, but he knew better I guess. That isn't the half of it. Tonight Aurelius Firebaugh busted into the jailhouse and shot Rufus and one of those Scandinavians and loosed Cole Morris and Ranny Brogan. They are now on the run with a posse of Skoll's boys after them.

Everybody has heard by now how Skoll got Cole and Ranny arrested on the charge of murdering that fellow Thorsen, and most see it for the bunco it surely is. Don't know if it's got to do with the row that went on at Skoll's place or what, but it has escalated far beyond all of that now. Some are saying Skoll's big boys chased the Q&M waddies all the way back to the Morris spread and burned them out of the big house. Nobody knows if any of them were killed or not, but most of the Scandinavians came back without anything to show for it.

I had thought this town had progressed beyond mob rule and night riding. Guess I was premature. Rufus and Judge Krumholtz are either in cahoots with Skoll or they have been bullied into cooperation. The Judge sits in his house and drinks while Ettie Krumholtz prays at the church with Parson Loon despite their difference in theological perspective. My wife is there too, and most of the other ladies in town.

I suspect they are all praying that the Lord reneges on the blessings they asked Him to lay on Skoll after he shot down Harley Crenshaw.

Well, I had been walking home after spending too much time handling John Gridley's 'case' and thinking how things were getting trumped out of proportion. Around then I heard the shouts of 'fire' and saw George Sagramore and the Negro woman he employed running about like a couple of headless turkeys in front of their grain shack, which was lit up and smoking like the Devil's own shitter.

Teller Carlson came running out of the Sunup with a bucket of water and the whore Whey-Belly Mary was right behind him with another. Dave Reed and Puff Tammany and Tim Morton all came running over, so I figured the fire would be well in hand. Funny how a fellow can rally an entire county to his call of 'fire,' and not turn up a single helpful soul if he shouts 'help.' I must have been the only one on the street headed in the opposite direction.

A few of the Scandinavians that had been sitting on the stoop in front of the jail went past me. I knew only that there was a fat chicken in the yard that I'd been imagining on my plate for the last week, and that after dealing with the intimate details of John Gridley's romantic life I felt like wringing its neck and treating myself.

I had just about reached the corner when I heard breaking glass and saw a figure throw up the window of the telegraph office and crawl inside. I'm no coward, but I've seen my share of fighting and want nothing further to do with it. Anyway there is nothing to steal in the telegraph office. Jake Krebb takes the cashbox with him after closing, and usually spends the day's profits at the Sunup unless his wife is there to intercept him.

Well, if I had taken the time to investigate the burglar at the telegraph, I might not have wound up in the fix I did.

Soon as I got to the corner, I saw a body of riders stop in front of the jail and go charging in with pistols out. It was dim in the lantern light, but by his hobble I recognized Aurelius Firebaugh out in front. There were two others besides him. I don't know who they were, though I expect they must have been Q&M sympathizers. Knew right away what their business was and tried to hurry past, not wanting any stray bullets to keep me from my chicken dinner. I could see through the window of the jail that Rufus had got up from his desk and filled his hand as soon as they kicked in the door.

"Empty your hand, Rufus!" Firebaugh said.

"They'll kill me, Alkali," Rufus answered.

"You dumb brush popper, what the hell you think I'll do?" said Firebaugh, and he fired.

Rufus fell to the floor, moaning and out of sight.

Then out of the dark doorway of the Picayune four men stepped quickly out into the street and headed for the jailhouse. They were Scandinavians (no bigger men exist in this part of the county) and they were armed.

Through the little lit window of the jailhouse I saw Firebaugh and his men stepping in totally unaware, hunting up Rufus' keys.

I did a fool thing then, and I haven't figured out exactly why. I dove behind the rain barrel that catches the run-off from the courthouse and gave out a yell for Alkali to watch out.

I didn't see all that happened next, but I heard Firebaugh's voice give a warning to his fellows in the jail followed immediately by an extended volley of shooting, both inside and out.

After that first exchange I dared a look and saw the four Scandinavians lying in the street. In the window of the jailhouse Cole was up against his bars with a pistol in hand. Alkali or one of the others had armed him and he had partaken in the fight.

I heard Rufus Shetland sobbing in the jail. Then:

"Cole, you alright?"

"Yeah. Get us out of this cage."

One of the men that had gone in with Firebaugh rushed up to the cell door and fitted a key into the lock. He looked like an Indian.

Cole stepped out and looked down at what I guess must have been Rufus lying there hurt.

"Confound you, Rufus," Cole said, "why'd you go and put up a fight? Do you work for Skoll now?"

"Not no more," Rufus answered. "That I'll admit. I just wanted to be sheriff, Cole. The Judge said..."

"You simple fool! How about the Judge? Is he Skoll's boy too?"

"I can't speak for him," Rufus answered, sounding pitiful.

"Hey we gotta go, Cole," hissed Alkali.

Cole lingered on Rufus for a moment before somebody passed him his hat, then the window was empty.

A horse came trotting up the side street right past my hiding spot. I plainly saw Alvin, and he was white as a sheet when he saw the dead men.

He looked like he was about to turn about and head out of town, but then the two men that had accompanied Alkali inside rushed out of the jail. Cole and Ranny Brogan were with them, Cole sporting a rifle and a bandolier of cartridges. Ranny tried to climb onto one of the big Scandinavian's horses, but it nickered and pulled away from him.

Then there was another voice I recognized. That of the Dutchman, Van Helsing. He said;

"Do not trouble with that mount, Ranny. It will only serve its master."

"I reckon you're right," Ranny said, and he and Alvin doubled up.

Alkali was the last to emerge, and he turned in the doorway and called inside in his usual blustery tone, "Keep quiet, Rufus, you damned turncoat, or I'll bust another cap on you."

Alkali took his time climbing onto his horse though the others seemed anxious to go, and I heard him remark, "We ought to go pay a visit to the Judge while we're at it."

"There'll be plenty of time for that later," Cole said.

"Alvin, did you..." Van Helsing began.

"Don't worry about me, I did my part. Just hope Ruddles gets the damn message."

"Hope? Hah!" said the Dutchman. "A more resilient man has faith."

"Whatever you say, Professor."

Then to my surprise, one of the Scandinavians I had taken for dead in the street took a shot at the riders. I don't know if he hit anything, but the next minute the whole lot of them went galloping west out of town.

By then the Scandinavians that had made for the fire came rushing up. The two men I'd believed dead got up from where they lay, and there were a lot of hot and angry words between both parties in their native tongue.

The Scandinavians seemed unsure of what to do, when two men on giant horses came up. One was Skoll, and the other, that red haired lawyer, Vulmere.

Skoll swung down from his saddle and stormed into the jail, ignoring the words of his men.

"Shetland! What happened here?"

Rufus answered in between nervous sobs. "It was Firebaugh and some others...they took 'em out of here and rode west out of town..."

Skoll was already on the porch and yelling at his men in the street before Rufus finished. All the Scandinavians went for their horses and Skoll and Vulmere mounted up. Just like Van Helsing had said, those big horses were as facile as lambs when the big blondes took hold of them. They went tearing out of town in the direction Cole and Alkali and the others had taken.

Rufus stood in the doorway holding his bleeding shoulder and called after them, asking what he should do next.

I slipped away in the dark.

That damn chicken has been granted a stay. There is a helluva lot going on here, and Skoll is in the thick of it. I don't like to think how Rufus became sheriff and how he is now under Skoll's thumb. I don't like to think about it, but I can't help it. It has gone and ruined my appetite. Turlough was a lazy bastard, but he didn't belong to anybody, not even Krumholtz. And after what Alkali said about paying a visit to Krumholtz...

I don't know, but I hate to just sit here.

* * *

Telegraph from Alvin Crooker to Marshal Stan Ruddles
Dated August 29th

M. RUDDELS,

INA BED WAY. STOP. SHERIFF SHITLARD HAS DEPUTISED FORINNERS. STOP. COLE MORIS IN NAIL. STOP. NORRIS HOUSE HAS BEENBUNNED. STOP. SEND HELF RAIGHT AWAR. STOP.

A. CROKER

Telegraph to Operator, Sorefoot, from Operator, Bastrop
Dated August 30th

MESSAGE OF AUG 29 TO M. RUDDLES INCOMPLETE OR UNCLEAR. PLEASE RE-SEND.

CHAPTER 16

From the Pen of Alvin Crooker
30th Aug

Won't be long now.

Don't know why I'm even writing this account, except to give me something to do. No doubt this will be lost as soon as Skoll's men make it down into the canyon. Van Helsing has pulled out those papers of Buckner's and is sitting in the firelight trying to decipher them. When faced with mortality I expect each man reveals his true nature in how he opts to spend his final hours. I write (and drink).Van Helsing reads and puzzles. Plenty Skins sits staring into the fire and singing quietly. Alkali, despite having lost his pegleg and sporting a passel of cuts besides, is running a rag through his pistols. Cole... Well, there my poetic theory fails. Cole is asleep.

And Ranny Brogan is dead.

I guess there is time enough to write about all that.

We weren't a mile out of Sorefoot when Skoll's bunch came after us. I don't know how many. All of them, I guess. Vulmere was there for certain. I could see his dark red head out front among all those blondes in the moonlight. Probably Skoll was beside him. We picked a helluva time for a breakout. At least the moon made the trail easy to see and the horses were sure footed.

We still had the advantage, our horses being quicker and lighter, but Ranny and I were doubled up, as were Van Helsing and the Indian. It wasn't long before we were lagging behind. Our horse's flanks lathered up quick. Soon I could hear the hooves of those giant horses behind us.

Then the shooting started. I've never pretended to be a man used to action. I was too young or too old for any wars, and any bravery under fire I've ever shown has usually up and bit me in the ass. The broken arm I got trying to 'save' Van Helsing is proof of that. I kept low against the neck of that horse as soon as the bullets started flying. I could hear them plopping into the dirt behind us. If our horse slowed a foot or more, those bullets would be relaxing square on our backs. The weight of the both of us got to be too much for the chocolate bobtail Ranny and I were on. It started panting like a winded bloodhound.

Then old Alkali, bless him, fell back and with the reins wrapped around his hook, pulled his pistol and took to firing behind us, discouraging the speed of the Scandinavians. Cole fell in line with him and did the same. The distance between our two parties became a no man's land of flying lead. We slowed, but our pursuers dared not gain any more ground. One tried, and had horse shot out from under him. He is probably still hoofing it.

It was a hell-bent ride and the horses were one and all spent when we finally got to within walking distance of Misstep Canyon, just north of the road that went past Buckner's shack. Our horse made a gurgling noise and fell dead, spilling Ranny and I to either side in the tall grass. The horse that carried Van Helsing and Plenty Skins died next, bleeding from its nose. Its game heart had burst in its breast.

Cole's and Alkali's ponies were no better off, and staggered as they were drawn up. Cole wasted no time in dismounting, and Alkali did the same. Their ponies wobbled off into the night, and if they fell somewhere out in the darkness we didn't know.

Now the strength of those slow, massive Scandinavian horses became apparent. They were galloping up the road, relentless as locomotives with their second wind.

Alkali, Cole, and Ranny took up positions behind the fallen horses and bade us all lie down in the tall grass unless we were shooting. We got low, but not a man among us would lay his head to the earth. The barrels of our weapons gleamed like hunting adders in the grass, and spat poison when the big horses came in range.

The Scandinavians rode into a perplexity of bullets, and I saw a few of them crash down. Then Skoll's voice bellowed a command in his guttural tongue and the other riders pulled back across the road and became fleeing, indistinct shadows.

Though one of the big horses lay twitching in the road, its blood black in the silver light of the moon, I saw no human bodies.

"Don't let up, boys," urged Cole, already reloading. "They'll be coming."

"Yes," said Van Helsing. "But not as men. Not on horses."

Plenty Skins nodded grimly.

"The Professor's right. They'll come as wolves."

Alkali glanced back over his shoulder.

"If we can get down into that canyon we can find cover and pick the sons of bitches off as they come down."

"They'll never let us," I whispered. "If we creep back they'll just get us in the dark."

"They'll get us if we stay, Alvin," Cole said.

"Not if one of us waits here and keeps 'em busy," Ranny said, and his voice was barely a whisper he was so scared.

"I'll stay," Alkali said almost immediately. He'd had the foresight to swing his pommel scabbards off of his horse before he let it go, and now he had one of the big irons in his fist. He was a game old buzzard.

"No, I think I better, Mr. Firebaugh," said Ranny, his voice breaking like a fishing line in his bobbing throat.

When we looked to see the cause of his distress, he lifted one hand from his side. There was a dark spot on his white shirt about three inches to the left of his stomach, and the front of his dungarees was oily like the hide of the horse in the road.

"Lord, Ranny!" Cole hissed, crawling over to where we lay beside each other, behind the cooling carcass of our pony. Out of the same instinct I suppose a dog at a dying compadre's side must feel, I inched away from Ranny. I got a splitting sensation in the middle of my stomach when I realized his wound might've been mine if it'd been me on the back of that horse.

"I musta caught it on the road. Didn't feel it till we fell."

Van Helsing was pushing me further away then, and peered at the wound.

"How is it, Professor?" Cole asked, his voice sinking.

"It don't matter!" Ranny sobbed. "I ain't goin' nowheres."

"We'll heft you," Cole muttered.

"Lord no, Mr. Morris. Them bastards'll get the whole lot of us. Ain't I enough?"

"Quiet boy..."

I looked at Van Helsing. He replaced the boy's coat over the wound and shook his head. There was nothing for him to do.

Somewhere out in the dark across the road a great noise went up, as if a whole chorus of men had raised their voices and screamed. It wasn't anything like a rebel yell. It was deep and angry and savage, like a chorus of angry bears. It ended even as we heard it. Sounded like '*Laayyy-diiing.*'

By his face, Ranny was fighting down hysterics.

Plenty Skins was crouched at the outer edge of us, back toward the canyon, ready to bolt.

"If we're goin'..." he said.

"Shut *up!*" Cole barked.

Alkali came over then and flopped down against the horse carcass. Without a word he laid one of his big pistols on the bobtail's belly. Then he took Ranny's own gun from its holster, checked the cylinder, and pushed it into the boy's hand. He lingered on Ranny's pale face for a moment, and it seemed like the young cowboy took something from the old bushwhacker's eye and strapped it to his spine, for he straightened though it pained him and sobbed no more.

"Sell it to 'em high, boy," Alkali growled.

Another bellowing yell went up from the Norgies out in the dark. It was terrible, and different from the last time. This time it went something like '*Dro-Maaaaaaa.*'

Then he pushed himself up and hobbled off toward the canyon.

Cole watched the old man disappear, then turned to Ranny and ran a hand over the nape of his neck.

Ranny nodded, suddenly calm.

Cole turned to us.

"Let's go."

The Injun was already gone.

A third scream went up, and beside me, Van Helsing said something that sounded almost like it.

"What?" I whispered.

"Glape-near," he said, and he was nodding his head to himself.

I didn't know what in hell he was talking about.

I opened my mouth to say something to Ranny, but he turned away from Van Helsing and I and took up one of Alkali's big Dragoons in his off hand and stared across the silent, silver dewed field. Van Helsing touched the boy's shoulder. I grabbed a hold of the old Dutchman's elbow.

"Come on, Professor."

Van Helsing pulled away from me, reached quickly into his shirt and pulled out the glittery cross on its silver chain. He slipped it over his head and dropped it over Ranny's. It hung up on one of his ears, but the old man straightened it. Then he turned to me and nodded.

We went side by side into the dark.

As we ran, he said that *glape-near* word again, as though it was too important to take with him to the grave if that's where we were running. He had to share it with me first.

"What?" I said again.

"Did you not hear? First *Lay-ding!* Then *Droe-ma!* Now *Glape-near!* The three fetters that bound the monster Fenrir! It must be that they break them to attain their change, metaphorically freeing their inner savagery — the wolf!" His face was lit up like a drunkard with a ten dollar gold piece, and he shouted all this to me in between breaths as he ran.

I vaguely remembered the story from the party, but then I had no more time to spare it any pondering.

The lip of the canyon came up without warning in its unnerving way, and under the light of the moon it was like the lands of hell down there, ghostly and cold looking in the gloom. The Indian was already over the edge, sliding lightly down the rocky slope, dropping like a nimble lizard from boulder to boulder. Alkali was proceeding more slowly, his false leg giving him a helluva time and sending the loose stones tumbling. Cole crouched on the rim and waved for us to hurry up.

As Van Helsing and I reached the others, a volley of pistol fire broke up the ominous quiet behind. Ranny's irons blazed somewhere back there, and I can only hope he gave a good account of himself. No gunfire answered his dozen or so shots, but suddenly his revolvers went quiet. The Indian and the Professor had been right. They didn't come after us like men.

I don't even know if they waited for Ranny's shots. It might be some of them ran right past him even as he cut loose. All I know is I saw them coming at us across the field, running on their hands like crazy apes. They saw us at the same time, and the whole bunch set up an ugly howl.

They didn't see our guns, or didn't care. We opened up into the onrushing line and still they came in their pointed cowls and hide shirts.

They were naked underneath. I expected them to break after the first discharge. Van Helsing and Cole and I were all slinging lead at them, but they didn't even pause. One of them tumbled to the ground and two others came leaping over him. They moved quicker than I thought a man on all fours could. I saw Cole turn his Winchester around and grip it by the barrel. One of the Scandinavians leapt at him and he stepped aside as if to let him pass, and brought the repeater down on the nape of the fellow's neck like an axe. The Scandinavian howled and went soaring over the canyon rim into space. His silhouette, more like a bristling animal's than a man's, flashed across the white moon for a minute, and then crashed somewhere far down below.

That was the last good look I had of anybody before two of those damned maniacs got to me. They had their claws strapped on, and my busted arm might have been shorn clean off but for the heavy wrappings. As it was, beating the lunatics away with my pistol was about as effective as pounding on a bull with a lady's handkerchief and yelling for it to behave.

I kicked and punched and tore, but one of their heads darted forward and I felt those hellish dentures tear a mouthful of skin and cloth from my shoulder. I think I must have shrieked, but I jabbed the long barrel of my gun like the point of a bayonet into the mess of fur and body that was weighing down on me and pulled the trigger. The son of a bitch that had bit me didn't slacken, but he did go twisting and snarling off of me, his wolf shirt on fire, I think more mad than hurt.

The other one grabbed at me and I had to slip my swaddled arm up to keep those devil teeth from snapping down on my throat, even as his claws ripped into my mangled shoulder. My pistol fell from my fingers and landed somewhere in the grass, and I hooked my naked trigger finger approximately where I figured those big black eyes to be and gave a jerk. I didn't gouge him properly, but I did manage to disrupt the eye holes of the mad fool's cowl. He roared like an upset lion, and spattered my face with froth, but in the instant of confusion I got away from him.

The only problem was, I scrambled right over the edge of the canyon. I fell free for about four feet before my neck and shoulders collided with the steep, rocky incline. Down I went, sliding and tumbling, praying I wouldn't go so fast or so far as to break my fool neck, and only being slowed by the occasional immovable outcropping. I careened off a protruding bush and led a route of rocks and pebbles right into some other poor soul who was making their steady descent, thus rendering whatever care they'd been taking a moot point. Like a rolling snowball, whoever I'd crashed into got caught up in my dangerous fall, and our combined momentum sent us pitching down the slope like a pair of sinful tumbleweeds riding a dust devil down the jagged road to hell. I don't know when we finally stopped, or if I was even conscious that we had stopped.

A big hand gripped me by my torn and bloody shirt front and growled, "Get up!"

It was Alkali I'd ploughed into, and it was a wonder that neither one of us had broken anything. I shouldn't say we didn't. Alkali's wood leg shattered on a rock during the fall. As I got to my unsteady feet and rubbed cautiously at my scraped and throbbing knees, he leaned heavily on me and I saw that only a sharp looking splinter poked through his torn pant leg.

I could see the old man plain, and he was a mess. His hat was gone and his thinly haired pate was a picture of cuts and scratches. His eyepatch had migrated to the center of his forehead in the scuffle, leaving his empty socket exposed. The good hand that held onto my bit shoulder and made it white hot with pain was bleeding too.

I didn't yell for the hurt though, because I was too busy marveling at the spot the Lord had chosen to deposit us. We were but three feet from a cliff that dropped off suddenly for seventy feet or more straight down.

I said a prayer of thanks that we'd stopped where we had, and Alkali, hearing me, said, "You best thank Barnaby Myers while yer at it."

"Who?"

"The blacksmith that gimme this hook back in Injun Territory."

He held it up, and I saw that it was slightly bent. He had thrust it out and used it as an anchor to slow our mutual descent. Back up the way we'd fallen, I could see the long furrow in the stony earth his hook had ploughed.

"Where's my damn rifle?" he snarled, looking all around.

I adjusted his eyepatch, slipping it back over the hole it had previously hid.

"I think it went over the edge," I said.

He cussed and inclined his gaze back up the slope as a clatter of gunfire rang out somewhere many feet above.

Dark shapes moved up there, and it was difficult to tell who was fleeing down the canyon side and who was pursuing. Those cussed

Norgies were having a real time by the sound of their barking and howling. It was like a bunch of bloodhounds had turned around on the hunters.

Someone appeared to the left of us then, very close, and Alkali ripped at the pistol still hung at his side.

"Hey, don't shoot!" It was Plenty Skins.

We relaxed and let the Injun get closer. He actually grinned at us in the dark.

"That was some spill you all took. I figured I'd find you dead."

"What now?" I mumbled.

"There's a quicker way down..." the Injun began, pointing to a narrow ledge trail that clung to the length of the canyon face and seemed to gradually ease downward.

"Not likely," said Alkali. "Where's Cole and the Professor?"

We heard gunshots then, and saw Cole firing up at the moving shapes. One of the figures ran past him and stopped. Alkali took aim with his gun, but then the shade on the slope produced a revolver and took to firing too. It was Van Helsing.

They made the remainder of their descent in the same way. One would stop and fire, allowing the other time to move further down, reloading as they ran.

Alkali waved his pistol back and forth in the air. Cole spotted him, and made for our position, bringing Van Helsing and a slew of wolf-men with him.

"Awright, let's git!" Alkali yelled.

Plenty Skins led the way, racing out onto the thin trail as if he were running across a broad plank walk in Dallas, and not some crumbling ribbon of a ledge with only sheer canyon wall on the right and the last and biggest step on the left.

I went next, with all the fear of a white man who knows there is no happy hunting ground waiting for him. I dug my fingernails into the rock like pitons and crept along that sliver of firm ground, trying hard not to spare worry to the drop and the horde of madmen speedily catching up with us.

"Go on, Alvin! Move it!" Alkali hollered. He stopped at the start of the trail and fired at the rolling, furred bodies coming like a wave, while Cole and Van Helsing scrabbled onto the trail and were soon crowding me from behind.

I found Van Helsing next to me. He was hatless, and his long English coat was billowing out over the nothingness. He'd stowed his pistol and like me, was doing his best to grab hold of the rock wall and sidestep quickly along.

I begged him not to rush me when his feet started brushing against mine. The Injun had slipped around a bend and was far ahead.

On the other side of us, Cole was supporting Alkali, and I was glad it wasn't me. Balancing on two legs was bad enough.

The Scandinavians reached the cliff we had come from and I thought for certain sense would come to them. But one of them came running on all fours, leaping over the stones and headed right for the ledge. Alkali fired squarely at him, the recoil nearly knocking himself and Cole over the edge. The bullet only grazed the charging wolf-man, but it was enough to upset his precarious balance and send him tumbling over. He bounced a few times off the wall down below and crashed among the rocks, never screaming once.

The other wolf-men howled and yipped and worked themselves up into a fearful lather. We could see them plain in the moonlight as we made our way around the bend in the trail. It was a bizarre sight. They fidgeted like stymied hounds that had lost the scent of the fox at the edge of the stream. They rushed back and forth on all fours, seeming to sniff at the narrow ledge trail and ran back to their pack to report. They nipped at each other angrily. They began to growl and shout in raging animal tantrums.

After a bit, one of the huddled figures rose upright and ran to the trail, hunched over like an ape. He shuffled along the same as we were, closing the gap between Alkali and himself.

Alkali took aim with his pistol, but either he decided against risking a shot that might dislodge him and Cole, or he was short on bullets, for he didn't fire.

The wolf-man got closer. His face was livid and his eyes big and black as smooth river stones. His fanged false teeth were bared and a loam of white froth was gushing from the corners of his lips. He growled low in anticipation, and we could hear his artificial claws scraping on the rock like dinner knives on a whetstone.

I reached the bend in the trail, which necessitated ducking underneath a jutting stone and swinging blindly for a half an instant over open air to get around. I felt my joints freeze up as soon as I crouched down. Had Plenty Skins managed this alright, or had he found nowhere to stand on the other side of this thing and simply fallen without a sound? I hunkered there, too scared to attempt the bend and too scared to straighten up again. Panic was bubbling up in me, and my hands seized up into claws as I fought this crazy urge to push off the rock and be done with it.

Van Helsing was standing over me, waiting to go, but his head was turned about and he was staring at the beast man about to engage Alkali. Cole too was looking back, his attention torn between finding the right foothold in front of him and keeping the old man up. He couldn't reach for his gun, which was shoved in its holster.

Then the crazed Scandinavian arrived and got a hold of Alkali. He seemed to give little thought to his own safety, but swung out with one great arm and raked his claws the entire width of the old man's chest, all the while hanging on to some invisible hold with one hand.

Alkali cursed him up and played his game. Gripping the arm that had wounded him, he put all his weight on his good foot and kicked out with the one nearest the beast man. The jagged splinter of wood left of his ruined leg jabbed full into the Scandinavian's side. The wolf-man's steady growling turned into a high yell of pain and wrath at the old man's audacity.

But with no leg underneath him and the other pinned precariously in the beast-man's torso, Alkali fell immediately. As he went, the harness around his knee unbuckled and he slipped out, leaving the broken peg protruding from the Scanindavian's side; a mass of wood and sweaty, writhing leather. Alkali was suspended for a moment by the trapped arm of the wolf-man, whose blood was now spilling down his naked legs in violent spurts from around the broken prosthetic. Then the Scandinavian lost his balance and went with the old man.

Alkali released his hold and grabbed at the tiny ledge as he fell with hand and hook, and Cole went down on one knee and latched onto his wrist with both hands, nearly somersaulting over the edge with both of them.

As it was, the wolf-man fell with the ruined leg, and Alkali dangled, hanging on by his will and Cole Morris' grip alone. Beside me, Van Helsing got a fistful of Cole's collar, and the three of them made a human chain.

Gradually and with no small effort they pulled Alkali back onto the ledge.

Behind us the wolf-men scampered warily back and forth on the outcrop. It was as though they had really abandoned their human intelligence and couldn't calm down enough to successfully manage the ledge.

From under the outcrooping over the bend in the trail Plenty Skin's hand swept up without any warning and pulled me under. I almost fell to my doom, but the Injun steadied me with both hands and pulled me up again. It seemed the trail broadened on the other side—not much, but it seemed like a great deal to me.

Van Helsing came next, then Cole, and with difficulty, Alkali. We could still hear the wolf-mens' bestial protests as we cautiously hobbled down the steep but manageable trail.

The moon was high when we reached the canyon floor and collapsed in exhaustion in the mouth of a short cave in the rock. They didn't follow us down the way we came, but we were wary, knowing full well they would find a way once they calmed down.

A long dried up sapling was uprooted to help Alkali hop along, and we built a low fire and counted our ammunition alongside our blessings. We have between the five of us two cap and ball pistols (one the Indian's and one Alkali's), and three revolvers of varying calibers, each with what amounts to about three to four shots a piece. Twenty bullets to keep us until dawn, and then what?

There is no doubt they will come, once they've regained their senses enough to reason it out. They'll find another trail. No one needed to state the obvious.

Earlier I posed the question as to how many of them were left.

"There's no telling," Cole said. "At least nine. I think there were a dozen working for Skoll, and three fell. I don't know if Ranny got any or not."

The mention of Ranny Brogan killed the talk for a few moments. Then Alkali rumbled, "We buried two on my place, and we gunned down three outside the jailhouse."

"We didn't see if the ones that were shot outside of the jail died or not," said Van Helsing.

"By God we shot 'em down," Alkali said angrily. "They're dead."

"He's right, you seen the way they drink bullets, Aurelius," Cole said. "There's just no telling."

Alkali mumbled angrily, something about the unfairness of it.

"And Skoll and Vulmere," Van Helsing said, "will be the most dangerous of all."

"What keeps them up?" Cole wondered. "I know on the way down I put bullets into a few, but they just kept coming."

"There are various theories about causes of the *berserkergang*. Narcotics, is one. A Swedish professor named Ödman theorized the ingestion of *amanita muscaria* – the fly agaric mushroom – by the Scandinavian warriors. Or it could be bog myrtle, which the Vikings used in *grut*, a spice in beer they often drank. I maintain it is faith, gentleman," Van Helsing said. "The berserks of old could sustain any number of wounds. They work themselves into a fury beyond normal ken. Have you noticed their eyes? The pupils seem to dilate more than normal. It is peculiar. Taken into consideration with this moonlight, they must see very clearly tonight. Indeed, moreso than on most nights."

"They foam like they're rabid," Alkali commented.

"Yes," agreed Van Helsing. "They are in a state of spiritual and psychological ecstasy, beyond reason. That is why they run into gunfire without any conscious thought of self-preservation. Belief is their weapon, my friends. They believe themselves possessed of a god's strength and a wolf's ferocity. They have convinced themselves of this, and not even a bullet will change their mind. That we have seen."

"If they can see in the dark," Cole said, "could they be blinded, like a frog in the dark with a lamplight in his eyes?"

Van Helsing shrugged.

"It may be. There is another chance...when their ecstatic state ends, there must be a period of exhaustion, as the intellect returns and the mind must deal with the damage and stress done to the body. They will feel the pain they ignored this night, and some may die yet from their wounds."

"Like the morning after a long drunk," I said. "Then why don't we go on back up?"

Alkali laughed.

"Think you're gonna go faster up that hike than you did down it?" He shook his head. "There's no way we'd ever make it."

We sat quiet around the fire. I thought about what Cole had said about blind frogs.

"It's like they ain't human no more," Cole said.

"In the state we saw them, they were not."

"You ever seen anything like this before?"

Van Helsing seemed to smile.

"Not precisely, but...something very much like this, yes."

"How? When?"

Van Helsing stared across the fire at Cole.

"With Quincey."

In spite of my pains and fright, I perked up.

Cole shared a look with the old Dutchman, and shrugged.

"Alright, Professor," he said. "Since I might not get another chance, tell me. What happened to Quincey?"

But Van Helsing shook his head.

"No. Such a story should not be told now. Besides, it will give us all another reason to live." He turned and grinned at me. "All of us. Eh, Alvin?"

I wanted to spit at him.

Maybe there's something to the Dutchman's talk. Maybe they won't even come until daybreak. I still wish we could sneak up out of the cabin, but Alkali's right. It'd take too long, and anyhow they're probably laid up somewhere up there, watching to see we don't try it.

I found that the brown glass whiskey pint I'd bought at the Sunup had proven itself sturdier than Alkali's old leg. It had survived its fall, and I cracked it open and wouldn't share. Nobody asked me to.

Cole drifted off to sleep while as I mentioned, Alkali lined up our pistols and began cleaning them and checking to see they were all in working order. Van Helsing got a hold of my shoulder, and dolled it up in a dirty bandage torn from his shirt sleeves, talking to the Injun as he worked. Now he's shuffling papers, as though he's on a field trip and has brought along his student's work to grade. The Injun took to humming, and then singing lowly.

Realistically there is little hope for us. We're outnumbered and short on cartridges and whole men. No one has asked me to confirm the message I telegraphed to Marshal Ruddles in Bastrop for help, but I'm sure fretting over it now. I was so damned hurried, out of fright and necessity. Was the message clear? Will Ruddles come in time?

I don't know when Skoll and his wolf-men will get to us. I hope I am passed out, though I guess a pint of whiskey won't be enough to get me there. At least I won't feel it when it comes...the way Ranny must have. I keep thinking about what Plenty Skins said about how they'd eaten Picker down at that burnt place in the canyon. The firelight moves like a shallow orange tide pool across our rock ceiling. I wonder how far away we are from that burnt place.

CHAPTER

17

Buckner's diary confirms that the dead man on Coleman's property was indeed one of Skoll's wolf-men. Picker and Buckner surprised and killed him, and Picker, fearing he had murdered a white man, took the fur mantle and cowl and went to his uncle.

I told Plenty Skins as much, after I had read it, and asked him to describe what had happened when Picker had come to him. He had been humming and rocking where he sat, looking into the fire. He fixed me with his eyes, and it seemed that something from the fire had made a home there and remained still.

"I knew the white man Picker had killed was no ordinary man," he said. "By then I had already had my dream."

Talk of dreams again.

"I told him the dream, and he got scared. I warned him to stay with me where I could protect him, but he run off. They musta been hunting him the whole time. He shoulda stayed with me. I coulda protected him."

Buckner's writings also mention some sort of goings on in the canyon. Drums, noises, a great fire. We have already seen the result of that night, but I cannot help wondering what it entailed (beyond the death of Picker). If Callisto was there — *the poor girl!* Will she be in need of psychological counsel when this is all over, if we do see things to a successful end and bring her from the dark influence of her husband?

I think of Mina Harker, and how, despite her ordeal, she came through the flames stronger even than I. I wonder how Callisto will be. A Mina, or a Van Helsing? My resolve is solid. God will deliver us somehow from this, if only for that woman's sake.

I turn my attention back to the matter of the ritual. It has been of some significance to them surely. Could it have been their wedding ceremony? Thinking of Callisto bound in her wedding dress among that pagan, wolf-clad horde fills me with outrage. I try to think back to my study of ancient Norse rites, and I endeavor to tie into those memories the facts of the ritual killing, the hearts, the bowl of blood, and the cannibalization of Picker, but without my library at hand it is quite useless. I can call up thousands of pertinent facts when I am prepared, but I didn't come to Texas expecting to encounter a single Norwegian let alone a cult of Odin worshipers. In my mind, every bit of vampire lore I amassed in my crusade against Dracula is rendered trivial. There are no hard facts to deal with here, only speculation.

I sense there is some pattern that I am overlooking. Nothing that will help us now particularly, but it does occupy my mind.

I asked Plenty Skins why he thought the wolf-man had been skulking around on the Morris ranch, for surely it was for the same unknown purpose the Skoll cowboys had been infringing upon the Q&M range land since the beginning.

"For the same reason Picker and Buckner were there," Plenty Skins answered almost immediately. "Hunting ground."

Picker and Buckner were warned off of Mr. Morris' place, but they went anyway to try and poison that mountain lion. So if the yellow haired wolves were warned off and kept coming, why do you think they did? The game was good. The cattle."

But, I pointed out, they had their own cattle, and the largest grazing land in the county in the property they bought.

"That ain't so," Alvin said. "Most of the cattle got auctioned off separate. Besides a few milk cows they just got the land itself."

Then it made sense. If one thinks of Skoll and his men as a pack of wolves (as indeed they believe themselves to be), then they would need a reliable food source. The cattle. The Q&M cowboys had suspected them of rustling. But in reality, they'd been hunting. And after being driven off the hunting grounds by Cole's men, they'd decided to take the land.

"Damn," said Coleman, from under the brim of his hat, where I'd assumed he was asleep. "Is that all they wanted? Cattle? I woulda sold 'em cattle and they coulda ridden the damn things naked on their own property for all I care. Hell, it's a free county."

"But they are not wolves. They are men, too. White men. They would not be content with what they could buy," said Plenty Skins.

I understand something of which he spoke. Skoll and his men are not fully wolves. They do not seek sustenance alone, but to glut themselves on ill-gotten bounty as their Viking forebears did of old. For them, danger seasons the meat.

Plenty Skins rose then, and took his ever present satchel from his shoulder. Even in the confusion of flight he had kept it with him. He opened it now, and took out the odd wolf hide apparel we had found him in. I watched him put it on, humming the same tune as earlier. He took out the turtle shell rattle and sat back down, facing the fire. He resumed his staring, and beat the rattle against his palm in rhythmic intercessions that were in time with his murmured song.

I asked him what he was doing, but he would not answer.

"Let him be, Professor," Alkali said, staring down the disembodied barrel of one of his guns. "You won't get another word out of him."

I asked Alkali if he understood something of what Plenty Skins was doing.

"Not a wit," Alkali admitted. "But I guess I know a death song when I hear one."

I didn't need to ask what that was.

Yet I am still not convinced we shall die here.

* * *

From the Pen of Alvin Crooker
August 30th

Skoll and his men came just before dawn.

The sky was as dark as a blanket of uncut denim, and the whole lot of us were finally starting to doze when a great screaming went up somewhere down the canyon, like the one we'd heard last night.

At first we all just sat and listened to it, like it was a weird siren song that kept us nailed put. But as soon as it ended, dropping off in the night, Cole was on his feet and shouting for us to get ready.

We all had our pistols nearby or in hand, except for the Injun. He'd quit his singing about an hour before and gone and sat at the back of the cave. Alkali laid a pistol down in front of him, but he just stared off into space like a man out of his head.

We took up places behind the big rocks across the cave mouth and got set to meet their rush. Van Helsing ran back to Plenty Skins and urged him to join us, but the red man sat the same as before, as if the Dutchman wasn't there shaking him.

Van Helsing gave up and ran for the rocks. As an afterthought, I scuttled over to where Plenty Skins was sitting and picked up the pistol that lay in front of him. I fixed him with what I intended to be a guilt-inducing glare, but instead found myself unnerved by his look of complete emptiness. It was as though he had so resigned himself to die that he was already on the brink. His eyes were large and unfocused, like they were seeing angels or the Indian equivalent. I got back to my spot near Alkali.

The racket they made seemed to come from all around us in that canyon. I kept looking over my shoulder thinking they were somehow creeping up on us. I only saw Plenty Skins, staring at nothing.

Then we saw a few of them, loping over the rocks. We directed a withering fire at them, and that was when the real body of them attacked from above.

They had crept onto the roof of our cave sometime in the night, and dropped down on our position in the cave mouth, engaging us hand to hand.

I heard shots all around me, but I was busy trying to catch my wind and keep it. My attacker landed full on my shoulders from a good height and I was breathless. I fought like hell to keep my arm and push him away.

Their shapes twisted crazily in the dying firelight and the hint of rising dawn. I felt his breath on me, hard and heavy, heard him growling. Then his artificial claws were in me, and I had my hands up under his chin, trying to keep his clicking dentures from my throat, even as his nails burrowed into my torso. I couldn't tell the sound of the ripping fabric of my shirt from the tearing of my skin. I tasted copper in my mouth and was convinced this bastard was going to be the end of me.

Somewhere a wild man raised his yell above the others and Alkali hollered back. A pistol fired, lonely in the loud rush of men's voices and the falling blows.

Cole screamed, "Goddamn you!"

That dark, fanged and bearded face I was squeezing between my white hands got closer. His jaw wrenched about, trying to nip at my fingers. My arms ached, the busted one crooning like a lovesick nighthawk. I couldn't feel the pain in my chest, but I knew by the flying fabric and the blood that he was doing his damndest to dig a hole right through me.

A howl sounded, different from all the rest. It was a real wolf's howl, long and keening, rising high in pitch and sliding through every man's ear and dancing a jig down each of his vertebrae. It even penetrated the scrambled brains of the blood-mad crazy that was killing me, for he went rigid in my hands and twisted his head away to look.

Then he was gone.

Something tremendous barreled into him and took his weight from me. I lay for a minute, staring at the ceiling with my arms still in the air, clutching at the empty space where he'd been.

I tried to sit up, but the pain was too much. I felt like I had a crocodile biting my belly. But something was strange. It was the noise. The hollering and the growling had stopped. I looked, and could see everyone plain, standing still and staring. Even the eyes of the wild-men were wide in their wolf-skin masks. I recognized Vulmere among them, his red beard blazing in the firelight, lips parted and drawn back around jagged teeth. His claws were dipped in blood, and he stood hunched like an animal about to break for the woods. All the men were aping him. Even Van Helsing. He was leaning against a big rock with his hair wild and blood across his face, his revolver in his hand and one sleeve torn and ragged. I saw Cole too. He was kneeling on the ground, and one of the Scandinavians had his arms around him, but they had both stopped wrestling, like a couple of little ones caught fighting in back of the schoolhouse.

Where less than a minute before the cave mouth had been filled with strife and chaos, now there was only a curious popping noise to my left.

Straddling the body of the Norgie that had been mauling me was a wolf. A tremendous, iron gray wolf, big as a young steer. Its legs were thick as a mountain lion's, thicker. They ended in huge black socks, each larger around than a big man's fist. I only saw it from the back. Its heavily muscled neck was inclined downward, and its muzzle thrust into the dead man's throat. Then, as I looked, it raised its head and saw me, a long thin strand of gore stretching from its black lips. Its eyes shone with fire, black as all evil. It had a huge head, with great ears that swiveled about constantly. One long tooth protruded from its lips like a red soldier's saber.

I got the strangest idea, and looked back towards the cave.

The Indian was sitting there still. Only his eyes were shut tight.

One of the wolf men yelled, and I looked back and saw it was Vulmere. His fists beneath his claws were bunched into hammerheads, and the veins were standing out alongside his red-rimmed eyes. His ugly teeth foamed and he shook like a man wrestling with the St. Vitus.

The huge wolf looked at him, lowered its head and flattened its ears. Its dark eyes narrowed and the lips split back to reveal rows of sharp red and yellow teeth.

Man and wolf-man rushed at each other. The wolf's huge claws scrabbled over the stones and Vulmere jumped gamely at him.

He caught around that wolf's head and hitched up his legs, digging his bare heels into the back of its neck and hanging on like a man trying to wrestle down a mustang the hard way. But the wolf's jaws clamped down on his shoulder. I heard the bones there shiver and split like timber. Vulmere gave a very un-beast like scream.

The wolf shook him like a puppy with a dishrag. His limbs flopped about like breeched fishes. One of his claw-gloves slipped off and stuck in the dirt in front of me, quivering. There was another crack, and the wolf flung Vulmere down. He lay in a tangle of sodden fur and right angles, twitching and gasping his last.

The wolf pawed at him with one great forefoot, then arched its back and let loose a terrible nose-to-the-moon howl.

Everyone in the cave mouth stood still in awe, frozen by the display and respectfully silent for its duration.

But when the monster lowered its head and licked its chops, the wolf-men surrounding it stirred. Cole and Van Helsing, Alkali and I were entirely forgotten. They growled, and, as if they were all of one notion, closed their circle and pounced on the huge animal.

Each of them attacked from a different angle. I counted five of them. They clung to its hide by their fists or by their teeth, and they alternately bit and kicked and stabbed. The monster wolf wheeled about like a bull, thrashing its head and kicking out, but the beast men held on like flies.

I saw Van Helsing take aim with his pistol and Cole rise up from the ground and grab him.

"You'll hit it!" he warned, and watched helplessly with the rest of us as our strange savior was overpowered.

Alkali was beside me, and his look was probably as worrisome as mine on him. His clothes were in ruins, and his exposed skin was slashed with crisscrossing red furrows.

"You alive, Alvin?" he asked.

I told him I thought I was. My eyes kept going to the big wolf. I was anxious for it.

Then there was another howl. But this wasn't the big gray's. It was higher, sadder, and it whirled ghost-like through the whole canyon.

All at once the wolf-men released the huge animal and backed away warily. The howl was still sounding. They stared wide-eyed at the huge wolf. It glared at them, breathing heavy and growling, bleeding from a half a dozen wounds that lent a scarlet shine here and there to its ashen pelt.

Cole and Alkali pointed their guns. This time it was Van Helsing that stopped them.

"Don't!"

The wolf-men retreated into the lessening dark, tearing off down the canyon. Cole shrugged off Van Helsing and fired after them. Alkali joined in, and their bullets ricocheted on the stones while the Norgies scampered off untouched. It seemed that as the howling dwindled, they were gone.

When I looked back, the big wolf that had saved me was gone too.

Then we all saw a dark shape perched up behind us on the cave roof, peering down with huge yellow eyes. It was a second monster wolf, though this one was obviously not as big as the gray. As the orange light filled the canyon and touched its face, it colored the animal water-at-midnight black. It whined once, then withdrew, quick and quiet as a ghost.

We said nothing to each other. Just stared, entirely confused and too ragged, I think, to move.

A voice echoed down to us from somewhere on the rim. It was Skoll.

"You live another day! But you had better leave! Today we are at our strongest!"

"Leave, nothin'," Cole muttered.

"Fiend!" Van Helsing bellowed up the rock walls, raging, turning around where he stood to address Skoll wherever he was. The red in his face matched the blood that was smeared across it. He looked like he'd just brought down an antelope with his teeth. "Villain! We're coming for her! Damn you!"

In answer, the canyon walls reverberated with Skoll's laughter.

"You are less than fools! You have been granted a boon this day! Don't waste it!"

"You son of a bitch!" Cole hollered back. "I'll see you and your bunch buried or burned!"

"You should have accepted my proposition, Mr. Morris! Now...I am not responsible for what happens!"

Alkali had my head in his hands and was jostling me. I was tired.

"Stay awake," he said. "Keep up."

I looked over at Plenty Skins' spot at the back of the cave to see if the red-skinned coward had slipped out during the fight. He was still there with his eyes closed, but dripping blood. It streamed down his face, over his wolf-hide cape, and was running over his bare ankles, pooling in his hands, which were one in the other, palm up in his lap.

Alkali must have seen my look.

"What in hell happened to him?"

Van Helsing was the first at the Injun's side. He crept up to him carefully, like he was a pile of rattlers.

Plenty Skins' eyes snapped open, wide and black and crazed.

I don't think a man among us didn't jump, and for me, that meant a lot of pain. A lot of pain meant I blacked out once more.

When I woke up, I was in the back of a funeral wagon with only a dead body for company. Cashman was driving, and when he saw I was awake, he told me the corpse was what was left of Ranny Brogan. The kid had made the big trip, but he had sent that big son of a bitch Walker on ahead of him.

Later on Doc Ravell told me after what'd happened at the jail, he'd gone straight to the telegraph office and wired Marshal Ruddles in Bastrop and told him in no uncertain terms that he had to be in Sorefoot with as big a posse as he could muster by sunrise. Then he'd gotten his old pony and ridden out to meet them in the dark, sleeping in the middle of the road till they showed.

Whether it was my line or his that brought help doesn't matter, I guess. Ruddles and twenty men rode all night and found Riley. They'd all gone straight into Sorefoot and arrested the Judge. Rufus had made a run for it south. Ruddles cut four marshals from his posse and set them on his trail. He didn't want to besiege the Skoll house until he was sure we were alright, so after commandeering Cashman and his funeral wagon and John Gridley and a few other men from town, he divided his men, leaving half to guard the town and taking out the other half hunting for us. Ravell said they found us hoofing it along the North Road. I don't know how Cole and the others got me up the rim of that canyon.

I don't know a helluva lot. By the clock here in the Picayune it is half past twelve. I'm told they deposited me in Cashman's wagon (I don't know if it was the only wagon available, or if they thought poor

Ranny and I were two of a kind) at eleven thirty and then made straight for the Skoll spread on fresh horses, intending to rescue Mrs. Skoll from her husband if they could. Even Alkali went with, I suppose still hopping on his sapling crutch.

I'm in a good lot of pain, but I have too much typesetting to do to give in yet. I'm leaving a few columns blank on this edition till I hear word. One of them is for the story about Quincey, which that goddamned Dutchman owes me. The other is the obituaries.

My only company is Useless. I don't know where the damn dog has been to, but he's curled up beneath my desk now, crushing a knob of bone, waiting for his master to return, I guess.

Just like the rest of us.

CHAPTER 18

From the Journal of Professor Van Helsing
30th Aug

May God help me. I fear I have doomed a poor girl and her unborn babe to death.

I will here record the events which took us from the bottom of Misstep Canyon to our present location.

As morning came full upon us and the light fell across Plenty Skins, who had to our collective displeasure spent the entirety of the skirmish seated at the back of our shelter, I saw that he was coated in blood. I went closer to him with trepidation, as I had not seen him stir during the conflict. He had only closed his eyes in solemn acceptance of death as it began. There was no question there was blood entirely coating him. It was no trick of the early morning light. It was his, judging by the open wounds I observed about his face and neck. There was a goodly gash in his right cheek and a scrape at his hairline, but there was no explanation as to how he had acquired his wounds. The berserks had not come near to touching him, as far as I knew.

Then, as I leaned in close, his eyes suddenly opened. I was close enough to see his pupils fluctuate, shrinking and growing again as though he had been pulled from a dark hole into daylight. He blinked, and held one palm up to block the early light across his face. He mopped the blood away there. He stared at his hands then, and looked up at me.

"They're gone," he said, rather than asked.

Before I could ask him what had happened, Mr. Firebaugh called me to Alvin's side. Our newspaperman had been grievously injured, and had lost consciousness. The berserk he had engaged had done its best to tear him open, and his cuts were very deep. I bound his rent flesh tightly with his own ruined shirt after cleaning the wound as best I could with the bottle he had been drinking from. He was delirious, and it was not certain he would survive.

I made it clear to Coleman and Firebaugh both the imperativeness that we deliver our friend to Dr. Ravell's care in Sorefoot with all expedience (where I could at least avail myself of his instruments, having lost my own in the fire at Coleman's). They both set out foraging for material to construct a litter to bear Alvin along. This gave me an opportunity to return my attention to Plenty Skins.

I found him stooped over one of the corpses, that of Vulmere. He straightened and lifted a grisly remembrance to the sky. Vulmere's red haired scalp, freshly lifted with his gory knife. Plenty Skins gave out a high, keening yip, like that of an excited dog. He turned in place, raising the scalp four times before turning to me, his own blood drying like chains of dark red lightning on his skin.

Though I found his barbaric display repellant, I understood that this was his sworn enemy and so did not dissuade him. When he was finished, I asked him pointedly what had happened during the fight.

"What I told you would happen, Professor. What the dream told me," he brandished the scalp at me. "I killed Red Hair."

"Do you mean to say, that monstrous wolf...was you?"

He hunkered down beside me, the very picture of a savage in his bloody wolf skins and bearing his trophy. I had seen that huge wolf, which existed in no field catalog of which I was aware, suffer several wounds at the hands of the berserks. One of them, a great slash opened on its muzzle, corresponded to a cut on Plenty Skins' face.

"I can't say what you saw," Plenty Skins said. "But I told you my dream." He nodded at Alvin. "Will he live?"

"His cuts are very deep," I admitted. "I cannot say if his internal organs have been damaged. Let me see your wounds."

He sat quietly as I wiped the blood from him and inspected his cuts. I could not say if they were self-inflicted. There was no flesh or blood under his nails. Nor could I explain the appearance of the great gray wolf, or how it had been the same shade as Plenty Skins' long hair and hide cape. I know he did not move from his space in the cave. There was nothing in the loose earth where he sat to indicate as much. But about six feet straight out from the spot, there were huge canine paw prints that began from nowhere.

Had the wolf then been some sort of psychic manifestation? But how could it take a physical form? I was swelling with questions, but there was much to be done and short time to do it in, if we were to save Alvin's life.

When Coleman and Firebaugh returned, Plenty Skins helped them weave together the dry branches they had found with strips of buckskin from his own clothes and fringe from his bundle. When we had secured Alvin into the makeshift litter, he stowed his wolf skins and shouldered the bundle.

Coleman and Mr. Firebaugh said nothing about the wolf, and nothing to Plenty Skins. But I saw their eyes flit across his wounds. Then Coleman and Plenty Skins and I bore up Alvin between us and hiked down the canyon, with Mr. Firebaugh limping behind.

The sun rose higher, but we were cool in the shade of the crevice. We did not make for the treacherous path we had come down in the night. With the litter it would be impossible. Instead we went toward the path we had brought our horses down days ago when we had first encountered Plenty Skins, dancing before his fire.

As we walked, I thought about the dizzying night, and remembered Skoll's words that morning. I asked Coleman of what proposition he had spoken.

"The day of the party," Coleman said, "right before the fight, Skoll took me out on the back porch and made me an offer for my land."

"Fair?" Firebaugh asked.

"It was fair, but I said no."

I glanced back at Plenty Skins. He had been right.

"I guess he aims to get it one way or the other," Coleman said.

We labored on through the morning. We passed the burned rock where the berserks had held their ceremony, and there stopped to rest. None of us had eaten or drank since yesterday, and Firebaugh said the water that had long ago carved out the Misstep had gone dry. We did not know to what end we struggled. It was sure that our horses were long gone, either wandered off or claimed by Skoll. Our canteens, still hanging from our saddles, were sorely missed.

We finally reached an ascending trail, and its easy slope was rendered tortuous by our shared burden. With no water, Alvin's condition became grave. His lips were split and cracked, and his fever high. He mumbled incessantly, words we could not discern. We endeavored not to jostle him, for fear of aggravating his wounds, and the walk up the trail was slow indeed.

We had no means to defend ourselves as we had spent all our ammunition. The nearer we came to the rim, the more assured we became that Skoll's men would be waiting for us.

Midway up the stony trail our fears reached a crescendo. We heard horses above, and the creak of occupied saddles, and men talking.

We lay low, trying to decide what to do. We could not descend again quickly and quietly enough to avoid alerting them, and we could not continue.

Then Firebaugh volunteered to continue on alone and try and bluff whoever awaited us with his empty pistols.

"You'd never make it, Alkali. They'd hear you comin' up and burn you down before you made it," said Coleman.

"They did not fear the guns when they *were* loaded, Mr. Firebaugh," I pointed out.

"Might give you the chance to get some cover," Mr. Firebaugh answered.

"Hell with that," Coleman said. "I'll go."

"I don't think it's them," Plenty Skins said. But no one paid him any mind. I sensed that Coleman and Firebaugh were nervous of him now.

"Well, I'll let you know. Get on behind them rocks over there," Coleman said, and before any of us could raise our voices in protest, he was going up the trail.

We struggled to move Alvin's litter out of sight, and lay around him behind a huge rock.

Mr. Firebaugh kept an eye on Coleman as he reached the top, slinking just under the rim with his gun out.

"What the hell's he doin?" Firebaugh muttered after a moment.

Peering around the stone, I saw Coleman stand up in full view and lift his hat.

Jubilant voices met him rather than bullets.

It was Ray Bixby, Tom Koots, and Paul Murtaugh, along with a few other young men from the Q&M I did not know by name. They had evaded Skoll's hunters in the night and hid out in the countryside. They reported that they were the last of the cowboys to have nourished hope that their employer was still alive. What members of their group had not been killed by the berserks had left the county and headed for their homes. All in all there were seven men, and their bedraggled clothes and dirty, unshaven faces were as pleasing a sight as a chorus of flushed faced children singing yuletide carols.

They had heard the gun battle of the previous night and found Ranny Brogan's body this morning, with the corpse of the towering Hrolf, who had born my invitation from Callisto to the Morris ranch. They had been deliberating as to their next course of action when Coleman had hailed them.

To a man they were ready for warfare, and reunited with their master they were like a pack of loyal hounds straining at the leash. They were happy to see Mr. Firebaugh too, and myself, though a few expressed unease at the presence of Plenty Skins, who remained aloof during the joyous reunion. We watered and ate in good company.

To compound our celebration, a body of horsemen we recognized from afar as not being of the Skoll faction turned off the North Road and came into our camp. Coleman's plan to have Alvin wire the United States Marshal of the nearby town of Bastrop had proven true. He arrived with four deputies and several men from town.

Marshal Stanley Ruddles was a weather-beaten lawman of angular proportion with eyes like an Irish hillside. He had ridden out after midnight last when the telegraph operator had roused him from his sleep, complaining about an unusual pair of messages coming in for him at an odd hour. Apparently Alvin's initial message had been unclear and Dr. Ravell, who had witnessed the rescue of Coleman and

Ranny from the jail had sent a second message personally. After learning of what had transpired from Dr. Ravell, Marshal Ruddles rescinded Sheriff Shetland's deputization of the Skolls. Shetland had eluded capture so far and was presumed Mexico bound, but Judge Krumholtz was imprisoned under guard pending an inquiry.

We were not of a mind to scold poor Alvin for his unsteady operation of the telegraph. I explained to Ravell the gravity of his wounds, and my own doubts that he would survive. His loss is yet another outrage which we must attribute to Sigmund Skoll, and I shared the group's intent to enact retribution upon him. The rage of the wronged had surpassed my own clinical curiosity and Hippocratic empathy for these Scandinavians and their psychological derangements. My only humanitarian thoughts were of Callisto.

Young Ranny's body was lifted ceremoniously into Undertaker Cashman's wagon, and Alvin was laid beside him. Mr. Firebaugh was urged to accompany Cashman and Ravell and their guard back to Sorefoot, but as usual he would hear nothing of it. He only demanded fresh loads for his weapons and a horse to carry him.

He was given both.

I warned the marshals what it was we all faced, and outlined the particulars of what they all could expect. They expressed disbelief, but Coleman and Firebaugh and some of the cowboys who had seen the berserks' powers to ignore pain corroborated my admonitions.

"I know it sounds crazy," Coleman said. "I know it. But the Dutchman speaks true. These Norgies are like wild animals. You can call it what you will, but they ran the lot of us down into Misstep Canyon and damn near wiped us out, and all without a gun between 'em."

"Awright, Cole," said Ruddles. "I ain't never known you to go tellin' windies, but it all sounds pretty peculiar..."

"They're a peculiar bunch alright," Firebaugh agreed. "I seen one keep fightin' with a hole in his neck and a bullet in his bread wallet. Damn near took me with him when he finally went. And if you don't believe us, Ruddles, you soon will, and you'll wish you had."

We were making ready to leave when Plenty Skins took me aside.

"I'm not going with you," he said.

This shocked me.

"You'll be safe with me," I told him. "I won't let them..."

"It's not that, Professor," the old Tonkawa said, shaking his head. "I'm all through here. Red Hair is dead, and the blonde wolves will follow. When too many white men are angry, too many things pass from the world that ought not to. It's up to the Great Hunter now, to keep his hounds in check. Remember the favor I asked of you, and when you go across the Waters back to the East, maybe you'll have learned something none of your books can teach."

He held my eyes for a moment longer, and there was something in his murky amber stare like the passing of the tide from a lonely shore. He gripped my shoulder in his bony hand, and smiled in satisfaction when I did not flinch away. He released me and went walking down the North Road with his bundle over his shoulder, in the opposite direction from where we were headed.

"Where's he going?" Coleman asked.

I didn't know.

I never saw Bill Plenty Skins, or any of his kind, ever again.

It was a long ride to the Skoll ranch, but we were confident that our sudden arrival would catch the enemy unawares. After their long night of mad fury they would be exhausted and spent in the light of day, and it was very possible we might even be able to capture them all without bloodshed.

Marshal Ruddles doubted they would be in the house at all.

"If these Norgies have any sense, they'll be headed to Mexico."

"They got a sense," Firebaugh said. "But they won't run."

He had gained a fighter's respect for their abilities.

With the marshals and the cowboys we had a sizable army to pit against Skoll, nearly twenty-five armed men to his half dozen.

"What worries me is the old Judson house," Coleman said.

"I know it," Ruddles agreed. "It is a damned fortress. If they do decide to make a fight of it, we could be in for a good long siege."

The house loomed as before on the flat plain. I had not realized before how very bare of cover the approach was. There were no trees, and as we rode into the immediate vicinity, a murder of crows took to flight from the tall grass, scattering across the sky like burnt leaves riding a sudden eddy and making for their home in the eaves of the big stone house.

"If they didn't know we were comin,' they know it now," Firebaugh complained. "Damn crows."

I was reminded of Huginn and Muninn—Thought and Memory, the two ravens who were the spies of Odin. The birds would return to their master's shoulders each night to whisper in his ears all the news of the Nine Worlds.

Skoll and his band had no need of birds though. They had waited for our coming, and if they could not come out to meet us fresh in all their savage, pagan regalia, they would make a stand these Westerners at least could appreciate. Rifle fire broke out. Puffs of gunsmoke erupted from the shuttered windows of the house, and we got down from our horses and formed breastworks. The rifles of the cowboys and the marshals spread across their horse's necks, and the siege was begun.

For nearly ten minutes the barrage of fire from the house did not stop. It appeared to come from three different shooters. Two on the ground floor, firing through ports cut into the closed shutters, and one from an upstairs window. I could imagine the three immense blonde riflemen seated at their positions, firing through their barricaded apertures, each with a man whose job it would be to provide his comrade with a freshly loaded weapon. Somewhere, perhaps in a closet, I could imagine Callisto, fettered and gagged, or worse.

Ruddles advised the men not to return fire as their bullets were landing far out of range of our position. It was his plan to wait for a break in the shooting and then advance close enough to utilize our own long arms. But then one of the deputy marshals slumped over, dead from a bullet in the chest, and our army was thrown into confusion.

It was possible to discern among the constant shooting now the report of a larger weapon coming from the shooter in the upstairs position.

"He's got a damned needle gun," Coleman said. "Stan, that son of a bitch will rub us out one at a time from that window if we don't do something to change his mind."

"If you got an idea, Cole," the exasperated Ruddles said, "don't wait to let me know."

Coleman looked around, then pointed out the pen where some of the giant horses were galloping about, frightened by the noise of the guns.

"Some men might be able to drag those water troughs over and use them for cover," he said. "We could spread the rest out and surround the place. With that buffalo rifle only able to cover one side of the house at a time, we might close the noose around 'em and give 'em something to duck."

"Them troughs ain't nothin' but clapboard," Firebaugh argued. "Why don't we put some men in the corral and just use the fence for cover? Then we can start layin' in from two sides at least. You can still move some men around the back to keep that son of a bitch busy."

It was agreed. Marshal Ruddles would lead four of his deputies to the corral, while Coleman, Ray, Tom, and Paul crept around back, and Firebaugh and the rest stayed here. I asked to go with Coleman, as I wanted to be among the first to penetrate the house. If there was a fight in close quarters, the men might be hard pressed to discern a woman from the enemy.

"Alright, Professor," Coleman said. "You can come with us, but you better keep your head down, 'cause we won't be stoppin' for tea."

Ruddles led his deputies toward the corral first. They went rushing along, hunkered down like aged men, their belts creaking and their weapons clinking. They moved in an orderly line and did not break, even as the ground around them exploded into little puffs of dust. Their mission was twofold. Not only were they attempting to gain position, it was their intent to release the penned animals and deprive the Scandinavians of a means of escape, lest they hold out till cover of darkness and then steal into the corral.

The men inside could read this plan from their vantage, and poured a discouraging fire in the direction of the marshals. But only the upstairs, large-bore weapon had any hope of reaching them, and it claimed only mud and dust.

Ruddles himself led the foray, and was the first to reach the gate. He knocked off the latch and swung it wide, as his men vaulted the four-rail fence and landed on their bellies in the deep, pungent earth.

The marshals began shouting, and the attention of the big Scandinavian horses was drawn to the egress. The chief among them, a huge, blonde-maned stallion, made a cautious inspection of the open gate, and then plunged through with a snort. His fellows did not hesitate to follow, and Ruddles gave the last one further encouragement by laying the barrel of his rifle to its tremendous rump.

I did not have time to admire the magnificent horseflesh in flight as I had at Firebaugh's. Coleman gave a harsh word of command and went running across the yard toward a position parallel to the southwest corner of the house. As we lurched to our feet, the marshals produced a distracting fire. They had crawled through the manure-laden plot to the corner of the corral behind the water trough, and were now in range to send bullets into the house. I heard the smashing glass and saw the shutters of an unoccupied window sprinkle with holes, and then I was running behind Tom Koots, my eyes fixed on the rushing ground.

The Scandinavians traded fire with the marshals as we went by unnoticed, but when we were within striking distance of our goal I heard a guttural exclamation from somewhere in the house. Bullets began buzzing past us like tsetse flies. I was reminded of Africa again, running through the brush as whistling missiles sought my destruction on every side.

In front of me, Tom Koots stopped and I barely avoided colliding with him. I ran past him without thinking, then turned my head to call to him. His hat had blown off and he had stopped to retrieve it. I saw him fall as a heavy bullet passed through his shoulder and emerged red from his lower side. Though I hesitated, something hot burst near my right foot, and I kept on. Coleman levered his rifle as he reached the corner of the house, and disappeared around the edge followed closely by Paul.

"Where's Tom?" Ray demanded of me over his shoulder, lingering.

I shoved him forward and told him to spare no thought on it.

We slid to a stop at a few feet from the edge of the back porch, crouching at boardwalk level.

"Where's Tom?" Ray repeated, going so far as to grab my sleeve when we were safe.

"If he ain't here, don't ask!" Coleman said, without looking back. The door leading off the porch was blocked by a heavy wagon whose left wheel had been hewn from the axle. There would be no access that way.

Coleman pointed to a cluster of old barrels that stood a few yards out, beside what appeared to be a door set into the side of a low hill. It afforded a good position on the house.

"There, next to that fruit cellar. See those barrels? That's where we're headed. C'mon, while they're still movin' to the back windows!"

We were on our feet again, running for the barrels, when the door to the fruit cellar burst open in front of us and one of the giant Scandinavians lurched out, still in his hide dress and drenched from head to foot in blood. One eye lolled in his head and he seemed barely able to stand.

Coleman brought up his rifle and fired three times.

The giant crumpled and lay still on his back in the doorway.

Coleman led us past the prostrate form and clambering over the smallish mound that was the roof of the fruit cellar, we fell behind the thick, rain-filled barrels just as the rear upper window of the house exploded outward and the barrel near my shoulder shuddered with the impact. The ground around it grew damp as the water escaped, and soon we were kneeling or lying in mud.

"Awright now, don't be afraid!" Coleman said.

Ray, the boy who had worried over Tom Koots, huddled with his rifle in his arms and sobbed like a child whose play had suddenly gotten out of hand.

"We got to keep their heads down, so start slingin,'" Coleman went on. "'Less you wanna spend the rest of your youths sittin' on your asses behind these God-forsaken barrels."

Paul reacted first, and, poking his rifle barrel through a gap in the cover, fired up into the house. Coleman stuffed ammunition into his weapon and joined in, and I added blindly to their volley with my revolver.

Ray stayed curled in on himself like a tortoise. We could do nothing for him.

A half hour passed before we realized he had been shot in the abdomen. By that time there was no hope for him, if ever there had been. I was reminded of young Ranny. The weight of another death to speed Skoll's descent into damnation.

In my heart I felt there was no hope that Callisto was yet alive. I could see her face, her dark eyes and curls, but she was pale as death behind my eyelids. The poor girl and her unborn child...was Skoll surely that insane that he would commit such an atrocity as the death of his own child and wife? Surely he was. Surely diabolism had been his intent all along. Doubly wicked is the crime that is perpetrated on the unsuspecting, on the innocent. All through the afternoon we called into the house for them to spare Callisto, to set her free. Our only answer was gunfire.

Then came a break in the shooting, when the sun was nearing its fall. For awhile only the sound of Ray's failing breath was to be heard.

Then:

"Van Helsing!"

I recognized the throaty voice immediately. It was Skoll. He called to me in Dutch.

"Van Helsing, are you alive?"

"What the hell's he sayin?" I heard one of the marshals shout.

"You know I am!" I answered.

"Who's that?" another of our men in front of the house called out, before I heard Firebaugh's voice calling for silence.

"You had better call them off, Van Helsing! Soon our power will have reached its zenith! Even you won't be spared!"

"Set your wife free, you villain!" I called. "Or we will burn the house down around you!"

Skoll laughed in a mocking tone.

"My dear Professor! Do you still think I hold my own wife against her will?"

His words gave me pause.

"Is she dead, then?"

He only laughed.

"Do you covet my wife, Professor? Is this the source of your paranoia about her welfare?"

I felt the hairs at the nape of my neck uncurl.

"You're insane!"

"There is a name for your condition too, Professor," he answered, amused. "I'm sure a learned man like you must be aware of it. Uther felt it, when he besieged Cornwall for what he thought was love of Igraine. But it wasn't love, Van Helsing. Shall I tell you what it was?"

"Dog!" I exploded, forgetting my Dutch and reverting to English in my wrath and embarrassment. "I won't banter with a madman! Release Callisto! Surrender your arms! In the name of God, spare her and your child at least!"

If it would have made a difference, I might have clapped my hand across my foolish mouth to trap the words I'd spoken.

"Abraham!" it was her, and her voice was tortured and hoarse.

"Callisto!"

"Abraham! *You promised you would not tell!*"

There were the sounds of a struggle coming from upstairs.

Coleman was staring at me. I think I drove my teeth into my knuckle. I tasted blood.

"So be it, Van Helsing!" came Skoll's voice again. "Tonight we will be at our strongest! None of you will live to see the morning!"

I entreated Skoll to speak further, but he said no more. I begged for Callisto's life, and turned to cursing him and all his men. When I was exhausted, I laid my head against the empty barrel, and felt Coleman's eyes upon me.

Later, the large bore rifle (Skoll's rifle, I felt sure) began picking off our horses, and John Gridley was entrusted to move them out of range. There was no more shooting after that, unless one of our party attempted to move closer to the house. Marshal Ruddles lost another deputy who was too brave, and Ray succumbed at last.

As the evening grew deep and the distended shapes of the long shadows lost their forms and began to spread like ink across the field, Firebaugh came around to our side. He took off his hat when he saw Ray lying still, and there was a bloody crease on the top of his skull I had not seen before.

He offered us whiskey John Gridley had brought, and Coleman and Paul drank, but I would not. I felt sickly, disgusted at how my own lack of sworn secrecy may have turned the already dark fortunes of a misled girl a shade blacker.

"How long did you know?" Coleman asked.

"Since the party," I answered.

"Will they kill her?" Paul asked.

No one answered. After a moment, the frightened cowboy spoke again.

"Will they kill us?"

"It's twenty to five now by my reckoning," Firebaugh said.

Silence for a few moments.

"I been meanin' to write a letter to my maw," Paul stammered. "I believe I'll be about it, while it's yet light."

The night will be upon us in another hour. No sound comes from the house. Paul has finished his letter. I can no longer see to write. The light is fading fast...

CHAPTER 19

Recovered from the Papers of Mdme. Callisto Terovolas-Skoll

Night is coming, and over the hissing of the lamp in this windowless room I hear the grunting of the men as they begin their ritual downstairs. The oil burns, and light is sustained, but for how long? The babies kick as though they wish to emerge and join their father in his pagan immolation.

They will come soon. Sooner than even I had thought.

Sigmund bade me witness the ceremony, but I wished to be alone. In truth I did not want to remember him thus. Rather, I would think on him as the gentle eyed man who approached me fearlessly in the dark forest, his blue eyes glimmering, so exotic, so new. How happy he had been to find me. He had fallen upon his knees and pledged himself to me, with his foolish heart's story of how he had seen me but briefly on a passenger ship.

'I know you for what you are,' he had said to me, heedless of my warnings. 'I have spent half my fortune to find you. I will not leave, unless it is with you.'

I would see him now as I saw him then. A proud, strong hunter, and I his mate among the undergrowth, with the broken light through the branches spilling down on us.

I do not want the last vision of Sigmund in my mind to be him stooped among his fellows, grinding his teeth and pulling his beard and striking the floor with his fists. Yet the noise of their chanting and growling has already ruined his idyllic portrait in the eye of my mind.

I can see him now as though I were there, watching him stamp his feet and shuffle on his hands in that primitive parody of the wolf's gait. I can see the hairs on his body rising...the tendons standing out on his naked arms like iron roots...the tidal foaming about his grimacing lips...and the unnatural widening of his irises. The black spreading to engulf the blue as though evil were swallowing good.

There is something in my love's religion that strikes me as more than barbaric. There is a falsity to their animalistic posturing, which is not so simple or harmless as mere self-delusion. Their grim one-eyed god, hanging from his tree, and beckoning for his worshipers to join him in death, favoring them only when they attain some new height of self-destruction. What manner of god makes such demands of his subjects? Sigmund assured me again and again that I did not fully grasp the profound nature of their beliefs, and I am convinced that I do not.

Surely they think themselves blessed by their Allfather this night. This cursed, vile night, which reeks of impending death.

Why did Abraham betray me? What did Sigmund say to him? Matters are worse for us all.

For now that Sigmund knows I am pregnant, now there can be no silent escape in the night. There must be blood and hell. He and his men will throw themselves into the bullets of the Americans in the name of protecting me and my sons, for sons they are. Of that I am sure. I do not need their goddess Freyja or her seior rituals to know this, as I did to prophesy that Vulmere would die. In truth, I do not even remember saying any such thing. Sigmund swears that on the night of our wedding in the canyon, when I was initiated as their volva — their priestess — consumed the sacrificial stew, and succumbed to delirium, that I did so.

I wonder now if Sigmund did not take advantage of my state and plant the seed of self-destruction in Vulmere's mind. I knew well that Vulmere plotted against my husband and coveted his position in the pack. He was hasty, and it was his rash vengeance against the man who had broken his nose which doomed him, I think. Sigmund was forced to comply in the plot to slay the man Searls and the constable by the influence Vulmere had over Judge Krumholtz and the new sheriff. Vulmere had swayed the pack against Sigmund's better judgment. But I think my husband got his own revenge. Faith is a powerful thing. Sigmund could have passed a false prophesy to Vulmere. Perhaps it was the man's own belief which slew him in the end.

Of the trance it was said I fell into following the night of chanting and eating that horrid stew in the canyon, I remember little. Flashes of dreams, really. Was there real prophecy there? Real power? I have never believed in such things. Had I been given some glimpse of the time to come, why could it not be about the fate of my children? Had I known they were to die here in flame, among these stinking cattle...But the only real visions I had were meaningless. Something about a large gray wolf, and about Abraham.

Abraham. He will die now, I should think. I could not bear to know he would be killed in the canyon with the others, not even for the dream of the land. Boundless, fenceless, game-filled land, where our dynasty could romp and hunt to the content of their wild hearts. It was a dream that brought us both across the ocean, each of us leaving forever our beloved homelands, where we were cast out. So much has been at stake. Life or death for my line, and the honor of my husband's.

And yet, I could not bear the death of one sad, funny old man. I ran all night to prevent it. I offered him an escape. I even extended clemency to his companions for his sake alone. But it was for naught. I fear I will not be able to do the same again. Abraham, why didn't you leave? If you had not come we might've all been happy, every one of us. Now, my children, my husband, what will become of them?

Will they see the world, and breathe its air but once—if at all?

My belly swells by the day. In three or four days they will be born.

I hear the resounding shout of 'Gleipnir!' down below. The last chain is broken. The men outside have lit brands of fire. I can smell it, even as I smell their dread, stinking and running down the intimate crevices of their nervous bodies. As I smell the heightened state of the men downstairs, as I smell my husband among them, and hear his heart beating fast as a diving kestrel's even as his throat rumbles for war. So, it is coming. I bid adieu. Though these words may never be read, I am sorry Abraham.

But I must stand with my love...

* * *

Narrative of John Amos Gridley, as told to Alvin Crooker

The proceeding was related to me in my office at the Sorefoot Picayune on September the first, by Mister John Adams Gridley, owner and proprietor of Gridley's Eatery. It is a true and factual account of the events of the night of August the thirtieth, year of our Lord, eighteen hundred and ninety eight. –Alvin Crooker, esq.

On the night of August the thirtieth, I was engaged in the siege of the Skoll house [formerly the Judson house], having volunteered to go along with a posse commandeered by Marshal Dan Ruddles of Bastrop to arrest the Scandinavians for the burning of Coleman Morris' house and the murder of Sheriff Michael Turlough, Early Searls, and Sean ['Ranny'] Brogan. Sig Skoll and his entire gang were fortified in the house with Mrs. Skoll [presumed captive] and had been firing on us throughout the day. Ray Bixby and Tom Koots of the Q&M Cattle Company were killed by bullets before nightfall, along with two of Marshal Ruddles' deputies [Tyler Freed and William Cannon] and three horses. Besides killing some of us, they ignored all demands by Marshal Ruddles and others for the safe release of Mrs. Skoll, and made a number of threats against our livelihood.

At this time I was engaged with walking the party's horses out of range of the shooting, for a rifleman inside the house had taken to killing the animals at extreme range, possibly with a Sharps or other long hunter's rifle, I would say of forty four, maybe fifty caliber. Being the least able to fight [due to a recent, sensitive affliction], I was elected to bring the horses back to a low ridge on the southeast corner of the property which overlooked the scene, and I had a pretty good view of all that went on.

When night came Mr. Aurelius [Alkali] Firebaugh hit upon a plan to smoke the gang out, and two of the Q&M boys [Way Parker and Bob Erb] set about breaking up the corral, which had been emptied of its horses, for burning.

There was a good lot of shouting coming from within the Skoll house at this point, but I was not close enough to hear clearly if anything was being said.

Alkali Firebaugh was in a position facing the rear of the house, along with Paul Murtaugh, Cole Morris [both of the Q&M], and a man called Van Helsing [Abe Van Helsing], while Marshal Ruddles and his deputies [Melvin Theiss, Sy Morant, Buster James] and Parker and Erb were out front. The plan was to light the front of the house and drive the gang out the back, where our best marksman would arrest or shoot them.

There was fear that the men would not be able to get close enough to the house to pile on the fuel, but whether it was the cover of dark or something else, Erb and Parker got it lit. As soon as the fire got up though, there was a hell of a commotion from the house, which I am hard pressed to describe. Some kind of call like a rebel's yell or a Comanche war whoop.

Parker and Erb had barely got away from the fire and back to Ruddles' line when the front door burst open The window shutters on the ground floor were flung apart and four large men came rushing out, jumping right through the flames and running across the front yard. With the fire in the front I could see pretty well that they were dressed all in furs, and were a frightening sight, like wild men. They ran on all fours, swinging along almost like apes.

This was against the plan and must have thrown Marshal Ruddles and the other men for a loop, or else they were afraid to shoot lest they hit Parker and Erb, for they did not fire. Two of the wild men singled out the two cowboys, and Parker and Erb both were dragged down and pounced upon. Ruddles and his men began firing then, for the two remaining men who were not otherwise engaged came right at them, though they appeared to be unarmed. I could hear them bellowing as they charged, and it was less like a man's war cry and more like the call of crazed beasts.

I did not fully see what happened next, for my attention was drawn to the back yard by the sound of a door slamming open. While the fighting continued in front, and the fire ran up the wall of the house, I could see and hear everything that went on in the back, thanks to the bright big moon that was out and the direction of the wind, which blew their voices up to me.

Two men came rushing out the back door, and Mr. Morris' group did not waste time but let fly with a good storm of lead that sounded like a brick of Chinese firecrackers. The two men kept coming, though it seemed they were taking hits all over, and actually reached their position before they fell, crashing into the very rain barrels Mr. Morris and his men crouched behind.

I heard a scream, high and long, and saw that one of the men had managed to wound Paul Murtaugh. Aurelius Firebaugh shot Murtaugh's attacker in the head. Then, leaning heavy on a spare [a makeshift crutch - his famous artificial leg had been lost], he dragged Murtaugh away from the barrels, as the water from them was spilt and wetting the ground where he lay.

Thinking the fight in the back had ended, I almost turned my attention back to the fray in the front yard, when I caught movement as another figure stepped out of the house and onto the porch. This one was dressed in the same weird way as his fellows, but he moved slowly and upright, in full command of his faculties. He wore a kind of wolf's head cowl, with eyes cut out for him to see through. This was Sig Skoll himself.

"Morris!" Skoll shouted, in his thick tongue. "You have defeated my pack. Stand aside now, and let me go, or at least my wife!"

"It's your wife we're here for, Skoll, you devil," Morris said back. "Lay down that long knife,"[he had some kind of sword in his hands, but no firearm], "and come peaceful. I'd like nothing better than to burn you down along with your house, you son of a bitch."

At this point, Van Helsing stepped up and called to Skoll, asking him again to let his wife out of the house before it burned to the ground, for the fire was on the wood roof now and blazing.

"Get back, old man!" shouted Skoll. "I don't want your blood this night. Callisto would never forgive me. But I'll have your head, Morris, if you do not let us pass."

Aurelius took aim with a rifle, making it three guns against Skoll now.

"Last chance, Skoll!" Aurelius warned.

Skoll waved his sword and charged off the porch, hollering.

Two shots struck him as he ran [one of the men did not fire], and like the others, though he was wounded, he kept on. The distance was so short from the porch to their position, that there wasn't time for another volley. Skoll chopped right at Morris with his sword and knocked his pistol from his hand.

I heard Aurelius call for Van Helsing to shoot as he himself had run shy of cartridges, but the Dutchman missed. Paul got up from the ground and pulled away from Firebaugh. He ran over and tried to tackle Skoll, but that sword came around and took the cowboy's head off his neck. Morris fought back, and I decided to lend a hand, and began working my way down the slope with the horses. I saw that Aurelius was fiddling with his rifle, while Van Helsing had turned toward the house, perhaps having it in mind to go after the woman still inside.

I saw a flash of metal, and realized Morris had got a big bowie knife from his scabbard and was wrestling to put it into Skoll, while Skoll had got rid of his sword and had his hands around Morris' throat.

I was running by this time, though in great pain from my sensitive affliction, and hollering all the way along with Aurelius for the Dutchman Van Helsing to do something to intervene. Aurelius had his rifle loaded, but couldn't find the right target among the two men, who were so tangled up in their combat on the ground as to be indistinguishable.

I reached the foot of the rise, but had to pause to allow for the pain. That was when I saw her [Mrs. Skoll] open the window on the upper floor and climb out onto the roof. I thought at first she would cry for help. She was in a white shift of some kind, and her long black hair was loose and blowing. The fire was close all around her, and she looked very bright among all that black smoke. In addition, there was a noticeable swell to her, which made it look to me like she was due for a baby.

I shouted for her to keep calm, and let go of the horses to get there faster, as I was afraid she meant to jump.

She called out her husband by name, and then pressed her face into her hands.

As I reached the back yard finally, I saw that Mr. Morris was standing up and Sig Skoll had rolled over with the big bowie knife stuck to the handle under his left arm. And that was how he finished.

Morris and Aurelius had not seen Mrs. Skoll yet, and I hollered for them to look as I joined up with them.

Mrs. Skoll was three ways distraught. When she took her hands away her eyes were red and running, and she opened her mouth and screamed. It wasn't a regular scream that came out. It started off as a womanly moan, but as it got louder, it seemed to break in sound and become like a dog's baying. It was so loud and unnatural I had to cover my ears.

She crouched there on the roof, and it seemed she was cursing us through her teeth, but I couldn't understand her words. Her hair was wild and flying and the ends seemed to spark from the closeness of the fire eating up the roof around her. Her shift caught, and she reached up with both hands and, taking hold of the sleeves, she tore it in half, flinging the blackening shreds both ways into the fire. It was plain then by her aspect that she was with child.

Aurelius Firebaugh reached us at that instant, and I saw him grab hold of Morris and shove him away.

A big twisting column of black smoke poured out from under the eaves just then, and Mrs. Skoll jumped off the roof, passing into it.

But it wasn't Mrs. Skoll that came out the other end.

It was a big black wolf with shining yellow eyes, and from where I stood I could see that its heavy paws were out in front of it like a bobcat pouncing on a javelina. Its long teeth were bared and its big sharp ears were flat against its huge head.

It would have flattened Coleman Morris if Aurelius Firebaugh hadn't been standing there in his place. As it was, the wolf knocked Firebaugh on his back and went running off across the back yard. In a minute it was gone in the dark.

Van Helsing regained himself and fired his pistol at the fleeing animal. We all just sort of stood there for a minute, not sure what had happened. There was a big hole in the middle of Aurelius' chest, and we saw right away that the wound was mortal. His heart could be seen pumping, and the blood was fleeing his body in every direction.

Aurelius cursed a great deal. He cursed me for not getting there in time, and he cursed Van Helsing for not doing anything while he was there. When Morris came to his side, Aurelius cursed him for not getting out of the way.

Then he shuddered, and it was as if he felt his spirit trying to escape. He grabbed hold of my sleeve, but he spoke to Morris, and there were tears running from his good eye.

"Take care of my place, Cole. Take care of Bernice's [a mare which had just dropped a colt] colt. You can sell off all them others if you can catch 'em, but keep them two. Will you?"

Coleman answered that he would abide the old man's request, and added, "And we'll get her for you, Alkali. We'll get her."

Whether he heard this or not, there is no telling. Having no more affairs to put in order, the old man gave up the ghost directly.

Marshal Ruddles joined us, with the news that Parker and Erb had been lost, but the rest of the Skoll gang had been wiped out. The house was burning spectacularly, but Van Helsing got up of a sudden and ran inside.

We all yelled after him, but after five or ten minutes, we decided he had been taken up by some kind of madness and had burned. He emerged a couple minutes later though, with a box bundled in his coat.

Though we demanded to know what was so important that he had risked his life in the burning house, Van Helsing would not answer. Marshal Ruddles did not ask what happened to Firebaugh, assuming it was one of the gang. I was excited over all I'd seen, and made to tell him and the others, but Van Helsing and Morris both stopped me.

We tied our dead over their saddles, having no wagon, and Marshal Ruddles declared his intent to take the dead and the living back to town and return to bury the Skolls. Morris said he would head out to Firebaugh's place, though it was very late, and Van Helsing volunteered to go with him.

That was two days ago now.

CHAPTER 20

From the Journal of Professor Van Helsing
August 31st

Day is risen, but the light of the morning brings Coleman and I no comfort. The prairie seems gray and dull and the sun is not to be seen. My friend Alvin may well have succumbed by now to the claws of the *ulfheonir*. Sigmund Skoll, our feared enemy, is dead by Quincey's knife, the same that slew Dracula. And Aurelius Firebaugh, that consummate frontiersman, is dead too at the hand of Callisto. She and her unnatural offspring live, but only until we find her.

Signs that meant nothing to me or were neglected in light of my fascination with her beauty are now as apparent as a rain of blood from a clear, bright sky. Her nearly joined eyebrows, her interest in Baring-Gould (what woman of her sort has ever heard of Baring-Gould ?), her sympathy towards Fenris in the old tale, and her incredible confession to me of being with child. All of these things seem to me now like shrill whistles of alarm. Was I deaf or blind to them all, or did I simply not trust my own mind?

The gestation period of the wolf is vastly accelerated when compared to the normal human pregnancy. It must be assumed that the term of the lycanthrope, the true lycanthrope, is at some halfway point. When I saw Callisto days ago I could barely discern her state. But on the roof last night...she will give birth any day now, it seems.

I told Coleman this.

He said nothing in reply.

It is his intent to avenge Aurelius, and mine to pursue the same course, both for the edification of science and the greater good. Plenty Skins was correct in his supposition that Skoll wanted the rangeland for game and for the cattle to rear his ghastly litter. But how long can a truculent predator such as a werewolf sustain itself on tame, stupid cattle? The tales of their ferocity and propensity for murder and cannibalism are legend. How long before Sorefoot itself becomes her hunting ground, and its citizens the innocent commissary of her hellish brood?

Thus is my failure compounded, as I see now that Skoll was not the greatest threat. He was but the deluded shepherd to her Ishtar, the Actaeon to her Diana. Skoll, or perhaps one of his pagan cult, found her in the forests of Arcadia and built (or solidified) their religion around her. What more evidence of the veracity of their doctrine would a society of *ulfheonir* need than the central figure of an actual shapeshifter?

As to her origins, who can say? If she comes from Arcadia as she told me, maybe she is descended of that ancient line of Lykos, who was cursed by Zeus (or so the mythology says) with the shape of the wolf for setting a dinner table of child flesh for the visiting god. More likely she is of some peculiar human subspecies originating in that region, whose existence was acknowledged in that ancient fable. There is the remote possibility that she is a victim of some curse or spell (or a willing participant), or perhaps an infection, like the vampire. Yet the fact remains undeniable in the gloomy light of this day.

Callisto Terovolas is a werewolf.

Whatever fondness I felt for her must be put aside in lieu of the dread business ahead. She has killed, and not only in defense. The tracks Coleman found outside of Buckner Tyree's shack, the queer fingerprint like paw marks, are that same as the ones we follow now. She will kill again.

Perhaps my infatuation with her is the product of some hormonal ability of hers. Do not the wolves of the forest communicate through scent manipulation and sensual reaction on some level imperceptible to human awareness? What if her power over me is deliberate, like the hypnotic power of Dracula's brides? Last night I hardly reacted to her brutal attack, even though I might have saved Aurelius' life. Of course, I may be seeking to salve my guilt, but what if the abhorrent stirrings of my imagination and the recent reeling of my subconscious mind in regards to her have been triggered by some recognition by my ego of the similarity between the bewitchments of the vampiress and the primal attraction of the were-bitch?

God, I ramble. Why has this been brought before me? Why must I consistently be the instrument through which evil is confronted and purged from the mortal world? It seems my lot in life is to confront what the greater number of humanity cannot know, to be faced with the darkest dwellers of deep imagination, and to feel the executioner's burden of terrible responsibility forever upon my old shoulders.

Why must it be Callisto this time?

I have been tested against hellish fires. If I have not dealt the final triumphant blow in all my battles, I have taken the commander's position whenever possible. I have put the sword into the hands of those more able. I have identified the Adversary wherever he has been, and made clear his foul intent. I have led men sometimes to death if it meant his eradication. Shall I forever be hounded by the denizens of the Beast in their many twisted forms? Must they now assume the shape of that which in my mind and heart has come to be so deserving of affection? An inestimable marriage of intelligence and purity and beauty in womanly form, which I have not known since before the departure of my own wife's sanity?

I see now that in Callisto, if it be not some unnatural symptom of a werewolf's guile, that she reminds me so very much of Mina Harker, as Mina reminded me of my wife, Diana. Strong, beautiful, and sensible. But so did the dark beauty of Dracula's bride strike me when I pried open her crypt. Must I stain my hands with another woman's blood?

Coleman and I are alone in this hunt. We dared not tell the others what we had seen, and we bade Mr. Gridley not to speak of it while we lived. I can only hope Alvin, if he lives, has not pried his eyewitness account from him. If he has I hope he has the wisdom not to publish it.

Coleman has asked me what it is we face. I see the trust in his eyes now, even as my own gaze passes over the heavy knife at his belt, the keen American blade that has sent two great evils to the inferno, and seems hungry for a third.

Callisto is as dangerous as any foe I have ever faced. I can only surmise her potential. Whereas in my pursuit of the vampire I had a vast store of folklore from which to glean the tactics I employed against him, there is comparably little in the lore of the werewolf to suggest how one may be defeated. They are spoken of as dying easily enough from the musket ball or the blade. It may be that in this form, though larger and faster and possessing of heightened awareness, she may be as susceptible to our bullets as any other animal (or woman). Perhaps moreso than even her berserk worshipers, who had their fanaticism to hold them up. Then again, what power may the waxing moon this night have over her and what power may she wield against us?

I have only guessed at her manipulative powers. At the party at Skoll's every man was at her beck. Was it simply because she is beautiful, or is there something preternatural in her allure?

And too, we must take into account that we are after a mother very near her delivery. An animal such as a wolf will fight viciously to protect its young. What we will face will be ten times the danger inherent in such a natural encounter. I think of the giant grey wolf in the canyon...and how a strong man like Vulmere could be rendered less than a rag doll in the span of seconds. I wonder to whom belongs the advantage? Two able armed men on horseback, or a lone, pregnant wolf woman? I wish Plenty Skins were with us.

When I saw her leap into the smoke and emerge in that terrible form, I did not want to believe. In my desperation to deny the fact, I even plunged headlong into the flaming house, searching for her. I moved through the burning furniture with no time even to lament the loss of Skoll's many priceless antiques. I called for her by name, struggling to be heard over the crackle of the fire and through my own strangled coughs. I fought my way through the heat as if it were a tangible enemy, and climbed even the dangerous stair, my coat drawn over my face to shield my watering eyes, which felt as though they were melting in their sockets.

I burst from one room to another until I recognized at the foot of a large bed the luggage I had seen her bear on the train. In her room I tore about like a madman, jerking open the closet and ripping the sheets from the bed, as though to find her cowering from the fire, ready to be saved. I found nothing but an open book on the night stand, the pencil laid aside by its author in the crease of the binding, the penmanship executed in a baroque, womanly hand, and in Greek. I took this treasure alone from that dying place, wrapping it in my coat to insure its safety as I made my way back down the fire-eaten stairs and finally exploded into the cool night air, coughing and feeling the blood rush from my face.

Here now is the only key to our prey. Our only guide to the werewolf. It will be more welcome than even my lost copy of Baring-Gould in the days to come.

*   *   *

From the Diary of Mary Weir
*September 1*st

Ben is due back from Austin in two days. This morning I found the chickens dead in the pen. A wolf or a coyote must have gotten them, but I don't see how, as the fence and wire were alright. I suppose it must have been an industrious predator, to have scrambled up and over the rail. When I found the pullets lying about, their white feathers soaked in blood and scattered all over the broken dirt, an overwhelming sadness poured over me like thick molasses. I dropped the can of feed and sat there crying on the step of the coop like a fool.

I wasn't crying for the chickens, for I had been planning to fry one of them for dinner tonight. I suppose I was crying for myself. With Ben gone the prairie is so lonesome. The wind through the tall grass at night climbs the walls of the cabin and seems to frighten the wood, making it groan dreadfully and leaving me wakeful in the big bed. Without the hens I feel I am the last living thing out here in all this big country. Aside from whatever animal is roaming about with a belly full of chicken meat, anyway.

If I felt like a fool crying in the pen, then I was twice as embarrassed when I saw that two men were looking down at me from their horses. I was embarrassed yes, and frightened out of my wits. I had been so unused to the sight of other people since Ben left a month ago that at first I had the crazy notion to vault over the fence rail and go running through the brown grass like a scared rabbit. I was so shocked by their sudden and noiseless appearance, I bolted for the only cover thereabouts, the back of the chicken coop. I don't know what I thought at the time, maybe that I would crawl underneath it, but the older of the two men raised both his hands to show they were empty and said something to me that sounded like:

"Pleace, dewt bee all armed."

Well, that stopped me right in my tracks, and I guess the look on my face must have tickled the younger one, for he grinned in a thin sort of way and said;

"It's alright ma'am. Didn't mean to scare you. Everything alright here?"

"Yah," said the older man, who had a kind of rusty beard and a great big cape-like coat, "Vote hast hep end to deez hens?"

I realized then that the old man was some kind of Dutchman, and now that I had more to go on, heard him right. He had asked me what had happened to my chickens.

I saw that they must have come up upon me while I was blubbering, and ran my sleeve across my watery eyes.

"Oh, coyote or a wolf," I answered.

The two men looked at each other.

"I don't know how it got in...the fence is fine and there's no hole underneath. Must've crawled over somehow."

The two of them stopped looking at each other only to look out over the whole prairie, as if they expected to see something other than nothing.

"You lost?" I ventured.

"No ma'am," said the younger man. He was about Ben's age, with straw colored hair and sun-dark skin, and eyes as blue as anything.

I think I took a couple steps back from the fence then, for if they weren't lost, then I assumed they must be looking for this place. They didn't look like anyone Ben would know.

"Are you here to see my husband? He ought to be around anytime now. He went down to the creek."

The older man cocked his head at me and had a strange look on his face.

"Is there something the matter with your well, lady?" he asked (I understood him better once I got used to his way of talking) gesturing to the pump beside the house. "Has it gone dry?"

The younger one looked at me for a minute, then took off his hat. The skin on the upper half of his head was a stark white from the red blemish of his hatband on up.

"Ma'am, I'm Cole Morris and this is Professor Abe Van Helsing. You needn't fear us. We've come upon you by accident, and aren't here on any mischief."

I felt myself go red at having been caught in a lie, and at the thoughtfulness of his courtesy.

"I'm Mary Louise Weir. I'm sorry. We don't get company out here. Please let me bring you some coffee."

"We'd be obliged to you, Mrs. Weir, if it's not too much trouble," said Mr. Morris, and he and his Dutch companion (surely I thought, he can't really be a professor. I guess it is a nickname, like how they call a bartender 'professor.') got down from their horses and tied them to the rail.

As I went into the house and began heating the water, I noticed through the window that they took a great interest in the chicken pen and the ground immediately surrounding it. They talked in low tones to each other.

When I brought the coffee, I asked them just how they had come out all this way and where they'd come from.

"Sorefoot, ma'am. We're hunting," Mr. Morris explained.

They did not look like hunters, which made me nervous again. They did not have the provisions or gear of men on a hunting trip.

"Madame," said the Dutchman, "did you hear or see anything unusual this night last?"

"No," I said. "Nothing. You can see a far distance from here all around, so anything coming is usually not a surprise. Until you, of course," I said lightly.

They did not smile. They seemed quite preoccupied with something, and drained their coffees quickly and would not have more.

"You're not hunting antelope," I observed. "What is it? Was it the same thing that killed my chickens? Is that what brought you here?"

"Mrs. Weir, when will your husband be back?" Mr. Morris said, ignoring all my questions. "Truly."

Again something in me cringed. Yet, I did not feel entirely threatened. There was an easy way about Cole Morris and a benign air to his companion that precluded my mistrusting them.

"Within a day or so," I said, almost with relief. I am terrible at lies, and I have been so lonely for company of any kind lately that I hate to think of driving off the only human beings I had seen in a month with fabrications. "He went to Austin at the beginning of the month for a cattle show. We want to raise cattle. Oh, just a few at first, maybe never more than that. But it's what we came here to do. Ben's father raised cattle back east in Vermont. Do you know anything about cattle, Mr. Morris?"

"Something about it," he said absently.

"Madame Morris," said the Dutchman, "it is imperative that you remain behind doors until your husband's return."

"What? Why?"

"There is a very wild animal loose," Van Helsing said. "Should it return and find no more hens to prey upon, it may be a danger to you."

The stern insistence in his eyes made me tremble slightly, like I had just felt a wind that had been through grave grass. I hugged my elbows.

"What kind of an animal?"

Van Helsing's mouth was open to answer, but Mr. Morris interrupted him.

"Lion," he said. "Gone rabid. It butchered one of my calves and mauled a horse. I believe it did get at your chickens sometime last night. Probably it won't come by here again, but better to be safe till your husband gets back."

I have never been much afraid of wild animals. The ones I have seen were mostly skittish, fleeting little creatures or the occasional cowardly wild dog, as afraid of an untoward look as they are a hurled stone. I had never known there to be any big wild cats out here, but Mr. Morris and Van Helsing did not seem to be lying. I told them I would indeed do as they advised, and gave them a handkerchief of biscuits I had left over from breakfast. My morning sickness made it impossible for me to enjoy them anyway.

They watered their horses from the well and then mounted up. Mr. Morris promised he and his man Van Helsing would pass back this way to look in on me on the return trip, after they had bagged the wildcat.

As they rode away over the rise, I felt lonelier than ever. The brief excitement of their news and their visit are gone and tedium has settled on me like dust. The house is so quiet now it is almost tangible, like the steady sound of rain though there is none. The noise of the chickens gossiping in the yard is even gone now. I will have to bury them away from the house so nothing else comes scrounging for their carcasses. How I wish and pray Ben would come home early...as I have every day, for the past two weeks.

CHAPTER
21

From the Journal of Shadrach Mueller
September 2nd

I met old Captain Quentin Morris' younger son today. It was not a particularly fortunate meeting.

It was just before noon and we were branding wild cows on the north forty when Ben Weir's wagon came up the road with two men I could plainly see were not Ben driving it.

I called Buster and Tripas over and told them to keep their eyes open, as I saw the two in the wagon had spotted us and were coming over. I wasn't sure if I was just mistaken about it being Ben's wagon (although you can't mistake his spotted old swaybacked gray Janey — it's the most pitiful animal in the county), but if these two were up to no good I wanted to be certain sure they didn't pull anything over on us. Besides, a couple of the 'strays' we had picked up had turned out to have Bob Billings' triple B brand (we weren't letting it stop us though, as I had warned Billings a thousand times to watch his cows better) and we were all a little jumpy at the sight of a wagon.

As it pulled up, I could see that it was indeed Ben Weir's rig with old Janey in the tracers, and with Buster and Tripas on either side of me, I asked plainly of the two strangers where they had got it.

The younger one, a light haired fellow of about Buster's age, touched his hat and said they'd found it about three miles to the south, and they had what was left of the owner bundled up in the box.

The older fellow, a rusty-bearded foreigner, added that they had urgent business to the northwest and were hoping we might be able to identify the poor corpse and take it and the wagon (and its goods) off their hands.

I still wasn't sure if they were shooting straight or not, but I bit and took a look in the box anyway. Sure enough, wrapped in the back was a sack of butchered meat with half of Ben Weir's face hanging ragged off a mashed-in skull. It looked like he'd been half eaten, or else trampled by a buffalo.

"Ben Weir," Buster said beside me, and the Dutchman gave a little sound of regret.

When we looked at him for explanation, the younger one explained they'd stopped at the Weir house on their way up north from Sorefoot, and Mary Weir had kindly given them coffee.

It was bad to find Ben Weir in such a state. Bad for Mary Weir too, who was all by herself and word had it, expecting.

"*Ay, que malo!* What happened to him?" Tripas asked, taking off his sombrero out of respect.

I shook my head.

"Did you find him in the wagon?"

"Nearby," said the younger one.

"Tracks?" asked Buster.

"It looks like a wildcat, or maybe a bear."

"Maybe the same thing that got to that Billings cow we found, huh Shad?" Buster said.

I shot him a look. I didn't want to touch on the subject of Billings' cows to a stranger when there were eight or ten Triple B steers waiting for the iron right here. But Ben did look an awful lot like what had happened to the cow we'd found on the far south range, torn and butchered, some of the bones cracked open and the marrow sucked out. It's odd business. There aren't any bears around that I know of, and no wildcat short of a striped Indian tiger ought to be able to do that to a cow, or a man. What troubled me more was that whatever had done this to Ben Weir hadn't touched Janey.

"Something been at the animals around here?" the young one asked.

I didn't like him asking me questions, so I answered with one of my own. I asked him who he was.

"Name's Morris," he said. "And this is Abe Van Helsing."

Well, I knew the Morris name directly, at least Quentin Morris, whom I'd served under against the Comanches out of Fort Elliot, and who

I knew had a spread down around Sorefoot. I also knew of his son Quincey, who had won a prize Winchester in a shooting contest in Ft. Worth, and asked him if he was that same boy. He told me he was the younger offshoot of the Captain, Cole, brother to Quincey. I hadn't heard Quentin had two sons.

I explained how I'd known his paw in the wars and his elder brother by reputation. I asked him what he was doing so far north with an old Dutchman for company.

"Headed for Austin," he said. "Van Helsing here was a friend of my brother's from back east, and I'm taking him up to meet a relative of his."

I looked the two of them over. They looked like they'd been out of doors for more than a while. The old Dutchman's beard was dirty while Cole's was sprouting in patches. Their clothes had more dust than a Denver pimp's prayer book.

"Looks like you shoulda took a coach," I said.

"Looks like."

I invited him and the Dutchman to come back to the place for a bite to eat, but though I could see in their eyes they wanted it, they said no. They had a lot of miles to cover, and had been delayed by bringing the body of Weir and his wagon over. They asked me what would happen to his widow, and I promised I'd bring her the news and the wagon and horse myself, though the body probably wouldn't keep much longer and our icehouse won't be finished for another week.

I saddled myself with a heavy burden agreeing to deliver this evil news to a lonely young mother to be. It's not something I would usually do, but for the Captain's son I make an exception. I don't know just what his game is, but if he and that Dutchman are going to Austin to visit a relative, then I am Daniel Boone's sister.

* * *

Journal of Abraham Van Helsing
September 2nd

Our spirits had descended to dark depths when we left the branding camp of Mr. Mueller and his men. Though I am confident that he is a man of his word, I would like to return personally to dear Mrs. Weir's home to express my condolences, if it is our fate to return at all.

That Callisto is responsible for the death of Mr. Weir is without question, just as it was certain that it was she who stole into the Weir chicken pen. Probably it was she who also fell upon the Billings cow. Why Callisto did not kill Mary Weir herself is uncertain.

We did not return to the place where we had found Mr. Weir lying near his wagon until dusk. We have lost a day of our pursuit. She ranges the same far flung distance of a full-blooded wolf, and it is difficult to keep up. I fear our sense of duty to Mrs. Weir (for it was with a grave and ironic surety that we knew it was her husband we found slaughtered, having found the bill of sale for a brand new baby cradle that was packaged in the wagon box) may have cost us our due vengeance.

Coleman asked me once more to tell him what had become of his brother Quincey. Unsure as I am of our future, I agreed to tell him. I do not know if there will be another opportunity.

Our campfire was the only light in the dark land when I finally finished the tale. In that impenetrable black beyond its glow, I took him to the Carpathians with Mina. It seemed that Texas faded away, and we were both of us with those devil women, circling in the outer dark like hooded scavengers passing seductively behind the veil of night. I did not dare to look Coleman in the eyes until I finished, and instead stared into the fire, replaying the events like flickering magic lantern pictures in the undulating flames.

When I did look up, it was to describe the penultimate hour of Quincey P. Morris' life. Coleman's expression was bereft of all emotion. When it was done, I did not know if we he would lunge across the fire for me and call me liar, or what.

We listened to the popping of the kindling and I chewed a bit of thick jerky while he unrolled his pallet and lay upon the ground, turning his back to the fire and me and laying his head on his saddle without a word.

As I finally lay myself down, he said, "It's a good thing you waited this long to tell me, Professor. I never would've believed you before now."

* * *

From the Journal of Abraham Van Helsing
September 3rd

After a murky day's travel under a gloomy, overcast sky, we took shelter in an abandoned sod house, some monument left by a long gone pioneer. Coleman says her trail is a day old. We are losing her.

As we bedded down, we lit a fire in an old iron stove and I read through Callisto's diary. Sifting through her more mundane entries and leafing through the most personal expressions of her life, I was able to piece together her history.

She had been born to a family of wealthy Arcadian vineyard owners and had been educated abroad. On the commencement of her nineteenth birthday she made mention of a 'Change,' the nature of which need not be related to surmise, I am sure. However, for posterity's sake, I shall elucidate. This change did not come as a surprise to her.

She writes:

'Tonight the Change came upon me. It was a horrid experience. I was sitting in my room reading Blake's Infant Sorrow:

'My mother groan'd! My father wept,
Into this dangerous world I leapt,
Helpless, naked, piping loud,
Like a fiend hid in a cloud'

when of a sudden there came a great heat upon me, though it was late in January and I swaddled for warmth beneath a heavy down blanket. My cheeks flushed and my dress was soaked almost instantly with perspiration. The fabric clung to me and I knew only that I had to get it off. I removed it with such vigor that I tore the garment to pieces. I threw the sopping remains away and happened to glance into the standing mirror in the corner. The hairs on my body were all erect and darkening. It was as though the shadows of the room were conquering my meager lamplight and claiming my flesh. What hair I had already spread up and down my body. My eyebrows, my scalp, the hairs of my nether regions, all of these seemed to pour and flow like oil across my skin. Soon, though I was naked, a man might have come into my room then and seen nothing. Even my breasts became dark woolen hills of black grass, and my limbs were coated in a shaggy suit of the same.

Then the pains began. The calves of my legs tightened as though cramped, and the agony flared so intense that I could no longer support myself. I fell to the floor and cradled them with my trembling hands. Under my fingers, I could feel my limbs shifting—elongating. I could hear the bones groaning. My feet tapered and stretched. Then something like a crossbow bolt seemed to erupt from behind the bridge of my nose, and I felt my face shifting, heard the popping of bones, and tasted blood in my mouth as my sharp teeth pricked my tongue. On my hands and knees I tried to scream for help, but my voice was distorted, like the strident, broken cry of some tortured thing. It frightened me into silence, and it was in silence that I bore the remainder of the Change.'

She goes on to write as though she had been well prepared for the event, as some daughters are made ready by their mothers for the inevitable transition into womanhood.

'Mother told me how the Change might come when I was particularly upset, especially during the nights of the full moon each month. She warned me at such times not to give free reign to every swing of my emotions, no matter how volatile. She told me further that I must not be afraid. That in time it would not come unless I called it. Until then, during the nights of the moon, I must lock myself in the windowless chamber, and leave off my clothes. Else, she tells me, I will ruin all my own and then have only Athene's second hand garments for myself...' —*Diary of Terovolas*

Apparently certain members of her family had been stricken (though she does not refer to her condition as negative in any aspect following the above-quoted passages) with lycanthropy since time immemorial. By the account of her family legendry, each generation bore forth a werewolf to atone for some great sin committed by the founders of their dynasty (the 'sin' against Zeus by King Lykos and his sons, perhaps?) The individual was traditionally protected, even to some extent revered, by the family as the bearer of sins, or the penitent. Like the traditional scapegoat of the Jews, which is driven into the wilderness. His or her health and prosperity ensured the survival of the next generation. Although, in one of its rages the werewolf might snatch babes from their cradles or bring down huntsmen in the forest, always the hunts of the authorities were deflected or sabotaged outright by the rest of the family...

'Last night I had a nightmare about chasing down old Antony, the drunkard who lives down at the base of the hill. I was naked and chasing him through the forest, and he seemed very much frightened. It was thrilling. I awoke this morning, very tired, and Mother came to me and told me Antony had been

found dead in the woods. Then she held me close and told me not to worry. I did not ask why.' —Diary of Terovolas

Yet, by Callisto's account, the Terovolas family was never burdened with the protection of their werewolf for long. In the previous generation, Callisto's own father Euandros had been the last penitent. He had disappeared in the mountain wilderness before she was three years of age. It seems the werewolf is not a human being afflicted with the spirit of a wolf, but a wolf's spirit born (and imprisoned) within the body of a human being. As the years progress, and the transformation (at first a painful and slow going affair, it eventually becomes easier and faster) is undertaken for more extended periods of time and at more frequent intervals, the individual becomes more acclimated to life as a wolf.

As the basis for this, I cite:

'The Change came so easy to me tonight! It was like nothing at all...'

And:

'I am beginning to feel ill at ease among my friends and neighbors, and even the grand old house begins to seem to me like a great breadbox in which I am shut up. At nights sometimes I awake in bed and am terrified to see the ceiling above me. The sheets of my bed seem to tangle like a net about me, and I kick them to the floor. "Where are the stars and where is the breeze?" *I think at such times, before I remember that I am human.'* —Diary of Terovolas

After that, the roles of clan and penitent are reversed, and it becomes the werewolf's burden to remain in the bosom of family.

'Why should I remain here? What purpose can I serve, except to endanger them with my nightly rovings? In the forest I can be who I truly am, and am not forced into a role which I cannot fulfill...that of a daughter, or a wife, or a lady in some spinning circle. Yesterday the ladies from the village came and I sat beside mother at the loom. The order of the patterns of the yarn and cloth seem like a maddening snare woven by the insidious shuttle. My soul is caught within it, thrashing like a fly in a web. Twice the other women spoke to me and Mother had to prod me to recognize them. I keep staring out the window, at the forest clustered beyond the edge of the vineyard...' —Diary of Terovolas

The mores of the human family begin to seem unnatural to the werewolf, and his or her company becomes something of a nuisance to the family...

'Today I was censured by Mother and Grandmother at dinner. Roasted lamb was served, and, forgetting myself, I clambered upon the table and began tearing into the meat with my teeth and hands. When Uncle Nikolas tried to pull me away, I bit his hand. I was quite unaware of what I was doing or indeed who I was...wolf or woman.' —Diary Of Terovolas

By the time of parting with her human family, she seems to have quite lost any pretense towards familial affection.

'Mother wept openly and the sound of it grated upon me. The eyes of Athene were glistening, and Uncle Nikolas told me they would all of them never forget me. It is not as though I am dying. I am only going to live in the forest as I feel that I should, as father did. It is only over the next rise, though I may go further back up into the mountains. I have promised to write them but I doubt I shall have much time for even this journal.' —Diary of Terovolas

It seems at this point, that she did not, for that entry is dated April the fifteenth, 1894, and the entries do not resume until May the eighteenth 1896.

Then the writing is stilted and full of imperfections, as though Callisto had been quite out of practice, or as though her human reason had deteriorated due to neglect.

'I am going home,' is all she writes, and 'I am' are the only words spelled correctly.

For the next year the entries are much in the same vein and it is difficult to glean any useful information from them. Why she returned to her family home from the wilderness is not known. But what she found when she returned was that poverty had struck along with sickness, and a great many of her family had died, along with her mother. While I do not know if Callisto was bereaved at this news, as her writing is vague and concerned only with the fact of the matter, she did not remain in Arcadia, but traveled for a time in greater Europe.

By the pattern of her travels, it seemed as though she were looking for something or perhaps someone. Always she shied from the established cities. She seemed to be gravitating toward towns on the edge of great wilderness. Freiburg, near the Black Forest. Inverness, in the Scottish Highlands. Even Sighisoara at the foothills of the Carpathians (whose geography I am all too familiar with).

'I have gone searching in this world,' she writes in her old way, as though her months of exposure to humanity had helped to return her to her former lucidity, *'and have found nothing but black smoke and buildings. I am going to my true home.'*

Wherever her travels took her, she eventually crossed the path of Sigmund Skoll, and struck perhaps by some preternatural instinct, he tracked her to her home forest. She writes of their first meeting:

'I did not know this man — only that he was a man and he was in my forest. He was dressed strangely, all in animal skins. By their lingering musk, I knew them to be wolf pelts, and thought that he must be a hunter. I Changed and came from the brushes, meaning to bring him down and taste his life over my tongue. I was hungry, there being nothing to eat but skinny hares for weeks. He did not run as so many others had. Instead he lowered himself to my level, so that I could see his lake-blue eyes, and he brought his yellow haired head beneath mine. Then it was that I realized that I had smelled him before. His had been the strange new scent I had found intermixed with my own markings on the trees and shrubs about my den. Who is this man, that he knows my true language? He was handsome enough, and despite the peculiarity of the situation, it was my time and so I allowed him. I had never known a man before, and he told me after, he had never known a wolf...'

Skoll had seen her briefly on a passenger steamer, and used his considerable resources to track her to her home forest in the Arcadian Wood. There he revealed to her the tenets of his *ulfheonir* beliefs, and though she secretly derided some of them, they developed a love for each other.

She agreed to join his pseudo-pagan society as a *volva*, a kind of sacred priestess. They lived together alone in Denmark for a period of a year, but the near discovery of their occult activities necessitated their flight from the country. Part of their rituals involved a kind of re-enactment of a Wild Hunt, and after several deaths in the vicinity of their cottage were capitalized by the disappearance of a constable out hunting, they made an expeditious emigration. Her reasoning of these slayings is the philosophy of a madman.

'We slew no one that was young and useful, only the infirm and the unwanted. The constable was an old hermit with spotted hands and a failing liver. I know because I tasted it.' —Diary Of Terovolas.

Callisto returned first to Arcadia while Skoll gathered up the rest of his cult and came here to America.

'I will wait for him and his men to send word that I may rejoin him in the West.' —Diary Of Terovolas.

They had come West for the abundance of open land, and Skoll had cultivated the persona of a foreign investor interested in cattle land in Austin, with the help of Vulmere. Then, when all was ready, Callisto was sent for. But their intent had not been solely to live in harmony and practice their religion away from prying eyes.

I found mention of what seems to be the ceremony that was enacted in Misstep Canyon, which Buckner Tyree heard or witnessed and at which Plenty Skins' nephew Picker became a sacrifice. It was not a wedding (Callisto and Skoll had been wedded just prior to leaving Denmark, and she had there stepped through a wolf membrane — an ancient pagan ritual designed to foster the birth of werewolves), but a vision seeking ceremony.

'According to their rites, they raised me upon a high seat of birchwood and girded me in cat skins. Then Sigmund's men set out into the dark and returned after an hour bearing the carcass of every animal they could find. Among them was a red Indian boy. They butchered him along with the animals, and took their hearts and boiled them in a stew with some hellbroth that I was expected to drink. I did so, for Sigmund's sake, but whatever agents were in it made me fall into some kind of swoon. I saw things which I don't entirely understand or believe.'

Among the visions she saw was the death of Vulmere.

In my study of the diary I have learned little else of interest and nothing of real use in our hunt. She makes no mention of the vulnerabilities of the werewolf. It may be as simple as a bullet in her heart, or it may be wolfsbane or an iron cudgel. I do not know.

But there is a nagging doubt in my heart now. In reading her words, I have come to know her more. While I cannot entirely ignore her crimes, I cannot entirely condemn her. For it seems, I understand her. But this is nonsense. Had I stumbled upon some personal narrative of Dracula's, would my heart have been softened too? Then what would have become of Miss Mina? She would have suffered the same fate as Miss Lucy. But then again, perhaps Quincey Morris would not have died.

William Blake has taken the place of Sabine Baring-Gould in my thoughts.

> Thro' the Heav'n & Earth & Hell
> Thou shalt never, never quell;
> I will fly & thou pursue,
> Night & Morn, the flight renew.

Later…

Before dawn we were startled awake by the screaming of our horses. I had barely risen before Coleman was standing in the doorway firing his rifle out into the lightening darkness. I was at his side in moments, in time to see a dark low form go galloping over the prairie.

"She must have doubled back, circled us sometime last night and found us. She might've been leading us all over the damn country," Coleman said.

Our horses had both been hamstringed and thrashed about on the ground, unable to stand. They were in great pain and there was no alternative but to put them down.

Our pursuit was at an end. As the second rifle shot echoed in the predawn stillness, I felt my emotions rise to a boil, and called out into the empty land.

"This is not ended! So long as we live, it cannot be! We will return with more men! You cannot wash the blood from your hands, no matter the distance you flee!"

Then I stood, feeling foolish.

But in a few moments there came an answer. Her voice was haggard, but a clarion in the quiet dim.

"Why? Abraham? Why? Have you and your companions not tormented me enough? You have slain my love and would put myself and my unborn children to the knife! They are all I have left! What sort of men are you?"

"You speak of injustice! How many have you killed and devoured? How many have you been a party to? Tyree, Searls, Picker, the Indian boy...to say nothing of your victims across the sea! I have read your diary, Callisto! I know everything!"

There was silence, and we thought she had gone. But then:

"You have read everything, have you? And yet you feel nothing! I was wrong, Abraham! You are a true man of science! No pity in your heart for one who must live between midnight and day — not a whit of understanding for one without a family or home among wolves or men! Come and take our lives, then, Abraham! But you will pay a dear cost! I will not so easily part with the only thing that is rightfully mine in this world!"

"And yet you have taken that very treasure from others without recourse!" I called back. "Who are you to decide the lives of men?"

"I am a hunter!" was her answer. "It is all I can be! The feeble old stag can understand this, and bears no ill will to the hunter. Why can't man?"

"Because we are not animals!"

"And I am not human! But come if you will, Abraham! Come, and die!"

I called her name, but she would not answer.

Coleman grabbed hold of my arm.

"Don't let her make you forget, Van Helsing."

"Forget? Forget what?"

"Aurelius. Alvin. Early. Weir..."

I nodded.

"I won't forget."

"She's out there right now," he said, and crouched down, running his fingertips over the crushed grass, which was dappled in the blood of our mounts. He looked up at me gravely. "We can get her tonight, maybe even before dark. But we have to go now."

We packed our rations and ammunition and left our non-essentials in the cabin. We are setting out on foot.

CHAPTER 22

Page from the Journal of Professor Van Helsing, written by Coleman Morris

Van Helsing pushed this book at me before he left and told me to write down what happened, so I am doing so, as there is nothing much else for me to do.

It is the night of September 3rd now, and I am writing this by firelight, about four miles northeast of the old sod house where the bitch killed our ponies.

It wasn't hard tracking her from the cabin through the tall grass. She left a good swathe through it that I believe even Alvin could've followed. There was blood on the stems here and there, so I knew I'd hit her this morning as she ran. Probably not much more than a grazing shot, or there'd be more blood. But she is slowing.

For the past three days she's covered a lot of distance. Now she's going at a pace even we can follow.

We struck a sandy wash a little after morning and then the trail got more scant, but thanks to the blood on the stones it wasn't impossible. We followed that winding wash for a good five hours. To old Van Helsing's credit, he never once slowed or asked for a rest. I don't know how much of what he told me about Quincey is the truth, but having seen what I've seen in his company, and comparing it to the grit he showed today, I can't help but wonder at this world and that there are men like Van Helsing in it.

He has shown me that there is a lot of possibility in this old life, not the least of it that my brother Quincey could change from a no-account shirker with a looking glass under his eyelids, to the kind of man who could stand up with his friends and show a lot of John Bulls and Dutchmen and goddamned vampires what it means to be a Morris. The kind of man I am proud to call my brother.

I wish I could have lived up to what he did over there, but I'm just a cattleman, not a soldier or an Indian fighter or some vampire killer. And I sure proved that I am no werewolf hunter either.

We came across a shallow creek that cut across the dry wash and stopped to rest. It was about dusk. I have been on my share of hunts along with Paw and Quincey and Aurelius, but I never stalked anything with the sort of sand to turn on me, and it showed when I threw my common sense out in the ditch and set my rifle aside to splash some of that cool creek water on my dry lips.

That mean bitch didn't spare the time it takes a fly to scat, but came down on me like the wrath of God on Sodom. I had just touched my fingers to my lips when the wind got knocked from me, and I found myself floundering like a drunkard face first in three inches of water with the stones biting into my cheek and her claws hooked into my shoulders.

She was heavy as a bull buffalo and by the angle and feel of my gun arm, she'd busted it clean when she'd jumped on me from the lip of the wash, where she must've been crouched behind a rock or shrub I'd missed. I couldn't fight her off. I felt a pain like hot hell in my shoulder, and heard the bones cracking.

Then I heard, through the snarling and splashing, Van Helsing's gun.

The bitch let out a yelp and pushed off of me and was gone. When I pulled my face out of the water, I saw her tail end splashing off down the creek as quick as an antelope. She was huge, with wiry black hair up and bristling between two sharp ears, but she was running with a limp, favoring her back right haunch as she rounded a bend and was gone.

Van Helsing tended me best he could, given that we'd left most anything he might've used back in the cabin with the saddles. My arm wasn't broken at all, but my shoulder was. She had bit me like a fanged mule, leaving a big open pit of blood and meat and splintered bones where yesterday I'd had a patch of skin the size of a green buffalo chip. It took a half hour for Van Helsing to set it right and bind it up in a sling for me to carry it in. By that time I was pale and tired and cold and hoarse from yelling for him to get after her.

As it was I swapped my rifle for his ledger and handed him my cartridges.

"I cannot possibly..." he began.

"Just up the creek, old man," I told him. "She'll be waiting for you, and you know it. Give me your revolver."

He did.

"When it's done, fire three shots. Bang. Bang. Bang. Like that. Then I'll know whether to use this or not," I said, gesturing at his revolver. I don't intend to wait for her to come back down the creek for me.

He understood.

I wished him luck, and he was gone.

About an hour has passed, and I haven't heard any shooting. I don't know what that means. I hope he at least takes that bitch with him. If not, I've got his pistol, with all six beans in the wheel in case she comes back. If she does, only five of them are for her.

From the Journal of Abraham Van Helsing
September 4th

When I found her, she was crouched in a hollow depression near the creek bed. She was naked, huddled with her arms cradled against her body. The long black hair was hanging down and laced with a collection of burs and thistles picked up in her flight like the souvenirs of a whirlwind tourist. Her long lithe limbs were painted with mud and her wide mouth, smeared with Coleman's dried blood, grimaced as I came with the rifle, hunched over under the weight of fear and curiosity and dread at what she knew I must do.

It was a feat of tracking unworthy of the quarry. The creek ran down from her, and I could see her blood clearly in the water before the sun faded and the moon was high. I was surprised to find her human.

"So," she said, in a cracking voice. "Now you have found me, Abraham."

"In truth," I said, "I had hoped to find you dead."

"To save you the task of seeing the life fade from my eyes? You are a coward."

I heard a whimpering then, and thought it was her. I moved closer, cautiously. Her bare shoulders, like molded alabaster in the silver of the moon, did shake, but I could see her downturned lips. They were pressed together, and no sound could escape, though tears ran from her furious eyes.

She lowered her head, and seemed to touch her chin to her chest. I heard her make some light, cooing noise. Then she turned her hateful eyes on me again, and their expression was like the flanged head of an iron spear in my heart. She flung her head proudly, and her hair fell behind her shoulders.

"I didn't want them to die by you," she said, her voice trembling. "But I couldn't do it. The human in me couldn't do it. If I was a wolf..." but she broke off.

Curled in her arms and pressed against her breasts were two small forms. One was a thin babe with tightly clenched eyes, working furiously and alternately grabbing the long strands of its mother's hair. And in the crook of her other arm, which was glistening with her own blood, there was a whimpering ball of fur, its white muzzle nuzzling at her nipple, its oversized paws kicking, its black pointed ears twitching, yet in the tight slits of its newborn eyes, every bit the sibling of the human child.

I said nothing, but looked again into Callisto's eyes.

"I had another litter once," she said. "Years ago, in the Caucasus. Their father was proud, strong. His voice was like a siren's song and led the chorus of the pack. The way it traveled down the mountainside...it was like he had sent his soul out into the world to look about." her eyes were far off, but then they snapped back, fixing me like thumbscrews again. "Men like you came to our den with fire. I was young then, and not entirely a wolf. I escaped. But when I saw the Slavs stretch their pelts on the drying racks, I swore I would never again leave a child...or a mate...to the hunters. Do you know how they killed my children, Abraham? There was a branch outside the den.

One they had gnawed so many times in their games...one of the hunters took it up, and broke open their tiny heads. They didn't even know enough to be afraid...just like these."

She glanced down at the pup and the infant. They were as oblivious to me or to the agony in her voice as any hungry whelp.

I thought of Plenty Skins' dream, and his parting words.

"How badly are you hurt?" I asked.

"If I die, it will be from your bullet," she said. "The one who killed Sigmund, he did not hurt me."

So the blood on the grass we had followed to the creek had been birthing blood. How long had she fled while in labor before she had burrowed this half den in the bank to drop her litter? It was miraculous the babies had survived.

I took a step closer to her.

She pressed herself against the dirt wall, shifting to shield her offspring.

"You won't take them," she snarled. "Not for your filthy science."

"No," I said. "I won't take them."

I pointed the rifle down the creek and fired. Once. Twice. A third time.

She stared at me.

I cannot fully explain my thoughts as I turned away. I cannot say why in the end I could not finish the task. Had it been Coleman in my place and I left bleeding in the dry river bed listening for those three shots that meant my life or death (and Callisto's), I am sure I would have heard them and have no doubt that they would have been genuine.

But what had driven me here? Revenge for my friends? Surely that was an element. Outrage? Madness? Jealousy? Love? Knowledge? All of these must have held some truth.

But for what then, did I turn aside from my vengeance? What in Callisto Terovolas' bizarre existence did not offend me to my core as had Dracula's and his wives'?

I know only that whereas the beautiful eyes of the vampire had been black as holes, the soul which peered at me through this were-woman's haze of rage was a mother's. I knew that the incessant sound of the suckling of her brood, wolf and human, was not unlike that of any other child. That sound, which seemed louder even than her angry words and my own murmuring sang to me in that moment. It stirred something in my heart, like a familiar scent or turn of phrase, which makes one think of better days.

It reminded me of my own son, whose existence is now almost lost to my memory, along with a blurred summer day in which I can yet see as though through unfocused eyes. I can nearly glimpse the silhouette of my dear wife, featureless and yet radiant in the loving glow of the birthing Natal sun, rocking gently in a creaking rattan chair with a small, soft bundle pressed against her chest.

It is an old memory. Long before the Zulu came. Long before those hated lances struck my child down like seeking adders. Before Dracula, or the undead, or werewolves, or madmen, or any number of abominations both human and inhuman which I have encountered since.

It is a memory from that day before I was driven from my own personal Eden, when I was simply Abraham. Not the Daktari, or the Professor, or the Dutchman. Merely Abraham, back in the days when King Laugh was the shrill, joyous sound my son made as he bounced upon my knee.

"You got her," Coleman said to me, smiling as I came into the firelight, very tired.

"Yes," I answered, settling down to inspect his wounds. "She is gone."

Finis

Professor Van Helsing's journal entries regarding his Texas excursion end here and resume following his return to Europe and a strange series of events involving the ill-fated vessel **The Demeter** *some months later.*

These events shall likely be organized and collected in a future volume, as warranted by public interest and allowed by the efforts of the editor, though not necessarily in chronological sequence, owing to the completeness of some notations delineating certain periods of the professor's career over others.

There are copious documents regarding Van Helsing's early years in Natal (complimented by my own writings of the time) and his experiences with Lawrence and Carter at the Tanis dig in 1911 for example, whereas his entries regarding the unexplained occurrences on a Dutch ship bound for Java with Helen Blavatsky in 1857, and an early sojourn in San Francisco's Barbary Coast region are both rather sparse, as of this writing.

However, organizing a man's entire life's work into a readable form is no small task, and day by day I am rewarded with new discoveries, all of which I shall share with the public as per my friend's wishes.

-J.S.

COMPILER'S AFTERWORD:

BEYOND THE BORGO PASS: THE VAN HELSING PAPERS

I, like most of the world, always understood Bram Stoker's *Dracula* to be a work of fiction. Seminal in the horror genre, surely, but entirely the product of Stoker's imagination.

I stopped believing this in or around the summer of 1997, when, between jobs and trying to make the rent on a two-bedroom apartment on Carmen Avenue in Uptown Chicago, I answered a classified ad placed by the University of Chicago in *The Chicago Reader* for a seasonal position.

This wasn't academic work, but a reorganizational project of the reference stacks at the university's Regenstein Library. This still makes it sound overly important though. In effect, I and about ten other part-timers were carrying boxes to and from the basement under the direction of a perennially bored student intern. It was back-breaking work, and tedious, but ultimately not without its reward.

In the course of the job, in one of the Reg's two basements, I happened across a dust-covered box of unopened packets postmarked from Purfleet, dated 1936, and addressed to the head of the archaeology department.

The label on the box had it earmarked for the library's Ravenwood Collection, but it had somehow been physically separated and omitted from the catalog. It had sat forgotten on the back of a shelf of totally unrelated material for at least half a century.

I have a curious nature when it comes to old things, and a knack for staying out of the way of supervisors, which was easy in the maze of the Reg with only a disinterested intern to answer to. Though I knew it could possibly cost me my job, I managed to pop one of the manila packets open with my apartment key and shimmy the old yellow papers out for a look on my lunch break, a ritual I would repeat without fail innumerable times on that job.

What I read shook me to my core. I say this without exaggeration.

Dr. Abraham Van Helsing, that stalwart vampire hunter I had seen depicted in countless films and comic books, portrayed by everybody from Peter Cushing to Mel Brooks, was real. It was like finding the logbook of the *Pequod* written in Ahab's hand, or reading Joseph of Bethlehem's name on a Roman census roll from the Augustan Age.

But the figure that emerged while studying these papers (and from fact checking later among the Reg's microfilm collections and via long years of independent research), was no two dimensional crossbow wielding, fanatical monster hunter, but a substantial man of letters, a serious academic, a contemporary and associate of Flinders Petrie, T. E. Lawrence, Madame Blavatsky, Max Muller, and a host of other scholars I (as a woefully undereducated liberal arts student) would only come to know later as I studied the man himself. He pitted his learning against the supernatural not by choice, but by chance, though his name has become inseparable from that pseudo-scientific offshoot, that embarrassing cousin of natural science now thought of as 'paranormal investigation.'

Not only was Van Helsing real, but so was Dr. John Seward, Jonathan and Mina Harker, Arthur Holmwood, and Quincey P. Morris (whose brother's grave I once visited at the old Fairview Cemetery during a research trip to Bastrop, and whose Bowie knife, the very same one he sank into Count Dracula's heart, was anonymously donated to, and is still innocuously displayed at, the Autry Museum here in Los Angeles).

It's hard to prove this, of course, outside of the papers, as most of the major participants in the *Dracula* affair faded into intentional obscurity, with the exception of Quincey Morris (who died) and Van Helsing himself, whose total eradication from academic record is almost Egyptian in its totality.

But he did live. One of my prized possessions is a 1907 Dutch edition of Arminius Vembrey's *Western Cultures in Eastern Lands*, one of Van Helsing's rare translations, which I unfortunately can't even read.

If I can confirm the existence of Van Helsing with a little research, then what about the things Van Helsing claimed to have encountered in his travels? Vampires. Werewolves. Ghosts. There are things Van Helsing says he tangled with which would make cryptozoologists and theologians alike faint dead away.

Now you see why I say I was shaken up.

But, you might say, the man spent time in a lunatic asylum. Who's to say he didn't write all his memoirs as some kind of therapy while convalescing?

Well, mainly because of the corroborative writings by outside parties. The papers collected with Van Helsing's journal entries (newspaper clippings, personal diaries, correspondences), some provided by the professor, some by Seward, and some gleaned from my own personal research into primary source documents, bear him out every time. It's unlikely that Van Helsing's writings are entirely fictional when they are substantiated by so many people from so many diverse backgrounds and stations.

For me, the world became an exponentially bigger place in 1997, squinting in the dim light at old typeface with the musty smell of antiquity in my nostrils.

I knew I had to continue Dr. Seward's work, see his ambition fulfilled, and tell the world about Van Helsing.

As the forward to this book points out, Abraham Van Helsing's longtime friend and colleague Seward first intended the initial volume of the late professor's writing to see the light of day in 1935, seventy-seven years ago.

For whatever reason (Seward suggests active resistance by the academic community, though by this time he was himself embittered toward the establishment), he failed to secure a publisher, possibly in the eleventh hour.

Seward continued to pursue the book's publication for the next five years, soliciting literary agents on both sides of the pond and mailing facsimiles to many of Van Helsing's former academic associates in the hopes of gaining professional support.

A succession of personal tragedies hindered his efforts, however. His wife of thirty-five years was sadly killed in the Battersea Park railway crash of 1937. Then, in 1938, the asylum in Purfleet he had co-founded and administered for close to fifty years closed its doors, forcing him into a retirement he had long resisted.

You have to admire the dedication of Dr. Seward, who from his writings and personal correspondences seemed to really feel he owed Van Helsing a debt. Seward was one of the parties who willingly provided personal records (in his case, phonographic recordings, mostly pertaining to his patient, R.M. Renfield) to Bram Stoker, which Stoker then used in the publication of his 'novel' *Dracula* in 1897.

Excerpts from Van Helsing's personal journal were included in that book (translated from Dutch, as are the ones that appear in these papers, by Seward), but among the descendants of Lord Godalming, there is still some question as to whether these pages were obtained with the professor's consent, or at least with his full understanding that they would be made public. Holmwood himself believed the account compiled by Stoker under the direction of the Harkers was solely intended for the edification of their young son Quincey.

The Holmwood family, in point of fact, assert that the fragments from Van Helsing's journal of the 1890 period are believed by them to have been copied by Seward himself during the professor's stay at Purfleet Asylum, or else by one of Seward's staff. The reason for this, the Holmwoods claim, was monetary. It is known that the asylum was in dire straits financially at the outset, and that it experienced a substantial economic turnaround in 1898, a year after the publication of *Dracula.*

As Seward wrote, Van Helsing had been ostracized by the academic world for appearing in *Dracula.* Even some colleagues who had previously shared in his adventures turned their backs on him publicly when their own reputations were endangered.

Everyone suffered a small degree of embarrassment at the hands of Stoker, of course. Lord Godalming was branded an eccentric, which was sort of inconsequential to an English lord. The Harkers were a private people, not well known in the first place. Being that publication was mainly their idea, and they shared in Stoker's profits and raised their son comfortably on residuals (under a new surname, legally petitioned for by Jonathan), it was little to them. Dr. Seward, by his own admission, deflected any criticism from his peers by pointing out the fact that *Dracula* was labeled as fiction, and claimed in private circles at the time to have nominally participated in it as a favor to Stoker, or as a lark. He wasn't known much outside the psychiatric community, and not well regarded outside of London, at that.

But Abraham Van Helsing, when confronted by his detractors, out of personal honor or perhaps naivety, denied nothing (note these events will be better understood and brought to light in a subsequent collection).

And that wasn't the end of his exploits, nor even, as I found, the beginning.

Van Helsing, by his own assertion (records are scant), was born in 1834 in Natal, South Africa to Voortrekker Arjen Van Helsing and his German wife, Konstanze Gottschalk. He died in Holysloot, North Holland in 1934 (This can be confirmed. I've seen his death certificate.) In between that time he was a seminarian, a husband and father, a Boer farmer, a scientist, a field scout and interpreter, a medical doctor, a philosopher, an amateur archaeologist, a mystic, a respected lecturer, instructor, and a world traveler.

It took me nearly thirteen years of fact checking and emailing, meeting and compiling (to say nothing of legal wrangling over the authenticity and ownership of the papers themselves) to release the first installment of the Van Helsing papers in accordance with the late professor's initial wishes.

In the end I was reluctant to do so. My own career after all, has been in novels, and in doing this I risk consigning the professor's true history to the realm of speculative fiction, just as Bram Stoker did (albeit unwittingly – Stoker believed the papers he transcribed and polished to be works of amateur fiction).

Yet I can only humbly submit the first collection of these documents and ask that the reader overlook the presenter and see the truth within. We are obliged to put out the stories that come to us.

Dr. John Seward's own efforts at vindicating his friend were cut short on September 7, 1940, when the German Luftwaffe initiated operation Loge and he was killed in the first strike of the London Blitz.

It is my hope that I, in accidentally uncovering these documents and laboring to continue Seward's work, have been passed his torch, and that in publishing them, I have at last done right by both men.

Edward M. Erdelac,
Valley Village, CA
May, 2012

ACKNOWLEDGEMENTS

Mr. Dederick Pietersen, Ransdorp, North Holland

Jefferson Carter, Braun Research Library, Autry National Center, Los Angeles, California

Dr. Byron McFynn Jr., History Department, Marshall College, Connecticut

Renee Ravell, Bastrop Historical Society, Bastrop, Texas

Dr. Jan De Vries, University of Amsterdam, Netherlands

Paul Ladbroke, Thurrock Local History Society

Oliver Ruddles, Bastrop County Records Office, Bastrop, Texas

Professor Stanislaus Laff, History Department, Empire State University, New York City, New York

Heleen Six, Curator, Allard Pierson Museum, Amsterdam, Netherlands

Professor William Wallace Spates III, Special Collections, Miskatonic University, Arkham, Massachussetts

The Herkein family

Edward Arthur Holmwood, 8th Viscount Godalming

Lady Godalming

Edward M. Erdelac is the author of the acclaimed *Merkabah Rider* series and *Buff Tea*. He is an award winning screenwriter and independent filmmaker. His stories have appeared in several magazines and anthologies on both sides of the pond. Among other contributions to the franchise, he wrote the definitive story about boxing in the *Star Wars* universe.

Born a Hoosier, he was educated in Chicago and now lives in the Los Angeles area with his wife and a bona fide slew of children and cats.

News of his work, misadventures, and extensive home video collection can be found at http://emerdelac.wordpress.com. He has also been known to putter around longer than necessary on Facebook.

Tied for 1st Place in the 2012 JS Horror Writing Contest.

Billy Moon would have given his life for rock 'n' roll stardom, but the Devil doesn't come that cheap.

Goth rock idol Billy Moon has it all: money, fame, and a different girl in every city. But he also has a secret, one that goes all the way back to the night he almost took his own life. The night Trevor Rail, a shadowy record producer with a flair for the dark and esoteric, agreed to make him a star...for a price.

Now Billy has come to Echo Lake Studios to create the record that will make him a legend. A dark masterpiece like only Trevor Rail can fashion. But the woods of Echo Lake have a dark past, a past that might explain the mysterious happenings in the haunted church that serves as Rail's main studio. As the pressure mounts on Billy to fulfill Rail's vision, it becomes clear that not everyone will survive the project.

It's time the Devil of Echo Lake had his due, and someone will have to pay.

"VERDICT This unique and unnerving read is a sure bet for horror and SF fans." - Rebecca M. Marrall, Western Washington Univ. Libs., - Bellingham - Library Journal

In the deepest reaches of space, on a ship that no longer exists, six travelers stare into the abyss...

Man has finally mastered the art of space travel and in a few hours passengers can travel light years across the galaxy. But, there's a catch—the traveler must be asleep for the journey, and with sleep come *the dreams*. Only the sleeper can know what his dream entails, for each is tailored to his own mind, built from his fears, his secrets, his past...and sometimes his future.

That the dreams occasionally drive men mad is but the price of technological advancement. But when a transport on a routine mission comes upon an abandoned ship, missing for more than a decade, six travelers—each with something to hide—discover that perhaps the dreams are more than just figments of their imagination. Indeed, they may be a window to a reality beyond their own where shadow has substance and the darkness is a thing unto itself, truly worthy of fear.

"The work is as tidy as the town and as pat as a familiar horror film." -

Publishers Weekly

Diagnosed with a brain tumor, Geoffrey returns to his hometown for a reunion of the Jokers Club (his childhood gang) with the hopes of unearthing the imagination he held in his youth.

Unfortunately Geoffrey's tumor quickly worsens, bringing on blackouts and hallucinations where he encounters the spectral figure of a court jester who had been his muse as a child. The jester inspires Geoffrey's work on his manuscript, fueling his writing at a ferocious pace. The dead and the living co-exist in the pages of Geoffrey's story, in a town where time seems to be frozen in a past that still haunts the present.

Will the pounding growth in Geoffrey's head be held at bay long enough for him to discover who is targeting his friends, or will the pages in his unfinished novel rewrite history?

"This is a novel full of visceral, intense moments. It will keep you holding on until the brilliant end." - Richard Godwin, author of *Mr. Glamour* and *Apostle Rising*.

An evil force is at work at the Hospital where Nathan is recovering from injuries he received at the hands of his Mom's abusive ex-boyfriend. Demonic looking men with pale faces and glowing eyes lurk in the shadows. Someone is harvesting skin and organs from living donors against their will.

In his dreams, Nathan can see these demons in their true form–evil creatures who feed on the fear and hatred they create in their victims. Nathan's only ally is the Doctor who cares for him. Bound together by their common legacy, they alone seem to share the ability to see the demons for what they truly are.

Together they must find a way to stop these creatures before they, and their loved ones, become the next victims.

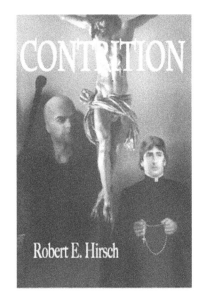

Robert E. Hirsch

In a tiny community on the Mississippi Gulf Coast, Brother Placidus finds little Amanda LeFleur sacrificed below a crucifix, in the attic of The Brothers of the Holy Cross. It is not the first body he's found there.

Assigned to the investigation is detective Peter Toche whose last case was that of a murdered child, a child that has been haunting his dreams, forcing him to face his worst fears and the evil that has targeted his town.

As additional victims are discovered, Tristan St. Germain, a mysterious man who was rescued by a parish priest from the waters near his home, may hold the key to the safety of all mankind.

Little Amanda was only the beginning...

"Faherty's latest novel provides readers with as much fun in a graveyard as the law will allow." - Hank Schwaeble, Bram Stoker Award-winning author of DAMNABLE and DIABOLICAL.

Rocky Point is a small town with a violent history—mass graves, illegal medical experiments and brutal murders dating back centuries. Of course, when Cory, Marisol, John and Todd form the Cemetery Club, they know none of this. They've found the coolest place to party after school—an old crypt. But then things start to go bad. People get killed and the Cemetery Club knows the cause: malevolent creatures that turn people into zombies. When no one believes them, they descend into the infested tunnels below the town and somehow manage to stop the cannibalistic deaths.

It's a race against time to find the true source of evil infesting Rocky Point, as the Cemetery Club ventures into the cryptic maze, to face their demons in a final showdown.

Lightning Source UK Ltd.
Milton Keynes UK
UKHW041006170720
366659UK00001B/47